"Well, we [barcode obscures text] **here**

"I heard you was t[...] [barcode obscures text] [...]e and Beau slid into her booth.

His expression made Betsy's flesh crawl; his words made her wish fervently that she was, as he put it, taken.

Before she could set him straight, a familiar voice sent her heart racing.

"You heard right, King. Get your butt outta that booth and your face outta my sight, because I'm not feelin' long on patience tonight."

Ben.

And one quick glance told her what he thought about finding her in a booth with two cowboys at the local honky-tonk.

His gaze locked with hers, then, taking her arm possessively, Ben turned to glare at the men. "You boys ever take a notion to get…friendly with this lady again, I suggest you think twice."

Dear Reader,

I'm in love with the American West and the entire Western myth. I could never resist a story about strong, handsome cowboys and beautiful, feisty cowgirls. When I began writing stories of my own, I became even more caught up in the Western mystique.

The natural result was a miniseries for Harlequin in 1993 about the Taggarts of Texas. Since several of my formative years were spent in the Lone Star State, I relished the opportunity to write the kind of books I love to read.

When I moved to the Centennial State a while back, it quickly became apparent that Texas and Colorado are "the same, only different." Both have lots of cows, cowboys and cowgirls, and some of the finest and friendliest people on earth. Other than weather, the biggest difference I noticed was that the only Coloradans who say "y'all" are transplanted Texans.

Naturally, I found another Western miniseries evolving from new surroundings and experiences: a May Day snowstorm, a trip over Independence Pass with my heart in my mouth, a swim in the world's largest hot-springs pool at Glenwood Springs...and the exploits of an old gray mare renowned as an escape artist.

All these adventures and discoveries—and many more—ended up in the three Camerons of Colorado books about a ranching family chock-full of rugged individuals. I hope you'll enjoy the stories of Ben, Maggie and Julie, and then...who knows where my love of the West will lead?

Maybe... Hey, maybe Thom T. Taggart of Texas and Etta May Cameron of Colorado ought to get together! Or what about—

Sincerely,

Ruth Jean Dale

Ruth Jean Dale

KIDS, CRITTERS AND CUPID

Harlequin Books

TORONTO • NEW YORK • LONDON
AMSTERDAM • PARIS • SYDNEY • HAMBURG
STOCKHOLM • ATHENS • TOKYO • MILAN
MADRID • WARSAW • BUDAPEST • AUCKLAND

ISBN 0-373-70678-2

KIDS, CRITTERS AND CUPID

KIDS, CRITTERS
AND CUPID

CHAPTER ONE

BEN CAMERON HAD SEEN stranger sights than a Colorado snowstorm on the first day of May, but this was a snowstorm with a difference. Out of its swirling whiteness slipped and slid a red BMW. And out of the trees and into the road directly in front of the out-of-control toy leapt a wapiti—a good five hundred pounds of bull elk.

For a moment it looked as if critter and car would meet up close and personal. Then the vehicle veered sharply to the left and went into a skid that carried it past the animal frozen with shock in the middle of the road. Ben held his breath while the vehicle slid straight toward the glass front of the Rusty Spur Café. Half rising from his stool at the counter, he grabbed Joey's arm, prepared to shield the boy in the event of flying glass.

At the last moment, the driver managed to swing the front wheels in a hard right and the car skidded to an uncertain stop at the curb before the vulnerable glass front of the café. Ben let out a long low whistle of relief.

"Man!" he said to no one in particular. "That was too close for comfort."

Four-and-a-half-year-old Joey glanced up from his mug of hot chocolate but said nothing. The boy's lower lip still trembled and tears sparkled on his lashes in the aftermath of a visit to Doc Kunkle for booster shots. Not that Joey ever had much to say to his father, but Ben had hoped that a treat on the way home might have earned a smile at least.

Nancy Wyatt approached with coffeepot in hand. The fifty-something owner of the Rusty Spur wore her usual uniform: jeans, boots, a checkered shirt and a big white chef's apron. Salt-and-pepper hair framed her face in a short spiky style that made her look like an aging pixie.

"What?" She peered through the window and into the swirling snow, recoiling from what she saw. "Lord have mercy," she said. "It's a good thing you parked around on the side, Ben. That fool's pulled in parallel."

Ben grimaced. "Not *pulled* in, more like *slid* in. I think we got us somebody driving more car than he can handle in weather he knows nothing about. I'll go a step farther—dollars to doughnuts, that car's got California tags."

Pretty safe bet; Californians were invading Ben's Rocky Mountains in increasingly alarming numbers. They paid too much for everything they saw, made a big mess and then went home. At least, some of them still went back where they came from. Since that last big earthquake, too many were staying in Colorado. Few of them knew what they were getting into, he thought with disgust.

"I should take you up on that bet just to force you to eat one of my doughnuts," Nancy said with wry humor, "but I won't. Probably just another tourist lost on the way to Aspen or Vail." She reached for his coffee mug.

"No more, Nancy. I've got to get back home before Jason sends out a posse."

"Aw, take your time. Joey's not finished yet." She slipped the mug from beneath Ben's resisting hand and refilled it. "That brother of yours keeps tellin' all of us how indispensable he is. Let him prove it."

Beau Turner, the only other customer in the café this late morning, slid out of his booth and ambled toward the cash register at the curved end of the counter, where he plunked down a bill. His eyes were bloodshot in an earnest pug-nosed face. "Good eats, Miz Wyatt."

He accepted the change Nancy offered, his hand trembling noticeably. Extracting a toothpick from the metal holder near the cash register, he glanced at Ben. "Calving goin' okay at the Straight Arrow this year?"

Ben shrugged. "Not bad. Your place?"

Beau's shrug mirrored Ben's. "Like you say, not bad. 'Course, our operation's not as big as yours. And with Grandpa gone..."

Ben and everyone else in town knew Beau's grandpa was in prison, put there for robbing banks and sundry other criminal offenses. The Turners' Lazy T wasn't much to begin with, and it wasn't going to improve in the care of Beau and his old man.

Beau glanced out the window. "You figure this snow's gonna amount to much? Sure wouldn't do our young stuff any good was it to turn into a real honest-to-God spring blizzard."

"Nah," Ben predicted. "Won't even be any on the ground this time tomorrow. These big fat sloppy flakes never hang on long."

"Good. That's good." As if taking Ben's prediction for gospel, Beau headed for the door. "See you around, then."

Ben watched the man out, his gaze making a natural transition to the BMW still idling in front of the café amidst blowing snow and billowing clouds of steamy exhaust. The driver turned off the engine and climbed out, moving around the front of the car with caution—and that was when Ben realized the driver was a woman.

Opening the passenger door, she lifted a child out of the car before shoving the door closed with one knee. Holding the child's hand, she started toward the café.

Neither was dressed for the weather or anything remotely approximating it. The woman wore slacks, high-heel shoes and some kind of lightweight hip-length jacket. She was bare headed, and snow clung to her short blond hair. Stepping from the parking area onto the walkway leading to the covered entry, she slipped. For the space of a quick breath, Ben thought she was going to fall. At the last instant she caught her balance, even managing to hang on to the child's hand.

Her close call spurred Ben to action. Jumping to his feet, he hurried across the room and through the entryway with its wet rubber mats and newspaper vending boxes. When he threw open the outside door, the woman literally fell inside. Ben caught her against his chest, feeling the lightness of her body in his arms. For a moment she clung to him, panting.

With snow-dusted blond curls pressed against his chin, Ben sucked in a quick surprised breath redolent of summer meadows. His hands curved over the soft suede of her jacket as he tried to help her regain her balance.

He felt a quick flash of sympathy. She must have had a harrowing drive. When unexpected weather hit, these narrow mountain roads even scared locals. There was also a strong likelihood she was lost.

He ought to stand her up, tip his hat and escort her into the restaurant—but he found he was in no particular hurry to do that. Only when he felt her hands fumbling for a hold on his arms did he do so.

Upright once more, she drew in a breath that sounded loud in the chilly silence of the entry and looked at him with an expression of utter delight. "Isn't this wonderful?" she cried. "Snow on the first day of May!" Her voice had a tinkly, silvery quality; her smile dazzled him. "I feel as if I've just fallen down the rabbit hole and come out in Wonderland."

So did Ben. This woman was gorgeous. From the top of her curly dark blond hair to the tips of her silly high-heel shoes, she was gorgeous. There was an expensive sheen to her, an understated elegance that spoke of money and privilege—and another world.

"Thank you," she added when he simply stood there staring at her. "You just saved me from a nasty fall." She stamped her feet to dislodge the snow still clinging to her shoes. "Did you see that deer?" she asked. "It ran right in front of me."

"Wapiti," Ben corrected automatically.

"Really?" She frowned. "It sure looked like a deer." She hesitated, then suddenly smiled. "What's a wapiti?"

Ben liked the ingenuous way she said it. "Elk," he translated.

"No kidding! I'd have sworn it was a deer." She shook her head. "Shows you what I know about animals, I guess."

He wanted to reach out and brush away the melting snowflakes in her tousled hair, but had the good sense not to; touching strangers fell squarely into the "politically incorrect" category. Before he could get his wits together, the little girl, who looked to be a bit younger than Joey, spoke.

"Mama, it's c-c-cold out here!"

"It sure is, sweetheart." The woman gave Ben a final smile. "Thank you again," she said, and took the child's hand to lead her toward the inner door.

Ben leapt to open it for them. The warmth inside felt almost smothering after the cold outside. It carried with it the aroma of coffee and bacon and the soup simmering for lunch. While the little girl led her mother toward a booth on the right, Ben returned to his seat at the counter next to Joey.

But he couldn't help watching the woman while she took off the child's blue velvet coat and got her settled into the booth. The little girl clutched a teddy bear even more tattered than the one Joey had left outside in the truck.

"Who's that girl, Daddy?" Joey tugged on his father's sleeve. "Who, Daddy?"

Ben blinked in surprise. Joey rarely touched his father voluntarily. "I don't know." He reached out to ruffle the boy's silky hair, but Joey ducked aside. "Are you about done with your cocoa?" Ben asked, pushing back his disappointment. "Uncle Jason's gonna shoot us if we don't get on home soon."

Joey picked up his cup and drank, but he was watching the girl with the tattered teddy.

Nancy moved around the end of the counter, carrying two glasses of water and a menu. Her back to the curious duo at the counter, she plunked down the glasses, then spread the menu before the woman. "Coffee right away?" she suggested.

"Please." Now it was Nancy's turn to receive one of those radiant smiles. "And Lisa Marie would like...?" She looked at her young companion.

The little girl cocked her head to one side and her face took on a dreamy expression. "I believe I'll have...a Seven-Up with six cherries and five straws." She spoke very seriously.

The beautiful young woman responded with equal seriousness. "And I believe you'll have...a glass of milk."

The child's lower lip thrust out. "*Ma*-ma!"

Nancy grinned. "One coffee, one milk, five straws, four crayons and one coloring book coming right up."

She bustled away while Ben tried to stop staring as if he'd never seen a woman before. He needed to get back to the ranch, he reminded himself; yet when Nancy refilled his coffee cup, he didn't object.

His interest and curiosity were getting the best of him. Maybe the woman wasn't just passing through; maybe she was here on purpose. Maybe... Nah. If he'd ever seen a lost tourist, she was it.

Nancy was back, laying the promised items before the little girl. "Anything else I can get for either of you?" she inquired.

The woman hesitated. "It's too early for lunch, but we didn't really eat a proper breakfast before leaving Denver." She gave Nancy a quick smile. "Did I see pie on the counter when I came in?"

"Yes, but you don't want any."

"I don't?"

"Trust me on this." Nancy and Ben exchanged amused glances. "I baked it myself, and baking's not my thing, as the kids say. I put it up there to snare the unwary, and those who wouldn't know piecrust from cardboard."

"I see." She obviously didn't. "Sandwiches, then?"

Nancy beamed. "I do good sandwiches."

The woman turned to the child. "Would you like a hamburger, sweetheart?"

"Yes, please." The little girl looked up at Nancy. "With pickles, please, but no onions. I don't care for onions."

Nancy chuckled. "At your age, neither did I. Want some french fries with that, sugar?"

"No, thank you. French fries are bad for my cres-cres-cresteroil." Her tone turned confidential. "Besides, they burn my tongue."

Nancy's struggle not to laugh out loud was heroic. "Then I'll bring you potato chips," she cajoled.

"No, thank you." The kid wasn't budging. She knew exactly what she wanted and would settle for nothing more and nothing less.

"But—"

"No, thank you." The little girl wasn't rude, but she sure was determined.

Nancy shrugged. "Okeydoke." She turned her attention to the mother. "How about you, hon?"

"A turkey sandwich?"

It was a question and Nancy answered it as such. "I can do turkey."

"On whole-wheat toast?"

"I can do whole-wheat toast, too."

Nancy started to turn away, then looked back at the duo in the booth. "Are you by any chance from California?"

The beautiful blue eyes widened. "How did you guess?"

"Intuition, pure and simple."

Chuckling to herself, Nancy headed for the kitchen, visible beyond the pass-through behind the counter. Her exit left Ben more or less alone with this beautiful creature.

I really should go, he told himself again. *Snow's about let up and there's no need gettin' Jason any more worked up than he'll already be.* He glanced at Joey, too quiet as usual.

At least this time there was a reason. The boy and girl were eyeing each other with considerable interest and many shy smiles. Joey didn't warm up to many people, grown-ups *or* children. Now he seemed as taken with the daughter as Ben was with the mother.

Aw, stay a while. What harm could there be in hanging around a little longer? The woman and her daughter would eat lunch, then get up and drive away and that would be that. Ben wouldn't get any more opportunities to enjoy just looking at her like this. He'd be a fool to pass up the chance.

Swinging his stool around, he contemplated his coffee cup glumly. Things had come to quite a pass when the sight of a pretty woman left him this discombobulated. Didn't say much for his social life.

For several minutes he ignored her, just to prove to himself that he could. When he looked her way again, she was whispering to the little girl and pointing toward the rusty spur nailed over the doorway.

Her interest in her surroundings came through loud and clear. She kept pointing out details of the room, things the child couldn't possibly care less about: the sign hanging over one of the big tables on the opposite side of the room that declared Liars' Table; the moldy old deer head mounted along one wall; the rubber checks pasted to the cash register next to the huge jar of pennies Nancy collected for some charity or other.

Everything the woman saw in this ratty little mountain café seemed to enchant her, which didn't make much sense to Ben. She didn't belong here; she stood out in these surroundings like the proverbial sore thumb. He glowered into his cup, irritated at the direction his thoughts had taken.

She was something real special. So was that great big diamond and the wedding ring on her left hand.

Shame. *Damned* shame.

She glanced up from her sandwich, and her wide-eyed gaze locked with his narrowly assessing one. A beautiful stain of color brushed her cheeks, and she looked away.

To hell with this. Ben stood up and lifted Joey off the stool. "C'mon, sport," he muttered under his breath. "Let's go see if we can make some time."

HE'D BEEN FLIRTING with her ever since she'd entered the little restaurant, unaware he was wasting his time. He was a big good-looking guy, but she wasn't in the market for a man.

Still, she took casual note of his lean denim-clad body draped over a counter stool next to the little boy. This rough-hewn cowboy was different from any man she'd ever encountered, just by virtue of being comfortable and at home in this place.

For this was a place unlike any Betsy had ever been before. Everything about it fascinated her, from the spur nailed above the door—she thought the thing was a spur, with its leather strap and big dangerous-looking barbs—to the booths of many colors and tables of many sizes. Nothing matched, yet everything was clean and comfortable and inviting.

She liked it, even if she didn't understand why. She was glad she'd stopped. This small café in Cupid, Colorado, was as good a place as any to ask her questions. Not that she really expected to find any answers. This was a long shot and she knew it, but for once, she didn't intend to let that stop her.

She could hardly believe she was actually here, after thinking about it for what seemed like such a long time. Even if it didn't work out, at least she'd always know she'd tried.

"How do you do," Lisa Marie said calmly.

Betsy blinked, wondering what game her daughter was playing this time. But when she looked at Lisa, she saw the girl's gaze firmly focused on some spot beyond her mother's shoulder. Turning, Betsy found the cowboy standing beside their booth, one hand holding a spindle-backed chair and the other resting on the little boy's shoulder. He grinned, and his teeth, white and even, flashed in his sun-browned face. His eyes, she noticed, were an unusual shade of gray, almost the color of slate.

"If I'm out of line, just say so," he began, "but you looked like you might be lost or...or something. And since my boy here's been giving your little girl the eye,

I thought we might as well come on over and introduce ourselves like civilized folk and see if there's anything we can do for you."

"You're kidding. Are you kidding?" Betsy thought she'd never heard such a corny line in her life, but she also found it somehow endearing. "I'm sorry," she added hastily. "I don't mean to be rude. You did save me from a fall, and I did notice the children watching each other." *The adults, too.* "The least I can do is invite you to sit down."

"Thanks. Don't mind if I do." He swung the chair around so that it faced out and straddled the plastic cushion. Resting his arms across the chair back, he leaned forward. He wore a plaid shirt with the collar unbuttoned, faded jeans and boots that were scuffed and well-worn. His gaze, from those silvery eyes, was steady.

Betsy put down the last bite of her sandwich and smiled at the children. "Scoot over, darling," she urged her daughter, "and let your new friend sit down."

"Yes, Mama." Lisa did as she was told without a trace of the shyness that had plagued her mother from the cradle. "My name is Lisa Marie," she added. "But you can just call me Lisa."

The boy sat down gingerly on the very corner of the bench seat. "Lisa," he repeated.

She nodded approval. "I live in California, but we don't have much snow there. I like snow. Do you?"

The boy stared at her as if she were some fabulous alien creature, and Betsy noticed his eyes were the same unusual shade of gray as the man's.

Who now nudged his shoulder. "Tell her your name, Joey."

"Joey! I got a dog. His name's Killer."

Lisa's brows rose. "I have a pink pony," she said serenely. "I'd let you ride her, but she doesn't like boys. I do, but my pony doesn't. I have a teddy—do you have a teddy? I have a blanky, but Mama made me leave it in the car."

The man looked amazed. "She's a talker," he observed unnecessarily.

"Poor Joey may not be able to get a word in edgewise." Betsy smiled. "I'm Elizabeth Ross, but most people call me Betsy. You've already met my daughter."

The cowboy extended one big brown hand. "Glad to meet you, Betsy. My name's Ben Cameron and Joey's my son, in case you haven't guessed. Welcome to Cupid."

She looked down at his hand, strong and callused, then slipped her own into the cradle of his fingers. His grip was firm and somehow overpowering; she felt the heat all the way up to her elbow and quickly extracted her hand. "I'm happy to meet you," she said. "But you're wrong about me."

He raised his brows skeptically. "Wrong how?"

"About me being lost. I'm not. I was just . . . a little confused by the weather. I'm not used to driving in snow."

"No kidding."

She returned his smile. "Honest. I'm on my way to Aspen actually." True, as far as it went. "This is the right way, isn't it?"

"It's *one* way but not a particularly good one, especially when it's snowing. You're headed for Independence Pass, and I don't think you want to do that."

"I don't?"

"Nope, and I'll tell you why." He almost drawled the words. "Independence Pass is more than 12,000 feet above sea level, and it's closed more than it's open this time of year. Even if they let you through, which I doubt, you'd regret it unless you're an experienced mountain driver—which I'm fairly confident you aren't."

She knew he was referring to her undignified arrival. "It was the deer's fault," she reminded him.

"Wapiti. But elk'll be the least of your worries on that pass. We're talking shelf roads—you know what they are? Hairpin curves with sheer dropoffs on one side and solid rock straight up on the other." His eyes glinted with something that looked like certainty. "Nah, you don't wanna go through Independence Pass, even when it's not slick as glass with fresh snow. Trust me on that."

She did. Just hearing his description made her shiver. She didn't like mountain driving under the best of circumstances. In the middle of a blizzard . . .

She gave in quickly. "I'm convinced," she said. "I'd rather spend another night in Denver than do something stupid or dangerous."

His nod indicated approval. "Is anyone expecting you in Aspen?"

"Well . . . sort of."

"Husband?" His pointed glance went to her left hand and settled on the diamond sparkling there.

She felt a pang of regret and doubted she'd ever get over that reaction to questions concerning her marital status. "I'm a widow."

"Oh. I'm sorry."

"Thank you." That response always felt awkward, but what else could she say? Her husband had died a little more than a year ago. She wasn't exactly reconciled to it yet, although she thought she was doing all right—considering.

She shot Ben a veiled glance; he looked thoughtful, his face in repose lean and strong and attractive. She couldn't see a single soft thing about either his rugged features or broad-shouldered body, certainly not the sensitivity that had drawn her to Evan.

She wasn't accustomed to dealing with men like Ben Cameron. There was something elemental about him, as if subterfuge wasn't even in his vocabulary. Instinctively she felt he would be a man of strong opinions openly expressed. She stifled a smile. Maybe she just thought that was how a cowboy was supposed to be, since this man was cowboy-poster material.

The front door flew open, banging against the wall with a clatter. Both Ben and Betsy glanced toward the commotion to see a young woman enter, a very pretty woman with dark shoulder-length hair. She looked around the room, her gaze zeroing in on Ben.

A girlfriend? Betsy wondered, but better judgment soon prevailed. From similarities immediately apparent—the dark hair and sensual shape of the mouth—this woman had to be his sister.

The newcomer tossed her purple corduroy jacket in the general direction of the coat rack and rushed toward the booth. Behind her, several men also entered the café, moving to a big table to the left of the door, the one beneath the Liars' Table sign.

"Ben!" The young woman halted beside him, not even looking at the other occupants of the booth. "I've got something to—"

"Hang on, Julie." Ben indicated his companions. "I want you to meet Betsy Ross and her daughter, Lisa Marie. They're passing through on the way to—"

"Betsy Ross?" Julie did a double-take. "Shouldn't you be home making flags or something?"

Ben groaned; Betsy tried to rise above something she'd heard a hundred times before. Lisa, however, was equal to the occasion.

"How do you do?" she said politely. "Do you know my friend Joey?"

Julie laughed. "I should—I'm his aunt." She winked at Joey, who grinned and winked back with both eyes at once. "Hiya, kiddo. How's it going?" Turning her attention to Ben, she said, "I don't have all day, big brother. Gene's on the warpath and—"

"Gene's her boss," Ben said in an aside to Betsy. "He's the editor of the *Cupid Chronicles*. That's the—"

"Ben, listen to me! I said I'm in a hurry!"

"—local weekly newspaper. Julie's a reporter."

"How interesting." Betsy smiled at the fuming young woman. "I always thought it would be so glamorous to work for a newspa—"

"It's not. I mean, sometimes it is, but mostly it's just plain old hard work."

Joey had crawled onto his knees on the seat. "Aunt Julie, can you take me and Lisa to ride my pony?"

"Sure, but it'll have to be later, okay? I have something important to tell your daddy, and then I've got to get back to work." She sucked in a deep breath and glowered at her brother.

"All right, Julie," Ben said with exaggerated patience, finally giving her his full attention. "The floor's yours. It better be good."

"It is." Simultaneously she lifted her chin and thrust out her left hand, displaying what could only be an engagement ring on her third finger. Her eyes—brown, instead of Ben's gray—sparkled with challenge. "Scott came by the office a few minutes ago and gave me this. We're officially engaged! We're going to get married and move to Denver!''

Betsy forgot all about being a nonparticipant. Clapping her hands with pleasure, she cried, "Julie, that's wonderful! You have my very best wish—''

The rest was lost in Ben's roar as he rose from his chair like Godzilla emerging from the ocean depths.

CHAPTER TWO

"YOU'RE GOING to do *what?*"

Julie lifted her chin another notch, adding to an already belligerent stance. "I'm going to marry Scott Hale and move to Denver."

"Over my dead body!"

"Don't tempt me!"

"Damn it, Julie!" Ben thrust a hand through his hair, fighting the urge to grab her and shake some sense into her. She was even more hardheaded than Jason, her twin, which was saying something. "The guy's a sidewinder. He's just after—"

"Watch it, Ben. Don't say something you'll regret."

"Sweetheart, you're the one who's going to regret it if you fall for this guy's line. Scott Hale is just another out-of-town opportunist cluttering up the landscape."

"He's the man I love and intend to marry! I'm twenty-one, an adult!"

"In the eyes of the law, maybe." Ben stood up abruptly, trying to overwhelm her with the force of his utter certainty. She was his baby sister and he loved her, but sometimes . . . "Julie," he said, "you don't really want to marry this guy. I don't know what the hell you *do* want, but whatever it is, there are better ways to get it than this."

She fell back a step. "You don't know anything about it. Scott proposed and I said yes. I *am* going to marry him. There's not a thing in the world you can do to stop me, so don't try."

"You tell 'im, Julie!"

Ben cast a sour glance at the leering cowboy seated on a stool at the counter, one of several who'd entered in the past few minutes, but the only one overtly listening. Johnny King was a wise guy just begging to be taken down a peg or two.

He must have seen that thought on Ben's face, for he hunched his shoulders and swiveled back around on his stool. Satisfied there'd be no further interference, Ben returned to the fray.

Too late, for all he saw of Julie was the purple flash of her jacket as she bolted out of the Rusty Spur. Disgruntled, Ben stared after her. One thing he didn't need was a new crisis with yet another member of his family. He was already involved in an ongoing clash of wills with Jason. Then there was his brother-in-law, Chuck Colby, a paraplegic whose health problems kept older sister Maggie at her wit's end.

Grandma was the only Cameron Ben didn't have to worry about—so far, anyway.

Turning toward Betsy with an apology on his lips, he saw her expression of disapproval. He straddled his chair again. "Sorry about that," he said. "Julie's got a short fuse sometimes."

Betsy's extraordinarily revealing blue eyes opened wider. "And you don't?"

"Hey," he objected, deliberately mild in his desire to return to their former friendly footing, "I'm head of the Cameron family. It's my duty to save my sister from herself."

"You don't think you were a little...heavy-handed? I know it's none of my business but..."

She hesitated, chewing on that full lower lip, and Ben said, simply to prolong the conversation, "What makes *you* different from everybody else? You're entitled to your opinion. Go ahead and say your piece."

"I'm not sure I should." She was very calm. "I mean, I don't know any of the background—"

"True."

"—and first impressions aren't always correct—"

"Also true."

"—but I had the very strong impression that your sister didn't really *expect* you to approve of her engagement in the first place."

Ben grinned. "Perceptive, aren't you?"

Her delicate brows arched. "Sometimes it's easier for an outsider to see what's really going on. You were pretty hard on her."

"Do tell." It was almost worth a fight with his sister to see Betsy play peacemaker.

"If you don't mind my asking, what have you got against this Scott—what was his name?"

"Hale." Ben's mouth curved down. "Scott Hale. You mean besides the fact that he's a phony bast—" He glanced at the children, busily scribbling on the coloring book Nancy had provided. "Phony opportunist?"

"Is he? Julie doesn't seem to think so."

"What does she know? She's only twenty-one years old, for Pete's sake. Too young to know when to come in out of the rain. Hale came big-dealin' it into town last year to open up a video store with his old man's bucks, drivin' a big car and throwing money around like he had it to burn. He's made moves on half the women in town. I was afraid sooner or later he'd work his way around to Julie, and he did."

"He must care for her," Betsy suggested, "or he wouldn't have asked her to marry him."

"He cares all right, about getting her into—" Again he stopped short with another meaningful glance at the kids. "This probably isn't the best time to discuss it," he said. "Not that I'm trying to hide anything. Hell, my life's an open book."

"Apparently your opinions are, too." With a wry smile, she dropped her paper napkin beside her plate. "I really do apologize for speaking out of turn. It's just that..." Just that like Julie, Betsy had had to fight for the man she loved, and she'd been younger than Ben's sister at the time.

Ben leaned forward. "Any chance you'll be hanging around Cupid for a while? I'd sure like to discuss this further."

"Oh, I don't think I'll—"

Nancy's voice interrupted her. "Anything else I can get you folks? More coffee? Dessert? Like I said, I can't recommend the pie, but I've got some bread pudding that's not half-bad.'' Gathering up cups and plates, she waited.

For Betsy, it was time to do or die. She must either speak up or pay her check, get back into her car and drive away. If she did that, she'd never know what might have been.

Her heart seemed to stand still, and she suddenly felt deathly cold. This didn't seem like a good time to bring it up, she thought a little frantically. The place was filling with lunchtime traffic and Nancy was obviously busy, even with the help of a couple of newly arrived teenaged girls.

Lisa stifled a yawn and looked at her mother with drowsy blue eyes. She could sleep in the car on the return to Denver, Betsy thought. This definitely wasn't the time to dredge up personal matters.

But if not now, when?

"I...I'd like the check please," she murmured, "and maybe..."

Ben and Nancy watched, waiting for Betsy to go on.

With a conscious act of will, she did. "...a little information? I wonder if either of you have ever heard of a woman named Joanne Thayer?"

Nancy gasped and all the color washed out of her face, the dishes in her hands wobbling dangerously. Ben took them from her and set them on the table, his glance concerned.

Nancy licked her lips, her gaze intent on Betsy's face. "You know Joanne?"

"She was my mother."

Nancy looked as if she was about to crumble. Ben stood and guided the woman into his chair, then squeezed in beside Joey. He looked as serious as Nancy did.

"Was," Nancy repeated. "That must mean she's...?"

Betsy nodded. "She died several years ago. I recently learned... I have reason to believe she might have lived here in Cupid at one time. I'd hoped to find someone who knew her—and I guess I have?"

Nancy's shoulders slumped. "You have," she whispered. She looked around almost helplessly. Nearly a dozen people were in various stages of dining: some ordering, some waiting for food or service, some already eating. "We can't talk here," she said.

Ben placed one big hand on Nancy's trembling shoulder. "Sure you can. With all these people around, you won't be so likely to come unglued. Your helper can handle the customers, Nancy. In fact—" he slid out of the booth "—why don't I take the kids out and let them build a snowman before this all melts? You'd like that, wouldn't you, Joey?" He lifted the boy out of the booth and stood him on his miniature cowboy boots.

Joey looked doubtful, but Lisa's blue eyes sparkled. "I would!" she cried. "Can I, Mama? Can I help build the snowman?"

Betsy's doubts must have shown on her face, for Ben gave her a rueful grin.

"Yeah, yeah," he said, "I know what you're thinking. What if this guy is some kind of nut case?

How about if the law vouches for me? Would that ease your mind?'' His gaze lifted. "Hey, Dwight!" he yelled. "Tell this lady I'm a man to be trusted!"

A bulky man sitting at the counter with his back toward them swiveled around on his stool. A bright silver badge gleamed on his shirtfront. "Whatcha bothering me for, Ben?" he demanded plaintively. "Can't a man eat his dinner in peace?"

"Just as soon as you vouch for me."

"Okay, I'm vouchin'. Now lemme eat." Dwight returned to his plate.

Ben gave Betsy an encouraging grin. "We'll be right out there." He gestured at the snow on the other side of the glass wall. "You'll be able to see us the whole time."

"Please, Mama, please?"

Joey added his entreaties. "Please, please?"

Nancy, who still looked distracted, nodded. "It's all right, really. Little pitchers do have big ears."

Betsy gave in with a sigh. "Okay, but stay where I can see her," she requested of Ben. She wasn't entirely comfortable with this arrangement but saw no way to avoid it.

Lisa pulled on her coat and Betsy buttoned it. "She doesn't have any gloves," she fretted. "Maybe this isn't such a good—"

"Joey's got extras in the truck." Ben said quickly. He herded the children toward the door. "Trust me, you got nothin' to worry about."

When the two women saw Ben and the kids happily packing snow just outside the café, Nancy turned to

Betsy and drew a deep shuddering breath. "You don't really look like her," she said faintly. "And yet there's something . . . that reminds me of her."

A great feeling of relief washed over Betsy. If nothing else came of this, not one single additional shred of information, she'd still count her detour through Cupid a success. "Then you knew her," she said. "You knew my mother."

"I knew her," Nancy agreed. "Joanne Thayer was my little sister." She reached across the table to touch Betsy's hand tentatively. "Now tell me everything, before I start bawlin' like a baby."

WHERE TO BEGIN? For a moment Betsy stared out the plate-glass window, trying to gather her thoughts. The sun was shining, to her amazement. Everything around here seemed upside down: snow and sunshine, strangers who felt like friends. For another moment she watched Ben show Joey and Lisa how to add snow to a mound he'd started, their attempts more enthusiastic than useful. It looked like a photo on a Christmas card: too good to be true.

"Honey, talk to me."

Betsy had to respond to the plea in the woman's voice. "I found out recently that my mother might have grown up here in Cupid," she began slowly. "I thought if I came here, I might find relatives, at least someone who'd known her or her family."

"Found out recently?" Nancy didn't look disbelieving so much as shocked.

Betsy nodded. "I thought Mother was my only family, and when she died, I never dreamed there was anyone else." Emotion almost choked her, and it was a moment before she could go on. "I'm an only child. My father died before I was born—"

"In California?"

"Yes. I thought my mother had been born in California, too. She told me she had no family, and I assumed that made her an orphan."

"How did you . . . ?"

"Something happened." Betsy bit her lip. "It's so complicated!"

"Take your time, honey. Just start at the beginning and tell me everything."

Nancy appeared to have herself under strict control now. She squeezed Betsy's hand, a gesture filled with more warmth and kindness than Betsy could ever remember receiving from her mother. The people coming in and out of the Rusty Spur knew Nancy, seemed to like her. Betsy knew instinctively that this woman could be trusted.

Still, it was an effort to go on, for she wasn't accustomed to talking about her family. "My mother never told me much about herself. I'm not even sure she told either of my stepfathers about her life before they met her."

"I hope they were good to you," Nancy said fiercely.

Betsy shrugged. "In a negligent sort of way, but I was never really close to either of them. The first one owned a chain of dry cleaners and was quite . . . well-off." What he'd been was rich, which was why Joanne had married him, but loyalty forbade Betsy from saying that. "Mother remarried six months after he died." She'd had to; he'd left everything to his first family.

"When . . ." Now Nancy seemed to be the one having difficulty finding words. She stared down at the scarred tabletop. "When did your mother die?"

"Six years ago, of a brain aneurysm."

Nancy wasn't even breathing. Someone called her name but she didn't seem to hear it.

After a moment, Betsy went on. "My husband died in an accident a little more than a year ago. After that, it was just Lisa Marie and me. I thought that's how it would always be until a few weeks ago." *A few weeks?* It still stunned her to realize how much and how quickly everything had changed. "My second stepfather contacted me. He was moving and had come across a box of Mother's old letters and papers."

"Ah." It was a sound of understanding.

Betsy nodded. "I found a letter from one of her closest friends, a woman named Holly Nelson. There was a lot of idle chitchat, but one paragraph . . ."

Reaching for her purse, she pulled out a creased envelope and extracted a letter. She knew the contents by heart, but she needed the prop. Half-reading, half-reciting from memory, she shared the fateful message: "'I always admired the way you knew what you wanted, then went out and got it, Joanne. For a girl from a little burg like Cupid, Colorado, you've done all right for yourself.'"

Nancy looked stunned; Betsy knew the feeling. She'd been more than stunned the first time she'd read those words. "I'd never even heard Mother *mention* Colorado," she said. "I tried to find Mrs. Nelson, but she'd moved and I hit a dead end."

Still, that old letter had opened some exquisite possibilities. Betsy, who'd longed for family, who'd fantasized about being part of a large and loving group, might have somebody somewhere, after all, somebody to whom she was connected by blood.

But what if she got her hopes up for nothing? Wouldn't she be better off to play it safe and forget the whole thing?

For days she'd vacillated, trying to decide what to do. Since Evan's death, she'd been forced to travel a long way toward independence, for she'd gone from a mother's domination to a husband's care without missing a beat. Her reaction to that unexpected letter told her too clearly that she still had a long way to go.

Then two things happened to spur her into action: a complicated situation with one of Evan's fans and an invitation from a friend to visit Aspen. It was clearly time to make a new start, so she'd left California—not for Cupid, not for Aspen, but for Denver. There she'd spent several days trying to screw up her courage.

Now it was too late for second thoughts. Lifting her head, she looked at Nancy. "I guess this means you're my aunt?"

And because she was staring straight into the woman's eyes, she saw the tears well up.

"I sure am, honey," Nancy said in a gravelly voice, "and that's not all—my husband John's your uncle. We never had any kids of our own so you'll forgive me if I... if I'm feeling a little... emotional."

Betsy nodded, feeling emotional herself. Suddenly she understood why Ben had suggested they talk right here in the middle of the bustling restaurant. Otherwise, she felt sure she'd have collapsed into a sodden mass by now.

She wasn't alone anymore. She had family. Everything was going to be all right.

I SHOULD HAVE KNOWN, Nancy castigated herself; *I should have known*. There was something about Betsy, some connection that Nancy had felt from the minute the young woman had walked into the café. She'd pushed it aside, vaguely intrigued but passive. Reaching across the booth for a paper napkin, she dabbed at damp eyes and then blew her nose.

"Lord, you must think I'm a basket case," she croaked. "I just realized—you said your little girl's name is Lisa Marie?"

Betsy, under control again, nodded. She, too, wiped wet cheeks with a paper napkin, but her smile was radiant.

"Do you realize she's named for your grandmother—her great-grandmother?"

Betsy's damp eyes opened wider. "My grandmother is named Lisa?"

Nancy laughed. "Marie. Your grandmother's name was Marie Thayer. It's such a shame you didn't get a chance to know her. She never gave up hope that someday Joanne would come back home." She lifted Betsy's hand and planted a kiss on the knuckles. "But you want to hear about your mother?"

"Yes, and then I want to hear about everyone else. This is so overwhelming. I never dreamed..." Betsy's face glowed. "I was afraid to let myself hope for too much. I kept telling myself that if I just found someone who knew my mother, I'd be happy. But to find an aunt! It's like a dream come true. So yes, I want to hear about my mother, and then I want to hear about you and my grandmother and everybody else."

Nancy wished she had a happier story to tell. "Well, for starters, Joanne ran away from home when she was eighteen," she said. "She'd been threatening to do it for a long time, said over and over that when she did that was it, we'd never see or hear from her again. She made good her word."

"But—" Betsy frowned "—why?"

Just like Holly's letter said, Nancy thought. Because Joanne knew what she wanted and wasn't going to let anyone stand in her way: not an anxious mother, not a strict and unforgiving father. Certainly not the mores of a little nothing town like Cupid.

Nancy chose her words with care. "Why did she run away? I almost think it was inevitable. She never belonged here—hated the town, thought the people were hicks. She was in hot water constantly with Dad, which was a strain on all of us. There's no denying that he was hard on her, but there are two sides to that story. He just had strong notions of right and wrong. Oh, the fights they had!''

Betsy frowned. ''That's really hard for me to imagine,'' she confessed, ''my mother fighting with anybody—I mean, anybody fighting with her. My stepfathers sure didn't, and neither did I. It just wasn't permitted. Now I find out...'' She shook her head, clearly puzzled.

''Sounds to me like Joanne grew up to be just like our father,'' Nancy suggested. ''He didn't want to permit it, either. Anyway, Joanne took off right after she graduated from high school. Dad wouldn't even let us mention her name after that, but Mom never stopped hoping she'd come back someday. In fact—'' how could she have forgotten? ''—when Mother died last year, she left the Rusty Spur to both her daughters.''

Betsy laughed incredulously and looked around the room. ''You mean my mother is part owner of this place?''

''That's right, or would be if she were alive. As it is—'' Nancy squeezed Betsy's forearm ''—congratulations, Betsy. You're the new owner of one-half of a slightly down-on-its-luck café in the Colorado Rockies.''

Betsy smiled at her newfound aunt. ''You don't have to do that. My mother died before *her* mother. Legally—''

"Who's talking legal?" Nancy looked affronted. "I'm talking *intent*. Your grandma would've wanted you to have your mother's share. Shoot, Betsy, she knew Joanne wouldn't have any use for a little hole-in-the-wall like this. It was a token of her love and forgiveness. Now her share is yours, and no back talk."

"But—"

There was a sudden pounding on the window. Betsy gave a start, momentarily confused. She felt drained, emotionally and physically, by Nancy's revelations; the interruption was welcome. She turned to see Ben, holding both children up to the glass. Lisa and Joey were gesturing excitedly.

Then she saw why. A snowman, or a reasonable facsimile of one—actually more a mound of snow—stood beside them, Joey's small cowboy hat planted on its head. The eyes were quarters, the mouth a happy curve of shiny pennies. Betsy grinned and nodded her appreciation.

Nancy motioned the trio inside. "We'll talk more later," she promised Betsy, lifting a corner of her apron to dry her eyes one final time. "My goodness, I feel limp as a wet dishrag."

Betsy did, too, but she knew that when all this sunk in it would be worth the emotional upheaval.

Ben herded the two kids over to the booth. "Sorry to disturb you, but they wanted to show you their masterpiece—and Joey needs to use the toilet."

Betsy slid around in her seat to make room. Little Joey was hopping up and down, his expression desperate. Nancy waved him on and the boy darted past.

Ben smiled at Betsy but spoke to Nancy with exaggerated innocence. "So how's it goin'?"

Nancy laughed. "Say hello to my niece."

Ben didn't seem surprised. "So that's how it is," he said. "Congratulations, Nancy. Looks like you got yourself a good one."

"That's the way it looks to me, too," Nancy agreed.

Betsy bit her lip. This was too much; she felt overwhelmed by the sheer improbability of it all. She'd almost turned back a dozen times during the hair-raising drive from Denver, stopping at the Rusty Spur only because she'd lost control of her car. Now that all seemed part of some greater plan to bring her here to this place and these people.

A faint smile curved Ben's mouth. "You all right about this?" he asked Betsy.

"More than all right." She must look silly, smiling so broadly her face hurt, but she couldn't seem to stop.

"Does this mean you'll be staying around for a while, after all?"

"I can't." That effectively wiped away her smile. "Aspen—"

"Aspen?" Nancy interrupted. "I thought that was just something you said because you didn't know what was going to happen here."

"I really *am* on my way to visit a friend," Betsy said firmly.

Ben leaned over the back of her seat. "I wasn't kidding about Independence Pass, Betsy. Chances are it's closed. Even if it's not, a tenderfoot like you's got no business tackling it. Hang around a few days, at least long enough to let them clear the road."

"Yes," Nancy inserted swiftly. "You're coming home with me and that's that."

"I couldn't." Alarmed, Betsy shook her head. She wasn't accustomed to putting people out, even people she knew. And despite her conversation with Nancy and the revelations that had come with it, she really didn't *know*.

But she did want to stay in Cupid, rather than return to Denver, she admitted to herself. "Cupid wouldn't have a motel or hotel?" she ventured.

Nancy gave an undignified snort. "No, but you don't need one. If you think I'd let any niece of mine stay at a motel, you've got another think coming."

Betsy frowned. "Please, I wouldn't feel right. We don't know each other yet. I just can't move in on you. I ... I'd feel more comfortable if there was someplace else I could stay."

"There is." Ben's announcement got their attention; he looked extraordinarily pleased with himself.

"Where?" Betsy asked.

"Right here."

She looked around, frowning. "In the restaurant?"

Nancy's face brightened. "Of course! I'm so rattled I'm not thinking. There's a bedroom in back here, just a little one but pleasant enough. Mom was always taking in strays, and she had it fixed up for those she wanted to help—but not enough to take home with her." She laughed. "She used it herself a time or two, when she was just too worn out to drag herself home."

"I really don't think—"

Joey had returned during the exchange and he suddenly said, his gaze on Betsy, "You're pretty."

"I... Why, thank you, Joey." Disconcerted but pleased, she smiled at the boy. He was a smaller version of his father, though there was something waiflike about him, too.

The boy shuffled his feet, but his gaze didn't waver. "M-my mama is pretty like you," he said in a painful whisper.

Ben sucked in a sharp breath. Joey's eyes flew wide and he retreated a step.

Betsy reached out and touched the little boy's cheek with gentle fingers. "What a nice thing to say," she told him softly.

Lisa sidled up to take his hand. "Let's go build another snowman," she suggested. "I never did that before and it's fun."

Joey glanced at his father uncertainly.

"Sorry." Ben sounded as if he really meant it. "Joey and I have to get on back to the ranch." He held out one hand, and after the slightest of hesitations, Joey took it. For a moment, Ben looked down at the boy's head with a sort of puzzled exasperation on his face. Then he smiled at Betsy. "I hope we get a chance to finish that conversation."

"We'll see." It was the best she could do, for she had no idea whether they would ever meet again.

Or even whether she wanted them to, since there wasn't a chance that anything could come of it.

CHAPTER THREE

THE STRAIGHT ARROW RANCH lay north of Cupid, the first five miles by paved two-lane road and the next seven on a narrow, winding dirt ranch road now dusted with snow. Ben drove quickly but carefully. He knew every inch of this road, every bump and pothole and turn, but he was still surprised when a battered old Ford pickup shot out into his path from the side road leading to the Turners' Lazy T.

"Son of a—!" Swerving, he managed to miss Newt Turner by a whisker. Newt waved cheerfully and didn't slow down. With a quick glance at Joey, Ben suppressed the desire to call down curses on the man's head and drove on.

Helluva strange day so far.

He rounded a curve in the road, and the red-roofed ranch buildings eased into view in the valley below. Ben smiled; he always smiled when he came back home, whether he'd been gone an hour or a week. He reckoned Camerons had been smiling at this sight since the first one came into the valley to homestead in 1887.

That had been Great-grandfather Robert, soon joined by Great-granduncle William. Putting together a herd, they'd built their own small cattle empire, selling beef without favoritism to miners and to the Indian Agency feeding the Utes run off the land by those same miners. Robert married and settled in for the duration; William eventually headed west, finally settling in Montana.

Robert was succeeded by his son, Grandpa Henry, whose widow, Etta May, still ruled the roost at the Arrow at the age of seventy-plus—she declined to be more exact. Grandma Cameron had outlived her husband and three children, including Ben's father, Glenn. Ben was head of the family now—had been since he was a button. Joey represented the fifth generation of Camerons on this land. When Ben thought of how close he'd come to never even knowing his son...

Joey shifted restlessly on the seat, and Ben saw the boy slip his thumb into his mouth. He started to say something but caught himself. Seemed like everybody in the world was united in the opinion that the less said about that particular bad habit, the better.

His gut tightened. He wanted desperately to reach Joey, but everything he did seemed wrong. What the hell was he going to do about his son? And Julie and Jason and...

The whole family seemed to be in a constant uproar. If they didn't have Ben to keep their feet on the ground, who knew what would happen to them, or to the Straight Arrow?

Ben drove across the small bridge spanning Horseshoe Creek, which marked the southern edge of the ranch compound. The road led between the main corral on the right and outbuildings on the left—bunkhouse and calving sheds, animal barns and pens. Everything looked solid and enduring to his critical eye and gave him a deep feeling of satisfaction.

He had preserved all this, made it better. He hadn't done it alone, but it had been *his* responsibility and he'd accepted it. No one was ever going to mess with what was his.

Pulling the truck up in front of the long porch fronting the two-story ranch house, he unbuckled his seat belt, threw open the door and jumped out. It took Joey a couple of minutes of fumbling but then he, too, with Ben's help, climbed out the driver's side. Without a word, the boy ran past his father and up the broad wooden steps to the front door.

Ben didn't follow immediately, just stood there looking up at the piney mountain rising behind the house, the trees providing a lush backdrop for the reddish brown log building with its spiffy white trim and red roof. Sometimes the possessiveness he felt for this land, this ranch, this way of life almost scared him. If everybody could know what it was like, feel the way he did, Colorado would be as crowded as California. Shivering, he put his head down and followed his son up the steps.

He hadn't even made it across the screened porch when a voice called from inside. "That you, Ben?"

"Nah, it's the Lone Ranger, Granny." He stepped into the living room and closed the door behind him. "Of course it's me. Who else would it be?"

Granny stood in the kitchen doorway to the right. She was nothing like the typical sweet little old grandma. At five foot seven, Etta May Lang Cameron was taller than either of her granddaughters and twice as feisty. Her face had only a few lines, and her dark hair only a few strands of white.

She grinned at her grandson and said, "Smart ass."

Ben scowled. "Watch your language." He cast a significant glance at Joey, struggling out of his jacket.

"Oh, pshaw!" Granny threw up her hands. "Come along, Joey. I've got a cookie and a glass of milk in here with your name on 'em." Together they disappeared into the kitchen.

The squeak of a wheelchair in the hallway to the left announced the approach of Chuck Colby, Maggie's husband. A former truck driver, Chuck had suffered a spinal injury in a fiery freeway pileup less than a year after he'd married the oldest of the Cameron kids. That had been ten long years ago, years he'd spent in a wheelchair with Maggie doing her best to take care of him and keep his spirits up. The doctors had told her straight out that he'd never walk again, but she'd refused to believe them, refused to let Chuck believe them. If you wanted a thing bad enough, and if you worked hard enough, you could get it, she insisted.

Maggie worked hard, all right, and she made Chuck work hard, too. But as time passed and the efforts went for naught, even she had to admit that in this case, hard work, grit and determination could not do the impossible. Chuck was an invalid and always would be. There would be no miracle for Chuck and

Maggie Colby. Accepting that truth made Chuck a bitter man, Maggie a resigned woman.

Now Chuck steered his chair through the doorway and stopped. He'd been a big, bold, broad-shouldered man before the accident, but today at thirty-five, he looked almost wizened, shrunken to fit his rolling prison.

Ben shrugged out of his jacket and tossed his hat onto the coat tree near the entryway. "Maggie around?"

"Nah. She got called in."

Maggie was a schoolteacher who rarely taught. Chuck didn't like her to be gone day after day, so for the past several years she'd been on call for substitute work at Cupid Elementary School.

"Seen Jason?"

"Just for a minute. He was swearin' a blue streak. He's not a happy camper, Benny-boy. He said he's workin' his tail off while you lollygag in town. They put a coupla calves in the hot box, and he was havin' a high old time trying to get some milk into 'em. Said he'd give it one more try, but if they don't catch on, they're goners."

"Two?" This was serious. Two premature calves in the incubator could also mean two dead cows. If the babies didn't make it, that could be four head lost. He'd hoped for a ninety- to-ninety-five percent survival rate for this year's calf crop, but now he doubted that would be possible. A calf born in snow or wind could freeze to death in minutes. But with no more snow than there'd been this morning, and temperatures no colder, he hadn't really expected much of a problem.

The front door flew open and Jason stomped inside. At twenty-one, he was maybe an inch shorter than his older brother—who was well over six feet in his boots—but had the same broad shoulders and big hands.

"So where've you been?" Jason yanked off his hat and jacket. "We been busier than one-armed paperhangers around here, calves droppin' like flies and running us ragged."

"Pressure gettin' to you, little brother?" Ben had been about to head for the stock barn, but if he'd still been needed there, Jason would've said so first off. Ben wouldn't insult his brother by checking up on the condition of the calves.

"You wish." Jason crossed the room to the massive stone fireplace, set catercorner against the far wall. Holding out his hands to the crackling blaze, he spoke with pride. "We got it under control. We got us two dogies, twins. One'll make it for sure. The other..." He shrugged. "If he's still hangin' in tomorrow, we got at least a fighting chance of pulling 'im through."

Ben nodded. Jason saw that gesture for what it was: approval. It was enough.

Jason glanced at Joey, who'd just come out of the kitchen with his ragged teddy bear in one hand and a cookie in the other. "Did the boy get his shots?"

"Yeah."

"Take all day, did it? I know doc's gettin' old, but that's slow even for him."

Ben gave his brother a shuttered glance. "We stopped by the Spur."

"So? That doesn't take all day, either. Something going on there?"

Ben was strangely reluctant to tell him. It was too complicated: Betsy, her daughter, their relationship to Nancy Wyatt—not to mention the bombshell Julie had dropped. He didn't feel like answering a lot of questions about any of it until he'd had time to think, maybe have a little talk with Maggie, his usual confidante.

So he said noncommittally, "The Spur was quiet. Joey was a big boy when he got his shots, hardly cried at all. I thought he earned a treat."

Jason grinned at his nephew. "Is that right, sport? Were you a big boy?"

Joey nodded slowly.

"In that case," Jason began, "maybe I'll take you with me when I—"

He was interrupted by Julie. She came bounding through the door with eyes already alight with the glow of combat. "Did he tell you?" she demanded of her twin while stripping off her jacket.

"Did who tell me what?"

"About my engagement!"

Julie thrust out her hand with its newly acquired diamond.

"Uh-oh." Jason glanced at his brother as if expecting an explosion.

Julie ignored the storm clouds gathering on Ben's face. "Granny, Granny!" She ran to the kitchen door. "Come see my engagement ring!" She whirled on Ben. "And as for you, brother dear..."

"As for me, what?" Ben picked up another log and tossed it on the fire, where it landed with a crash of sparks. "You already know how I feel about—"

"*And as for you,* who was that woman you were with at the Spur? You been holding out on us, *Ben*-jamin?"

"What woman?" Jason's eyebrows shot up.

"Nobody," Ben said, his voice a warning growl.

"Ha!" Julie tossed her head. She spoke to Jason, ignoring Ben. "Midtwenties, real cute if you like the fancy blond-and-blue-eyed type."

"I do, I do," Jason said enthusiastically.

"Was that her kid?" Julie demanded of Ben.

Jason's face fell. "She's got a kid?"

"Yes, her daughter," Ben said.

"I'm not too crazy about kids," Jason muttered doubtfully, "except for Joey of course. She'd have to be awful cute for me to overlook my convictions on that score."

Julie looked appalled. "Jason," she said to her twin, "you are *weird.*"

We're all weird, Ben thought, listening to them argue. The Cameron family was one big mostly happy and rambunctious bunch of rugged individualists— but they were weird. Sometimes he thought they'd rather fight than eat, and sometimes those fights were physical as well as verbal. Nevertheless, he loved and felt totally responsible for every single one of them.

IT DIDN'T SEEM possible to Betsy that she, who had eaten in some of the world's finest restaurants and even studied briefly at the International Institute of the Culinary Arts of America, was suddenly half owner of a little hole-in-the-wall diner—or that it pleased her so much. The Rusty Spur was an anachronism in her frame of reference, opening every morning at six and closing every afternoon at two, or whenever the last of the lunch crowd left.

Nancy explained. "When Mom was alive, she kept the place open until seven or eight most nights, but I just don't have that kind of commitment. I'd probably have closed it for good by now if the town didn't need it so much." She finished washing down the counter and looked at her newly acquired niece. "Besides, this place was Mom's pride and joy. It was her salvation after Dad died."

"How so?" Seated at the counter, Betsy paused in the task of refilling an odd assortment of napkin holders, everything from orange plastic to stainless steel.

"This place was *her* dream." Nancy leaned her elbows on the counter. "It wasn't Dad's, so she had to wait until he was dead to go for it."

"I'm all in favor of people going for their dreams," Betsy said. "Did..." She couldn't call a man she hadn't known existed a few hours ago "Grandfather," so she substituted, "Did your father have a dream?"

Nancy shrugged. "Who knows? When Joanne and I were kids, he ran a little grocery store over on Third Street, where the feed store is now. Mom helped out, of course, and so did I when I got older."

"And my mother—did she help out, too?" Betsy had never been able to talk about her mother with anyone who'd known her in her youth. It felt strange even to ask the questions.

Nancy laughed. "What do you think?"

"I think she'd have hated it."

"You're right. Joanne didn't want anything to do with the store. It was just one more thing for her and Dad to fight about. He'd accuse her of thinking she was too good to work there, and she'd just laugh and say he was absolutely right—she *was* too good. For a while, she did have a job at the soda fountain on Main Street, though, where the Rocky Pizza Place is now."

Unable to imagine her mother ringing up groceries or stocking shelves, Betsy could easily see her concocting ice-cream sodas and flirting.

"Mom didn't much care for the grocery business, either," Nancy said. "She never told Dad, but the first thing she did after he died was sell the store and buy this place. She loved to cook and she loved to talk. Everybody in the county knew her and loved her, and they came to her for a lot more than food. She handed out advice and comfort, and even a dollar or two in a pinch."

Betsy closed a napkin dispenser. "I wish I'd known her," she said with a sigh. "I wish she'd known Lisa." She glanced at her daughter, seated in a booth with a box of straws and several dispensers. Lisa worked with a concentration far beyond her barely-four years.

"So do I, honey. So do I." Nancy cleared her throat. "Come on, I want to take you two home and feed you a good supper."

"All right." Feeling shy, Betsy closed the final napkin holder and slid off her stool. "May I see the bedroom here before we go?"

"Sure thing." Nancy led the way to the back, past the kitchen and down a short hallway. "This whole area used to be storage," she explained, "but I can't tell you how many people have slept here since Mom converted one corner into a bedroom. Like I said, it's small but comfortable."

She opened a door to the left of the exit and waved Betsy inside. The room, not more than ten by ten, had space for a double bed, a footlocker and a narrow chest of drawers. Everything was clean and bright, the walls painted a cheerful yellow, which matched the predominant color in the piecework quilt serving as a bedspread. The single window had both a roller shade and cheery yellow-and-white curtains, assuring privacy.

Betsy, who'd dreaded finding a closet with wall-to-wall bed, was relieved. A night or two here wouldn't be so bad.

They left the café by the back door. Betsy, holding Lisa's hand while Nancy locked up, looked around with disappointment. The snow was disappearing, leaving the streets wet and shiny. A few white patches remained beneath trees and in the shade of buildings, but that was about all.

Nancy made sure everyone was securely belted in before starting her minivan. "I thought I'd give you a quick tour of the town on the way home," she announced. "I actually only live a few blocks from here, so we'll take the long way."

Pulling out of the parking lot, she turned left, then made a quick right. "This is Main Street," she announced, "such as it is. The rumor that we roll up the sidewalks at nine each night is a bald-faced lie. We don't roll 'em up till ten."

Betsy had expected a sleepy little village, but Cupid bustled with pickup trucks and cars of all ages and descriptions, some parked nose-in at the curb, others double-parked for drivers to have quick conversations with pedestrians. Dogs ran barking across the street, kids strolled the sidewalks and tossed a ball around on the field next to the elementary school, which dominated one side of the first block of Main Street. On the other side was a two-story professional building, and next to it a real-estate office. Every kind of architecture was represented, from old restored structures to relatively new buildings of concrete and glass.

Nancy drove slowly, pointing out the local sights: the home of the *Cupid Chronicles,* the weekly where Julie Cameron worked; the bank, established in 1921;

a hardware store across the street from a furniture store; City Hall and Rocky Pizza.

"The jail's a block over on Aspen Avenue, behind the hardware store," Nancy explained. "At the south end of Aspen there's a grocery and general store, but on the north end the residential district begins. That's where John and I live."

Just then a pedestrian stepped to the curb and hailed the minivan. Nancy stopped, effectively blocking the traffic lane, and leaned toward the passenger window opening with a soft whir. Betsy pressed back against the seat, trying not to block Nancy's view or that of the man who walked into the street to peer through the window.

"Nancy, don't forget we need your ad copy by noon tomorrow."

"Sure thing. Gene, I want you to meet my niece, Betsy. She's from California. Betsy, Gene Varner, crusading editor of the *Cupid Chronicles.*"

"Your niece!" The editor's bald head gleamed but not as brightly as his smile. A beefy man in his early fifties, he had an alertness appropriate for a journalist. "Welcome to Cupid, Betsy."

Welcome to Cupid. Betsy loved the sound of that.

Laughing, Nancy waved him off and continued the tour. "Now up here is the Y." She made a sharp turn at a fork in the road. "Not much more to the town. There's a gas station down the road a piece, and a honky-tonk called the Hideout. This road we're on is Lovers' Lane. There's something I want you to see...."

She pulled to the curb and pointed across the street. "See that house? That's where your mother and I grew up."

Betsy caught her breath. The house was a beautiful restored Victorian with soaring turrets and a big wraparound porch. What a wonderful place to grow up in, she thought.

They drove on, Nancy keeping up a running commentary. "Gene, who you just met, lives there now. Mom sold it to him when he first came to town. It was just too much for her to handle after Dad died."

They moved slowly past one old house after another, in various states of repair and maintenance. Some were showplaces; others looked ready to fall down. Behind the lots rose an evergreen-covered mountain; the right-hand side of Lovers' Lane was devoted to a park with natural landscaping and children's play equipment. The road ended in a sharp curve to the right that turned it into First Street, with the Rusty Spur Café visible a block away at the corner of First and Main. They'd traveled in a loop.

The last house on Lovers' Lane was little more than a cottage. It stood alone, separated from its neighbors by overgrown vacant lots on both sides. Betsy's heart skipped a beat. What a charming place, she thought, but how forlorn it looked! The old-fashioned porch was most inviting; even the nondescript brown paint seemed right, a proper backdrop for sunny yellow daffodils nodding bravely above snowy flower beds.

"Who lives there?" she wondered aloud, not sure why she would ask the names of people she couldn't possibly know.

"No one, as of next week." Nancy drove the van back around the curve in the road. "I wanted you to see it because your grandmother spent her final years there. I expect I'd have sold it if anyone had shown any interest, but I just never got around to listing it. There's a salesman who's been using it on weekends once or twice a month, but it's yours, if you want it... if you'll stay."

"Oh, Aunt Nancy... Aunt Nancy—" How strange it felt to say that.

"Think about it," Nancy said quickly. "Mick will be out in a few days and you can take a look at it then."

Betsy's mouth went dry as she listened to her aunt's explanations. A powerful feeling of déjà vu swept over her, the strangest feeling somehow that she was destined to live there.

But that hardly seemed possible. She was going to live and work in Aspen—if Chase Britton would give her a job.

LISA PROMPTLY FELL in love with Nancy's big old gray tomcat, Chester. But then, Lisa loved every animal she met, even those who didn't return her affection. Fortunately Chester did, and the next time Betsy saw him he was wrapped in a bath towel and cradled in the arms of his young admirer. The expression he turned on Nancy seemed disbelieving, yet he made no move to escape, which he could easily have done.

Betsy was trying to think of a way to ask Nancy about Joey's mother when John, Nancy's husband, returned from a fishing expedition. He greeted Betsy and Lisa as casually and cheerfully as if his wife dragged home long-lost relatives every day.

"John's retired from the gas company," Nancy explained while he shed his outdoorsman garb. "He spends most of his time fishing and the rest of it hunting. If it's wild and he can shoot it or trap it or hook it, we eat it—that's the rule around here."

But not tonight. Tonight, Nancy served chicken-fried steak and mashed potatoes.

John forked another piece of meat from his plate and gave Betsy a conspiratorial smile. "Better eat or she'll quit cookin'," he advised.

So Betsy and Lisa ate, feeling more at home here with every passing minute.

After dinner, Nancy pulled out the family photo albums. For the first time, Betsy saw a chronicle of her mother's early life: Joanne as infant, toddler, child and teen, with parents, sister, various boys.

"I never dreamed," she whispered, touching a fingertip to a picture of Joanne in her midteens, the centerpiece of a crowd of clowning teens.

Nancy removed the photo from its corner mounts. "Take it, hon."

"Thank you." Betsy blinked hard and cleared her throat. "It's been a long day, Aunt Nancy. Lisa and I should be getting back to the café so we can all get some rest."

"Please stay. Look—Lisa's already asleep." She pointed at the little girl curled up in an armchair with Chester.

"I...I really can't. I need to be alone, to think about everything that's happened today." Betsy slid the photo into her purse, careful not to wrinkle it. "I thank you for asking, though."

Nancy looked as if she might argue, but didn't. Without further fuss, she drove the two back to the café. While Betsy carried Lisa in, Nancy grabbed Betsy's small overnight case, which was all they'd need. She even hung around while Betsy tucked Lisa into bed. At last the two women stood quietly in the darkened hallway outside the bedroom door.

For a moment, they looked at each other. Then Nancy pulled Betsy into her arms. "I already feel like you're the daughter I never had but always wanted," she whispered. "Welcome home, honey."

That was when Betsy realized she wasn't dreaming. She really *had* found something very precious, something she'd thought never to have again.

She'd found a place to belong.

BEN, BUSY WIPING DOWN another shivering newborn calf, heard the door creak open and looked up to see Maggie enter the barn. She clutched one of her brothers' old denim jackets around her, hunching her shoulders as if she was still cold, despite the mildness of the night.

She looked tired. The naked bulb on the ceiling cast deep shadows under her eyes, emphasized the hollows beneath her strong cheekbones. Still, she managed a smile. "I figured I'd find you here," she said, squatting to stroke the trembling calf.

"You look beat, Maggie."

She shrugged. "No more than usual. It's you I'm worried about, Ben. You were so quiet at dinner I figured something must really be bothering you." She grinned suddenly. "Something beyond the obvious, that is."

"You mean Julie." Ben stood, then picked the calf up bodily and carried him to his mama for a snack. This was the red heifer's first offspring. She was having a little trouble getting the knack of it, so they'd installed her in the barn where they could keep an eye on her.

Turning back to his sister, he saw she'd taken a seat on a hay bale and was waiting for him to go on.

So he did. "Don't you ever get sick of hearing your little sister sing the praises of a guy you know is nothing but a sidewinder?"

She looked uncomfortable. "Sometimes."

"Admit it, Maggie. You don't like him any better than I do, and neither does Jason."

She sighed. "Okay, I admit it. But what good do you think it'll do to keep harping at it? You've got to lighten up, Ben."

"Do I?" He shoved his sweat-stained Stetson back on his head, his frustration close to overflowing.

"I know you feel responsible for the whole kit and caboodle of us—"

"I feel responsible because I *am* responsible," he cut in. "If I hadn't shirked my responsibilities—"

"I won't listen to that!" Her dark eyes flashed fire. "You're human, Ben. I'm not going to hold that against you, even if you do."

"Suit yourself. But I can't stand by and let Julie throw her life away on a guy who's just trying to get her into the sack."

"You...don't know that for sure."

His glance sharpened. "What have you heard?"

"Nothing," she denied quickly.

For a moment he stared at her. He didn't believe her but made a conscious decision not to pursue it. "Okay," he said shortly, "if you say so. But then we got Jason and all his big plans to go rodeoin' this summer. And Chuck complaining because you have to work and can't be available to wait on him hand and foot twenty-four hours a day, instead of just fifteen or sixteen. All that bellyaching at supper was enough to turn anybody's stomach."

"Usually you're right in the thick of it, giving everybody hell, instead of sitting there like a bump on a log. Which makes me wonder if...there's something you're not telling me."

"Like what?" He stared at her, his eyes narrow.

"Like...that woman Julie saw you with at the Spur."

He shrugged suddenly tight shoulders. "What about her? She's Nancy's niece, but she's on her way to Aspen. I'll probably never see her again."

Maggie stood up and gave him a hug. "I hope you do," she murmured, "her or somebody else. You need a life of your own, Ben. You haven't had anybody special since way before you got Joey." She pulled back, smiling at him. "As for the family, taking responsibility isn't the same as taking over people's *lives*. You've got to give us at least a little rope."

"And watch you all hang yourselves? I don't think so."

Talking quietly, they strolled back to the house through a star-bright night.

CHAPTER FOUR

"MAMA? MAMA, where are you?"

At Lisa's sleepy cry, Betsy turned quickly from the only window in the small room and moved to the side of the bed. She didn't know how long she'd stood there in her nightgown, peeking past the curtains at the sleeping town. She'd never imagined any community could be so silent and peaceful, even in the hours between midnight and dawn.

She reached for the thrashing child and stilled her with a gentle hand. "It's all right, Lisa," she crooned. "Mama's here, sweetheart. Go back to sleep."

Lisa Marie quieted beneath her mother's reassuring touch. She swallowed loudly, mumbled something, flopped over onto her stomach and went back to sleep.

For several minutes, Betsy sat there, stroking her child and murmuring. When she was sure Lisa Marie slept soundly, she eased her own way beneath the covers and stretched out, only to lie stiff and alert. Not frightened, exactly; not frightened at all by her surroundings. But perhaps a little frightened by her situation.

The responsibility was hers and hers alone. As the only child of an overprotective mother, she'd never been required to do much of anything alone, including make decisions; in fact, she'd never been *allowed* to make decisions. She'd gone from her mother's keeping straight to Evan's. Her husband had protected her from most of the realities of life, just as he'd been doing since they met in elementary school. She'd had her beautiful home, her adorable daughter, time to pursue her interests, time to share with the man she loved ...

And then he'd died. Even now, a year later, it seemed impossible that someone so talented, so famous, so close to realizing all his dreams, could kiss her goodbye and walk out the door, never to return. Without an anchor in her life, she'd tried to be strong for Lisa Marie but wasn't sure she'd succeeded. The first few months had been a blur, and she'd only hauled herself back to reality when things began to go wrong. Little things at first, but then bigger things, and finally, something big enough to nudge her into taking a step no one who knew her could possibly have predicted.

She hardly believed it herself: that she'd pulled up stakes, broken all ties with everything she'd known and struck off on her own to make a new life for herself and Lisa Marie. Perhaps that life would be in Aspen ...

Or maybe it would be in Cupid, Colorado. Wherever, she was on her own.

Was Ben Cameron married?

Her body went bowstring-tight. That question had lurked in the back of her mind all evening, but she hadn't been able to think of a graceful way to ask it. She was curious, nothing more.

She had no intention of becoming emotionally involved with that man or any other, and she doubted she ever would. Losing her mother and a husband she'd adored, being on her own for the first time in her life, she'd discovered something: she wasn't the fragile creature she'd always been led to believe. She could be her own woman and make her own decisions. She'd admit she wasn't very good at it yet, and she'd made some mistakes, but she was learning.

Which was a good thing, for she didn't have forever to get her act together. Despite appearances, she wasn't rich or even comfortably well-off. Evan had set up a trust fund for Lisa's education shortly after her birth, and Betsy would never touch that. She had an expensive car, a classy wardrobe, a valuable diamond ring—and a rapidly dwindling bank account. The lifestyle of a star did not come cheap, and Evan's years of fame had been horribly few.

Betsy needed an income, and she needed it fast. She opened her eyes in the dark, trying to see the closed door, envisioning the little café on the other side of that barrier. Half of it was hers, Nancy had said. But did Betsy, a stranger, have any right to an inheritance from a grandmother she'd never known, whose heart her own mother had apparently broken? Nancy seemed to think so, but Betsy wasn't so sure.

Anxious and uncertain, she rolled onto her side, moving carefully because she didn't want to disturb Lisa. She'd grown used to sleeping alone since Evan's death, but she hadn't learned to like it. At first she'd kept herself strictly on her own half of the bed, as if by saving his half he'd eventually return. That hadn't lasted long, however. Soon the sight of a half-slept-in bed was more than she could bear, and she'd taken to sleeping restlessly, tossing and turning and tearing the sheets from their moorings, throwing the blankets onto the floor.

A happy medium no longer existed for her, and so she lay, tense and aware of the soft and warm little body beside her. Eventually she dozed; awakened to lie there willing sleep to return. Surely dawn would break soon.

It didn't. Perhaps it was the whirl of thoughts and worries she couldn't control, or perhaps it was a strange bed in a strange town, but she simply couldn't sleep. After what seemed like an eternity of trying, she crept from the bed, dressed quickly in the dark and slipped out of the room.

By the subdued night-lighting in the café, she saw that it was only a little past two. She groaned; now what? If she didn't find something to distract herself, she'd go crazy.

Walking behind the counter, she hesitated only a moment before proceeding to make herself a pot of coffee. She found what she needed by trial and error, opening and closing cabinets and drawers. Soon a welcome fragrance accompanied the drip of coffee from the machine into a waiting glass carafe.

Ah, that was better, she thought, sipping. Maybe if she had a piece of toast to go with it . . .

But all she found was a loaf from a commercial bakery, when what she wanted was a thick slice of good homemade bread. The Rusty Spur had no biscuits or muffins, either. There was a piece of apple pie beneath the domed keeper on the counter, but Nancy had warned against that, Betsy recalled. Looking at the dry brown filling, she shuddered.

Either Nancy didn't have time to bake or didn't enjoy it. Betsy, on the other hand, adored baking, everything from classic birthday cakes to elegant European desserts, from quick biscuits to fragrant yeast breads. Although her stint as a student at the International Institute of the Culinary Arts of America had been cut short, she'd spent years studying at the feet of her mother's various cooks. If she was confident of one thing, it was her abilities in a kitchen.

She'd never found a better way to combat stress than kneading a lump of dough. Surely Nancy wouldn't mind if she helped herself to whatever she could find in the kitchen, especially if the result could be served on the breakfast plates of hungry customers.

Bread, muffins, biscuits, maybe even a pie . . . Ben Cameron looked like a man who'd appreciate a good piece of pie. Her steps suddenly purposeful, Betsy hurried into the kitchen, trying to remember what she'd been told about baking at higher altitudes. Less yeast, less sugar—yes, that was it.

Happily she went to work.

NANCY SAW THE LIGHT on in the café while she was still a block away. Quelling a moment's panic, she reminded herself there was no cause for alarm. Betsy had no doubt turned on the light. Maybe she'd needed to make her way to the washroom, or maybe Lisa had wanted a drink of water. No problem. Nevertheless, Nancy jumped out of her van and hurried to the back door with the key already in her hand. She'd feel better when she knew for sure.

Betsy and Lisa should've stayed with me last night, she fumed, fumbling in her hurry to fit the key into the lock. Betsy was family; not for a minute did Nancy doubt a single detail of her story.

The door finally slammed open, banging against the wall. Nancy stepped inside, ready for anything.

Anything except what she got: the fulsome aromas of yeast and cinnamon and coffee. "Betsy!" she called. "What in the world . . . ?"

Instantly Betsy appeared from the kitchen, cheeks flushed and streaked with flour, her smile glorious. "Good morning!" she exclaimed. "I hope you don't mind. I couldn't sleep. Just let me get that bread out of the oven and we can . . ."

She disappeared again and for a moment, Nancy stood riveted with surprise. If ever she'd met a woman who *didn't* look like she knew her way around a kitchen, it was Elizabeth Ross. Joanne hadn't even known how to boil water and liked it that way. Stunned, Nancy walked into the kitchen.

Marie Thayer had been known far and wide for her biscuits, and she'd also baked a mean pie and an occasional loaf of bread—but never in the history of the Rusty Spur had such an assortment of baked goodies been assembled. Nancy stared, impressed.

Betsy shook a shiny loaf of golden brown bread from a pan, lining it up with several others cooling on a wire rack. She cast her aunt an anxious glance that was curiously ingratiating. "Do you mind?"

"Mind!" Nancy gestured. "Look at all this! I'm tickled pink, and the breakfast crew will be, too. My only worry is that you'll spoil 'em and they'll think they can expect this kind of treatment all the time."

Betsy placed the empty bread pan in the deep sink with the others. "I guess I did get a little carried away, but I was enjoying myself so much I didn't know when to stop." She picked up a serrated bread knife and sliced off the end of one hot loaf. "Want to test it?"

Nancy accepted the slice of bread and stared down at it, noting the even texture and golden crust. She might not know how to achieve the same results, but she recognized quality when she saw it.

The yeasty aroma made Nancy's mouth water. Was there anyone who didn't respond to that smell? She took a bite of bread, savored it, then closed her eyes and sighed. "This," she said, "is wonderful. How in the world did you learn to *do* this, Betsy? I know it wasn't from your mother."

Her niece looked startled, then embarrassed. "Once upon a time, I wanted to be a pastry chef," she confessed. "I used to beg mother's cooks to teach me, and for a while I even studied at a culinary institute. Then Evan—that was my husband—had a friend who owned a restaurant. He introduced me to his chefs and they let me hang around sometimes."

"Well, this is the best bread I've ever eaten in my life, and that includes my mother's." Nancy popped the last morsel into her mouth and brushed crumbs from her fingers. "But, honey, I feel bad about you being up all night and working so hard. Is anything wrong? Bed not comfortable? Something scare you or upset you?" As she spoke, she moved around the room, setting up for the six-o'clock opening.

Betsy shook her head. "I like to cook but I *love* to bake, that's all. As long as I'm here, I'll do my share of the work."

Nancy paused in the act of tying a long cook's apron over her jeans and white blouse. "If I work you too hard, you may take a notion to move on. I wouldn't want that."

Betsy looked on the verge of making some protest, so Nancy rushed on. "Here." She fished in her jean pocket and pulled out her key ring. "Why don't you take this and go on over to my house? You can shower and be back for breakfast before Lisa Marie even wakes up."

Betsy took the key but looked uncertain. "What about John—Uncle John? Won't I disturb him?"

Nancy smiled to hear her niece call him that. It obviously didn't come natural to her, but she was trying. Poor little thing really didn't know what family was all about, that was for certain. "Sweetie, Uncle John's long gone. I don't know what critter he's after today but it better be runnin' or swimmin' for its life."

"If you're sure, then . . ."

"I'm sure."

"I wouldn't want to be a bother."

A lump formed in Nancy's throat and she swallowed hard, but she was fighting a losing battle. "We're family," she murmured. "You'll never be a bother to me, and I hope we never will be to you. As far as I'm concerned, you can do anything you want anytime you want." She dropped a quick kiss on Betsy's cheek. "Now run along before we start bawling like a couple of babies."

BETSY SHOWERED QUICKLY, threw on a clean pair of jeans and a yellow cotton sweater, a minimum of makeup, and was back at the café in less than an hour. She entered as she'd left, through the back door, moving quietly down the short hall and into the café proper.

More than a dozen people were seated at the counter, at the Liars' Table, in booths. Among them was Lisa Marie, perched on a stool at the counter next to a burly man wearing a blue uniform and a badge. Betsy recognized him as the man who'd vouched for Ben yesterday.

Lisa Marie saw her mother and smiled. "Mama's here!" she called. "Aunt Nancy, Mama's back!"

"Here she is now, boys!" Nancy's laughing voice reverberated through the room. "I want you all to meet my niece, Betsy. She's the one who spent half the night slaving over a hot oven, all for your dining pleasure."

Spontaneous applause startled Betsy. Embarrassed, she tried to smile, to act as if she was accustomed to such glowing acknowledgment.

The man sitting next to Lisa Marie grinned. "So you're Joanne's girl," he said. "Well, I'll be."

Betsy caught her breath. "You knew my mother?" She could hardly believe it. Her mother had emerged from this secret world, which Betsy had discovered only through sheerest chance.

"Honey," the lawman drawled, "everybody in town knows the Thayers. Me'n your mother went to school together." He thrust out a meaty hand. "I'm Dwight Deakins, marshal around here. Glad to meet-cha, Betsy."

"Th-thank you."

"This is my *friend,*" Lisa piped up. "He's the *law* in these parts."

Everyone laughed, and then Nancy took Betsy's arm. "Let me introduce you to a few people," she said proudly.

Everyone in the café met Betsy with smiles, pausing in the serious business of swigging coffee or shoveling in pancakes or eggs or the fruits of Betsy's early-morning labors. Each seemed to have some personal comment to add: "I was your mama's Sunday-school teacher, years back, but I don't believe she could make a muffin this tasty..."; "Joanne and I sat next to each other in Miss Phipps's English class, and I don't know which of us got into more trouble..."; "Your mama was the prettiest girl in town, and it looks like you take after her in that department...."

It was both wonderful and frightening to Betsy, and far too much to take in all at once. In the space of a single day, she'd apparently gone from complete unknown to local celebrity. Not only was her mother well remembered in Cupid, Colorado, but Betsy herself had made a ton of points with her nocturnal baking spree.

Introductions completed, it seemed only natural for Betsy to pitch in and help with the morning rush. A cheerful black woman named Cora Witherspoon was doing the cooking while Nancy worked the counter and the floor. Without asking, Betsy picked up the coffeepot and made another circle of the room, refilling cups and retrieving dirty dishes. It wasn't the first time she'd waited tables, she thought with amusement. No need for Nancy to look quite so startled.

JULIE GRIPED at Ben every mile into town. Joey, squeezed between them on the bench seat with his thumb in his mouth, never uttered a word.

"I don't know why you couldn't just let me use the pickup while my car's in the garage," she sniped. "You're supposed to be working at home today. You pull another disappearing stunt like you did yesterday and Jason'll have your hide."

"Can it, Jewel." Ben turned off the dirt road and onto the paved.

"Don't call me Jewel! I need wheels today—I mean, I think I will. Gene said something about sending me to interview that kid who just got back from a student-exchange program in France, and he lives way out in the boonies. How am I supposed to—?"

"It's Gene's story. Let him figure out a way to get you there." Ben drove past the gun shop, then between the Spur on one side of the street and the gas station and fast-food drive-in on the other. He couldn't tell if Betsy's BMW was there or not, hidden among the pickups. He'd awakened this morning with a burning urge to know if she'd stayed or gone. Appeared he wasn't going to find out without going inside—as if he hadn't planned to all along.

He pulled over and stopped in front of the bank, which was directly across Main Street from the *Cupid Chronicles* office. Julie threw open the door hard enough to jar the entire vehicle.

"I won't forget this, Ben Cameron," she promised, hopping out of the cab. "Just because you're mad at me about Scott is no reason—"

He didn't wait for her to finish, just drove off. The forward motion of the vehicle ripped the door from her hands and slammed it shut on her howl of outrage. Truth was, he wasn't concerned with Julie and her problems at the moment. He had other things on his mind, like the beautiful blue-eyed blonde who'd come skidding into his life yesterday out of a snow-storm. Was she still around or had she already skid-ded out?

He parked in front of the Rusty Spur and led Joey inside. Lifting the boy onto a stool, Ben slid onto an-other one and looked around with a casualness he didn't feel. He didn't see her. He saw Cora cooking, Nancy waiting tables, but he didn't see Betsy Ross.

Well, hell. He'd driven all this way, irritated his sis-ter for coming, irritated his brother for going, and Betsy wasn't even here. He was never going to see her again, he was sure of it. What had he been thinking, classy woman like that, obviously pampered and pet-ted—a Californian, yet. She wasn't going to hang around a little one-horse town like this, even if she *had* just discovered a long-lost—

"Joey's daddy, Joey's daddy! Is Joey here?"

Ben felt a tug at his sleeve and glanced down. Lisa Marie stood beside his stool, her expression implor-ing.

"Joey!" she repeated. "Where's Joey?"

Ben's smile felt broad enough to split his face. Where Lisa was, Betsy could not be far behind. "Right here, little lady." He leaned aside so she could see the boy on the next stool.

The two kids grinned at each other, Joey shy and Lisa not. "Can you come sit with me, Joey?" the lit-tle girl asked hopefully.

"Can I, Daddy?"

"Sure."

He watched them stake out their territory at the far end of the counter with much giggling and chatter. Joey needed a friend, among other things. What did Joey's daddy need?

"Coffee, cowboy?"

Betsy's light voice brought him sharply around on his stool again. There she stood, a tousle of dark blond curls and laughing blue eyes, every bit as sexy and sweet as he remembered. She held a coffeepot aloft in one hand, and her brows rose in question. She looked even better today than she had yesterday, he decided. Somehow she seemed more...natural. Her ivory skin glowed, her blue eyes sparkled, her breasts rose beneath the pale yellow sweater.

She wasn't wearing a bra.

Something twisted in Ben's gut. He could see the clear outline of her nipples. He tried to look away, anywhere else, but couldn't seem to do it.

She knew what was going on. When she reached to turn his cup right side up, her hand trembled. When she poured the coffee, a little splashed over the rim of the cup and onto the counter.

"Oops, clumsy me," she said, and this time her voice was a little breathy. "I'll be right back to clean up my mess."

She hurried away without acknowledging his stare, either positively or negatively. Some women he knew would've slapped his face for staring at their breasts that way; others would've breathed deeper, stood taller, and all but dared him to do more than look.

Betsy Ross had done neither. He'd embarrassed her, he was sure, but she'd chosen not to acknowledge his interest. Now what the hell was that supposed to mean?

It meant she wasn't having any, he decided when she returned, wearing one of Nancy's big white aprons tied up tight almost to her chin. There wasn't a damned thing to see now except...that beautiful oval face with its high, lightly flushed cheekbones and full sensual mouth, which trembled every time he looked at it.

She wiped up the spill.

He toyed with his coffee cup. "Glad to see you're still in town," he said.

"Nancy can be pretty persuasive." She concentrated on wiping down the counter.

He sipped at coffee he didn't want. He'd been up since four, had had a half-dozen cups already. "So, have you decided to hang around a while?" he asked hopefully.

She shook her head but still didn't look at him. "Lisa and I will be heading to Aspen as soon as I help Nancy clean up after the breakfast rush."

He couldn't believe what he was hearing. "Independence Pass—"

"It's open," she said quickly, looking up at last. "I checked. If I take it slow and easy..."

He stared at her. "You're nuts."

Her cheeks flushed more brightly and she lifted her chin, but her tone remained even and reasonable. "I'm sorry you think so."

"You don't know what you're getting into," he insisted. "That pass is brutal."

"Be that as it may, it's between here and the place I want to go, and I'll just have to chance it." She frowned. "I mean, how bad can it be? It's a public road, for heaven's sake. Everybody who drives it can't be a Colorado native."

"What's so all-fired important in Aspen?" he grumbled.

"A job, I hope."

"A job?" Nancy had approached without either of them noticing. "Honey, you want a job, you've got one." She added to Ben, "You taste that bread?"

"What bread?"

"The bread this girl made about four o'clock this morning. Or the pie. She made pie, muffins, you name it."

Ben tried to hide his astonishment. From the brief flare of resentment in Betsy's eyes, he'd done a lousy job of it. "Pie? I don't think I've had a slice of really good pie at the Spur since Miss Marie died," he said truthfully.

"You don't have to humor me," Betsy said loftily. "I was... bored. I wasn't trying to impress anyone."

Which told Ben she sure as hell had been. He hoped it was him. "Bring on that pie," he told Nancy, "and then I'm going to drive this stubborn woman to Aspen."

"What?" Nancy and Betsy exclaimed simultaneously.

The younger woman deferred to the older. "Am I wrong," Nancy asked, "or is this not calf season at the Straight Arrow, like it is everywhere else?"

"Jason can handle it," Ben said, grinning at Betsy. "Your turn."

"You can't drive me," she said, "because I'm not sure I'm coming back. So how will I get my car?"

Nancy, who'd opened the pie case and taken out a big juicy slab of apple pie, almost dropped it. "Why wouldn't you be coming back?" She put the pie in front of Ben, and he immediately dug in.

"I'm hoping I'll be offered a job," Betsy said.

"Just because it's offered doesn't mean you have to take it." Nancy sounded hurt. "Honey, you've got a job right here as half owner of the Rusty Spur. I told you that."

Betsy chewed on her lower lip. "I'm really not sure about that," she began. "It doesn't seem right, walking in off the street and taking over. You don't even know for certain that I'm who I say I am. I could be a . . . a con artist or something. I could be—"

"My niece." Nancy looked completely unperturbed. "Blood will tell, sugar lump. Now, why don't you let the nice man drive you to Aspen so you can refuse this job and hotfoot it right on back? What do you say? I'll keep Lisa and Jocy here with me."

"But—"

"You young people run along, you hear?"

Ben scooped the final forkful of pie into his mouth, knowing this was beyond a doubt the best pie he'd ever eaten but reluctant to say so for fear she'd think he was trying to hit on her. Which he was.

"I hear," he told Nancy, standing up.

Still Betsy hesitated, looking at Ben through half-lowered lashes. "Don't you have to get back to the ranch? Won't your wife be—"

"No wife," he said.

"Joey's mother—"

"No mother."

He'd spoken harshly; she looked taken aback, so he added, "Just a brother who's perfectly capable of holding down the fort." His tone turned coaxing. "C'mon, it'll be fun."

"Well...okay, but I'm not promising anything." She removed her apron. "It depends on what my friend in Aspen has to say."

Nancy nodded. "Understood. But you can't blame me for hoping, can you?"

Me, neither, Ben thought, then realized he'd better hope that when he returned home hours later than expected, Jason wouldn't set upon him with a pitchfork.

Even so, he had a hunch it'd be worth it.

CHAPTER FIVE

INDEPENDENCE PASS was not for the fainthearted, Betsy quickly discovered. Clinging white-knuckled to the edge of her seat, she held her breath while Ben negotiated the maze of hairpin curves leading up at an incredibly steep angle to the 12,500-foot summit—one of the highest in Colorado, he told her matter-of-factly.

She'd insisted they take her BMW, instead of his truck. Despite his initial reluctance, he changed his tune fast enough once he got behind the wheel. The red convertible was almost two years old, a gift from Evan, and it had fit her like a glove from the start. Apparently it fit Ben just as well, for he quickly got that aggressive expression common to men enamored of a great set of wheels.

They entered yet another sharp curve, this one with a steep drop-off on one side of the narrow two-lane road, a soaring cliff on the other. Betsy swallowed hard and closed her eyes.

Ben chuckled. "Don't look at the road," he advised. "Look at the view. It's spectacular."

"I would, but it makes me dizzy," Betsy groaned. "How did anyone ever get the insane idea of building a road here?'' She opened her eyes just a crack. The way ahead looked temporarily reasonable, so she sat up straight again.

"Miners used this route to bring in supplies by burro train," Ben explained. "This was the only link between mines in Aspen and smelters in Leadville."

"I didn't know Aspen was ever a mining town. I thought it was just, you know, skiing and glitz."

He looked strong and confident in profile, maneuvering the car with ease on the treacherous mountain road. "Just about every place in Colorado was connected with mining one way or another. Between gold strikes and silver strikes, it's been boom or bust all over the state, and usually both. With Aspen, it was silver. The strike came in the 1880s, and everything was rosy until silver prices collapsed in 1893. After that, it was downhill until the 1930s and 1940s, when someone got the brilliant idea to build ski runs." He glanced at her with unveiled curiously. "You've never been to Aspen, I take it?"

She shook her head. "Actually I haven't traveled out of California all that much. I lived in New York City for a little while, and I've vacationed in Mexico and once in Hawaii, but that's about it."

"And now you want to take a job in Aspen?" He shook his head as if he couldn't believe it.

"What's wrong with Aspen?"

"Nothing, if you're a snow nut. Do you ski?"

"Well . . . no."

"Ever lived in snow?"

"No." She grimaced. "I can learn, Ben. I'm not made of glass, whatever you may think."

"Shows, does it." He had the good grace to look and sound embarrassed.

"How about you?"

"How about me what?"

"Have you spent much time in Aspen?"

"Not hardly." His brows soared. "Aspen's a little rich for my blood. But there was an old codger on my mother's side who was a miner. He went in with the first big wave. Didn't strike it rich but he came out with enough to set himself up in the freight business in Denver. He was an exception, though. Most of my family's been ranchers, not miners."

Betsy couldn't imagine what it would be like to know so much about your forebears. "So you actually live on a ranch."

"You couldn't tell?"

"How am I supposed to know a drugstore cowboy from the real thing? Anybody can buy a ten-gallon hat and a pair of boots."

"True. Sad but true. Yep, I live on a ranch, fourth-generation rancher, in fact. My ancestors homesteaded 160 acres more than a hundred years ago. Today, with leases and all, our operation covers better than eighty thousand."

She gave him a blank look; the numbers meant nothing to her, though the family history did. "It's all yours?"

"Not exactly." The road funneled into another series of corkscrew curves, and he slowed the car. "I've got a brother and two sisters and a grandma. And Joey, of course. The Straight Arrow's a family affair.''

They were still on the upward slope; would they ever reach the summit? She tried to concentrate. "The Straight Arrow—that's the name of your ranch?"

"Yep. My great-grandpa had a reputation as a straight arrow, because he was so honest in all his dealings. He planned to call the ranch the Double C because he started it with his brother—two C's for two Camerons. But before he could register the brand, his brother moved on to Montana and the Straight Arrow moniker caught on. At least, that's what Grandma always said."

"Do your brother and sisters and grandmother all live there?"

"That's right. There's Julie—you met her—and her twin, Jason. Maggie's a year older than me, and there's also her husband, Chuck. And Grandma and Joey, of course." He frowned. "It's like a zoo, if you want to know the truth."

Betsy couldn't imagine; she simply couldn't comprehend so many adults living under the same roof. "What about your parents?" she asked finally.

Ben hesitated a split second too long before answering. "My dad died when I was seventeen and Mom went not long after. How about you?"

"Me?" She blinked in surprise.

"Nancy told me this morning while you were in the ladies' room that you didn't know you had family in Cupid until recently."

He said it casually, as if it was an everyday occurrence for people not to know their relatives. "My mother had a grudge against her family, and she carried it to the grave," Betsy said slowly. "There's nothing she could ever have done to hurt me more, not even—" She stopped just short of saying, *not even her attitude toward Evan*. She was feeling comfortable with Ben, but not comfortable enough to get into all that.

He flashed her a sympathetic glance. "Still, here you are. Guess it was fate, Betsy."

Without warning, he whipped the BMW into a parking area on the very top of the pass and stopped. Climbing out, he walked around and opened her door, then offered her his hand. After a moment's hesitation, she took it, and his warm fingers curled around hers almost possessively.

He drew her out of the car, and she came hesitantly, looking into his face with a certain discomfort. His nose was straight, almost aristocratic, and his well-shaped mouth stretched in a smile that revealed strong white teeth. She frowned, less than pleased to realize the direction her thoughts were taking.

"Close your eyes," he commanded.

Automatically she obeyed. She felt his hands slide up her arms as he turned her slowly and carefully in a half circle; she sensed his nearness, could almost feel his body heat. His hands cupped her shoulders, and his breath fanned the tendrils of hair near her ear.

"Okay, you can open your eyes again."

She obeyed, then caught her breath at the panorama before her—green mountains and meadows, blue skies and fluffy white clouds. She breathed deeply of air so clean and fresh it seemed to go to her head. Suddenly she felt almost dizzy.

"It's the altitude," Ben said softly, tightening his grip on her shoulders and guiding her back the few inches separating them until her shoulder blades pressed against his chest. "We're a couple of miles above sea level, and the air is thin up here. Just take deep breaths and hang tight. It'll pass."

"I'm not sure I want it to pass," she confessed breathlessly. Somehow it seemed permissible for her to enjoy his loose embrace under these extraordinary circumstances. "I feel as giddy as if I'd been drinking champagne."

Glancing around, she saw one tiny yellow blossom poking bravely through a patch of snow, but no trees. None. They were above the timberline.

Ben must have noticed her interest. "That little yellow flower is a snow buttercup," he said. "It's first to bloom in the alpine zone each spring, but this is early, even for it."

"Early, and wonderful," she said sincerely. "Thank you for stopping."

"You're ready to go on, then?"

She wasn't, but the light wind was icy and she was beginning to feel chilled. "I suppose we..." She felt him tense. "What is it?"

"Look up there."

He pointed toward the clear blue sky and she saw it: a huge bird gliding gracefully with the air currents. She let her head fall back onto Ben's shoulder, so intent on following the spectacle in the sky that she neglected to pull away as she normally would have. The bird soared nearer and nearer to where they stood transfixed.

"That's a bald eagle," Ben murmured, sliding his arms down to curve beneath her breasts. Every move he made seemed as natural, under the circumstances, as breathing. "Beautiful, isn't it? I hear they're making a comeback."

"Wait a minute." She watched the graceful swoops and turns, thinking she should distance herself from him but taking no immediate action to do so. "Wild things aren't my strong suit, but don't bald eagles have white heads?"

His soft chuckle sent tiny vibrations traveling down her spine. "They do—white tails, too—but not until they're four or five years old. That one's just a baby."

They watched until the eagle turned in another direction and became, eventually, no more than a tiny dot in the distant blue. Betsy's brush with the wonders of nature was over, and she straightened and stepped away from him.

"Something wrong?" he asked cautiously.

"Nothing," she said firmly, because of course she wasn't going to allow either of them to read anything into their recent intimacy. "That was wonderful. Thank you so much."

"No need for thanks." His eyes narrowed fractionally and his mouth tilted up at one corner. "I...enjoyed it, too. Time to move on?"

She nodded, suddenly tongue-tied. Heaven only knew what he'd made of her willingness to stand in his arms on the top of the world. She'd have to tell him how things were the first chance she got.

The drive down the other side seemed both quicker and safer than the drive up, and she supposed perhaps she'd gained a bit more tolerance for the mountains. Ben didn't say anything, just concentrated on his driving; she didn't say anything because she was still a little stunned by what she'd just seen—and how she'd felt in his embrace.

Soon they descended into the bowl where the storybook village of Aspen lay. Even she, who knew nothing about skiing, recognized the trails blazed down the mountainsides, bare streaks through thick pine forests. They crossed a bridge at the edge of town—over the Roaring Fork River, according to a sign—and entered a Victorian mining town with all the glitz and glamour of—

"Good grief," Betsy said, breaking the silence. "This reminds me of Disneyland!"

Ben laughed. "Never been there, but from what I've heard, that's a good comparison. The old stuff is window dressing for the new in this burg. I wouldn't live here if they paid me."

"I doubt you'll ever be put to the test on that one," Betsy teased. "Oh, look, there's a mall with jugglers and street musicians. And a horse-drawn carriage!

Come on, Ben, admit that Aspen has a certain charm.''

"No way," he growled. "Don't you wonder what these people do when they want to buy a pair of underwear?" She'd been teasing, but he, apparently, wasn't. "Where'd you say we're goin'?"

"It's a restaurant called Chase Britton's. It's…" She grabbed the small purse by her feet and pawed around for the directions Chase had sent her months ago. She was sure he never dreamed she'd actually take him up on his invitation. As she directed Ben through traffic, she felt her hands grow cold, her breathing accelerate.

What if Chase hadn't meant it? What if her sudden arrival embarrassed, instead of pleased, him? He had, after all, been closer to Evan than to her. Probably he'd just been being kind. If Ben wasn't with her, she'd be tempted to turn around and run back to Cupid. At least she knew she'd be welcome there.

Ben made a sharp right-hand turn and slowed the car "Damn," he said. "Will you look at that?"

It was exactly what she'd expected, a cutting-edge glass-and-chrome restaurant so tony that she had to look twice to find the name of the establishment. How Ben had spotted it back against the mountainside, surrounded by a forest of evergreens, she couldn't imagine. But he had, and unless she wanted to embarrass herself, she had to follow through on her announced intention.

He swung the BMW around to the discreet parking lot in the back and into a space practically camouflaged by greenery. Betsy took a deep breath and met his gaze. For a moment the connection held, almost as if some special electricity drew them together. Then he raised his brows and shrugged.

"Let's go," he said, opening his car door and moving around to assist her.

There was nothing to do except square her shoulders and march up to the enormous silver door.

THE HOSTESS GREETED THEM with a professional smile. "Two for lunch?" she inquired, plucking a couple of enormous tasseled menus from a holder.

"No, thank you. I'm here to see Mr. Britton, please."

Did Betsy's voice crack just a tad? Ben frowned. He might feel as out of place as a gambler at a church social, but *she* looked completely at home here in her white slacks and red silk blouse, face carefully made up. Her earrings sparkled; they had to be diamonds.

The hostess raised one brow, but her polite tone didn't change. "Is Mr. Britton expecting you?"

"Just tell him it's Elizabeth Ross."

"As you say." The woman picked up the handset of a silver space-age telephone and tapped one digit with the tip of a fingernail long enough to spear olives in a deep jar. "Mr. Britton? There's an Elizabeth Ross here, who—" She blinked, tapped daintily on the disconnect button, then hung up. "I don't know what happened," she said. "Apparently we've been disconnected."

"Betsy!"

A tall, decisive-looking man hurried down the hallway with its plush carpeting and muted lighting. Walking straight up to Betsy, he swept her into a hug that lifted her off her feet. Ben frowned; this Chase Britton was too damned confident, grabbing her that way.

"Chase!" Laughing, Betsy drew back as if a little embarrassed. "I was afraid you'd have forgotten your invitation to visit."

"Not a chance." He dropped a light kiss on her cheek. "But why didn't you tell me you were coming? Where's Lisa Marie? Come on back to the office so we can talk."

So he knew Lisa, did he? Ben was liking this less and less. Worse, the guy wasn't as old as he ought to be to own a place like this. Despite the sprinkling of gray at his temples, he couldn't be much more than Ben's own thirty. This was not the kind of competition Ben welcomed.

Betsy resisted the tug on her hands. "Chase, I'd like you to meet Ben Cameron. He drove me here today, or I probably would've chickened out trying to get over Independence Pass."

The man frowned. "Independence Pass? I don't get it. Didn't you come from California? The pass is east of here."

"We came from Cupid."

"Cupid! Now I'm really confused." He thrust out his hand. "Whatever. Glad to meet you. Cameron, is it? I'm Chase Britton."

They shook hands, and then Britton indicated the hallway from which he'd emerged. "Let's go back to my office where we can talk," he said again, leading Betsy away but including Ben with a glance.

The office was bigger than the entire Rusty Spur. What it must have cost to decorate would've bought several country cafés with change left over. Everything was black and gray and silver, from floor to furniture to window coverings—Ben couldn't think of those silver shades as *blinds*.

There wasn't a thing in here that bespoke the personality of the incumbent except for a small silver frame on the glass-and-silver desk. Ben scooted around to see who or what had found such favor; a woman, he hoped, preferably a wife. He was disappointed to discover it was a photograph of a girl of perhaps eight or nine. Britton's daughter, Ben bet; she had the same sleek good looks.

Britton drew Betsy down onto a black sofa with silver inlays on the arms. "Now," he said, taking both her hands in his, "tell me what you were doing in Cupid, and where Lisa Marie is, and when you're going to move to Aspen and get away from all those bad memories."

Ben felt a sharp stab of something that bore a vague similarity to jealousy. This guy obviously knew a lot more about Betsy and her life than he did. Furthermore, this man was hanging on to her as if he intended to keep her.

Betsy explained, adding information new to Ben: how she'd come into possession of her mother's let-

ter, how she'd gone first to Denver where it had taken
her a few days to get up her nerve to drive to Cupid—
in a snowstorm yet.

Britton groaned. "You were lucky, sweetheart.
You're not used to our weather. You've got to be more
careful."

Betsy smiled. "It worked out all right," she said,
her tone gently chiding. "Chase, I've got to make
these decisions for myself now—for myself and Lisa.
And it was worth it, because I found my family. I've
got an aunt and an uncle in Cupid, and a whole town-
ful of people who knew my mother."

"That's great!"

Betsy nodded eagerly. "So great I'm thinking about
hanging around there for a little while so I can get to
know everyone."

Ben, leaning against the desk with his legs crossed
at the ankles, watched the little scene and felt more
and more like an intruder with every passing moment—but dynamite couldn't have blasted him out of
there.

"I see." Britton shot a pointed glance at Ben. "Is
Mr. Cameron one of your long-lost relatives or just a
newfound . . . friend?"

"Friend." Betsy apparently read nothing whatsoever into the question. "His family and my family
have known each other forever. When Ben found out
I planned to drive over Independence Pass today, he
insisted on doing it for me—and I've got to admit, I'm
glad he did." She gave Ben a quick bright smile.

Britton stood up. He wore carefully tailored dark trousers, shiny loafers and a knit shirt with a tiny embroidered something-or-other on the pocket. "We've got to talk about this," he said, "but first, let me get you something to drink. Coffee, tea, something from the bar—name it." He glanced at Ben. "You, too, of course."

Betsy considered. "I think I'd just like an ice tea," she decided. "I've felt so dehydrated since I left California."

"A beer for me," Ben drawled.

Britton's dark brows soared. "Any particular kind?"

"Any of the Colorado microbreweries will do fine."

While Britton used the telephone on the desk, Ben walked to the sofa and sat down next to Betsy. *Losers, weepers,* he thought, meeting Chase Britton's surprised glance.

THE DRINKS CAME, along with an array of beautifully arranged munchies. Betsy couldn't resist the stuffed mushrooms. "Mmmm, wonderful," she said. "Just like those at your other place."

"Exactly like." Chase pulled a chair up on the opposite side of the coffee table and sat down. "Betsy, I meant what I told you in that letter of mine all those months ago. About your learning the business, I mean."

Betsy knew he couldn't begin to appreciate how relieved she was that she hadn't made a mistake coming here. He was just as cordial as he'd been when Evan was alive—and just as attractive. She'd never known a more urbane and sophisticated man than Chase Britton, and she'd always liked him enormously.

"Thank you," she said sincerely. "I may take you up on that eventually, but for the moment . . . it's important for Lisa and me to spend some time in Cupid, I think."

He nodded. "I can understand that. But I also know how interested you've always been in the restaurant business. Sweetheart, I'm offering you a chance to work with my chef and learn from him. He's good. Studied in Paris, among other places."

"It sounds like a wonderful opportunity—"

"I'll work with you, too, teach you the business end. Say the word and you're on the payroll."

It was a tempting offer, one she'd have jumped at before learning of her ties to Cupid. "Maybe later," she said at last, adding with a smile, "I don't think I told you that my aunt owns a restaurant in Cupid. It's a little diner open for just a few hours each day. Right now I know she can use my help."

Chase looked regretful. "I'm sure she can. A diner, huh? Some of these little places tucked away in the mountains serve spectacular down-home cookin'. Maybe one of these days I'll drop by for a little sample."

"Just make it before two o'clock," Betsy advised, "because that's when the Rusty Spur closes."

"I'll do that." Chase glanced at Ben, then back to Betsy. "Tell me, sweetheart, how are you *really* do-

ing? You look wonderful, much better than the last
time I saw you."

Betsy remembered that time very well. "That was
just a few weeks after Evan's funeral," she reminded
him. "It was hard, Chase. I wasn't sure there for a
while I was going to make it, but for Lisa's sake..."
She shrugged and drew a deep breath. "I've never
been on my own before in my entire life. Never." She
shook her head, almost unable to believe what a babe
in the woods she'd been.

"I know," Chase said. "Evan told me. He worried, even though he expected to be there to take care
of you and Lisa forever."

She was going to cry. Just as she'd found it emotionally draining to hear from people who knew her
mother, she found it equally unsettling to hear from
someone who'd known her husband so well. She
blinked and swallowed hard, wondering if she'd be
able to force words past the lump in her throat. And
discovering she wouldn't have to, for Ben leaned forward.

"Betsy'll do just fine. She told me herself she's not
made out of glass." He glanced around, his expression unreadable. "So how long has *this* place been
open? I gather not long."

"About ten months." Chase looked puzzled by the
distraction.

"What kind of food?"

Chase raised a dark eyebrow. "Continental.
Betsy—"

"We haven't eaten since early this morning," Ben interrupted. "Are you hungry, Betsy? These little doohickeys—" he gestured at the tray of hors d'oeuvres "—are good, but they're no meal. Maybe we should eat before we head back over the pass."

"Perhaps we should. Would that be all right, Chase?"

He was instantly transformed into the gracious innkeeper. "Of course. We'll get you taken care of right away—on the house of course. For old time's sake, but also because I'm trying to tempt you." He gave her a teasing smile. "Just come this way..."

He ushered them through the door and back down the shadowy hallway. Walking at Ben's side, Betsy felt the slightest brush of his hand against hers and darted him a questioning look.

He winked.

"THE COLORADO FREE RANGE Chicken's a specialty," Britton said. "The Seafood Bisque is also exceptional."

Ben examined the most ostentatious menu he'd ever seen, wondering what a chicken's land rights had to do with how it tasted on a plate. "You got a hamburger in here anywhere?" he asked.

Chase slipped the menu from Chase's hand expertly. "A hamburger it is. French fries with that?"

"Is there any other way?"

Betsy closed her own menu. "That sounds good," she said. "Hamburgers and french fries for two."

Ben's jaw tightened. She was patronizing him, trying to save him from an embarrassment he didn't feel. Okay, he might feel awkward and uncomfortable on the chrome-and-black leather chair, and a bit put off by such plush surroundings, but embarrassed? Hey, he'd been to town before.

Betsy, on the other hand, was obviously in her element. "Will you join us?" she asked their host.

"I'm afraid not." Chase looked genuinely regretful, all his attention on beautiful Betsy. "I've got a business appointment I can't put off. But we'll see each other soon."

"Promise? You'll come to Cupid?"

"Promise. And just remember, I'm here if you need me." Taking her hand from where it rested on the table, he raised it to his lips.

Ben looked quickly down at the linen napkin in his lap. Was Chase Britton the kind of man who appealed to Betsy? If so, he, a rough-and-ready rancher, was wasting his time and rousing his brother's wrath for nothing.

BETSY DID NOT ENJOY the meal, although it was expertly prepared and served. Even Ben agreed it was a great hamburger with all the trimmings, served on a fresh yeasty roll with golden brown planks of potato on the side.

The problem was that for the first time since she'd left California, Betsy felt publicly vulnerable. As more and more diners arrived, she found herself sinking lower and lower into her chair.

What were the chances she'd be recognized? she argued with herself. She was not a celebrity, nor had she ever been one. True, she'd be recognized in a heartbeat if she walked into Spago on Sunset Strip or Jones in West Hollywood, but here in Colorado surely she was safe.

Ben was looking at her with a peculiar expression. She didn't think he'd been impressed by Chase, which was no great surprise. The two men were as different as night and day. Ben might be a diamond in the rough, but Chase was a polished gem. It was a relief to know she could still count on—

She felt a sudden tingling sensation between her shoulder blades, and her heart stood still. Slowly she turned her head.

Three young women were standing beside a table across the room, whispering, staring. All it took was one glance for Betsy to realize they knew—or thought they did. They were exactly the kind of hip young things who'd latched onto Evan and made his life a torment. They wouldn't do the same to her; she'd be gone before they worked up their nerve.

Jumping to her feet, she said to Ben, "Can we go now?"

"Sure. Is something the matter?" He dropped the last french fry back on his plate and stood up.

"Please, let's just go!"

Betsy bolted for the door. Ben dropped bills on the table for a tip and followed, wondering what the problem was. He'd watched her withdraw into a shell as the meal progressed, and there was no reason to think it was the food. Now Betsy was running for the door as if pursued by a pack of wolves.

Ben caught up with her on the landscaped sidewalk outside. "Slow down," he complained. "There's no need to..."

She turned and a look of horror suffused her face. Someone brushed against him, and he moved aside automatically. Next thing he knew, three young women were circling Betsy like dogs working cattle. She took a step back, bumping into the hood of the BMW.

One of the women, an expensive-looking blonde, spoke. "Weren't you married to Evan Ross? I'd bet anything I saw you with him at the premiere of his first movie."

"I just *loved* Evan Ross," another gushed, pressing closer to Betsy, who looked about ready to fly apart at the seams. "When he died, I wanted to die, too. You were the luckiest woman in the world, being married to Evan Ross."

"She was married to Evan Ross, the actor?" Another trendy-looking female paused on her way to the restaurant door.

Betsy's face looked frozen. "No, you've all made a mistake. I—I'm not who you think I am."

The woman stepped closer, eyes narrowing thoughtfully. Then her face broke into a wide smile. "Betsy, it's me, Laurel Chamberlain. You remember, we met at a party about a year and a half ago? My husband Steve was an assistant director on Evan's last picture?"

Completely dumbfounded, Ben stared at the drama unfolding before him. Betsy looked at him over the heads of the four women, and he saw pure panic on her face.

He didn't take time to try to figure out why he felt so betrayed. Acting on instinct, he pushed to her side and slid an arm around her waist. She sagged against him gratefully.

The four women took an instinctive step away, and he spoke straight to them. "You've made a mistake, ladies. I'm Ben Cameron and this is my wife—" he fumbled for a name "—Crystal." Damn! Of all the names to come up with. "You'll have to excuse her," he added for emphasis. "She's shy."

Quickly he deposited Betsy in the passenger seat, climbed into the car himself and drove away. Once safe, she groaned and let her head fall back against the headrest.

"Thank you," she whispered. "I can't believe that just happened."

"You're welcome," Ben said, feeling like a fool. He'd had no idea her husband was some kind of celebrity. Now that he knew, he didn't like it a helluva lot. Over his better judgment, he asked, "You want to tell me what that was all about?"

CHAPTER SIX

BETSY DIDN'T *KNOW* what that was all about. Oh, she understood it well enough from the fans' point of view, but it was her reaction that mystified and frightened her. Because she should have been prepared. She'd known that sooner or later someone would recognize her, yet the minute she'd driven across the California border, that fear had magically disappeared and she'd felt liberated.

A false feeling, she now realized.

She didn't want to talk to Ben about it, though. She needed to rethink her situation.

It wasn't as if she had anything to hide. Staring through the window at Aspen whizzing past, she struggled to come to terms with her feelings as they neared the edge of town. At last she shifted in her seat and looked at him. She had to force herself to break the strained silence. "What you did back there...I appreciate it more than I can ever say."

He shrugged. "You looked like a doe caught in headlights. It was no big deal."

"It was to me." She found herself fumbling for words. "Ben, honestly, haven't you ever heard of Evan Ross?"

"Yeah," he said irritably. "He was your husband and he died."

"He was more than that. Most people knew him as an actor." She thought of the scene just played out in Aspen and shivered.

"An actor." Ben said the word as if he found the concept impossible to comprehend. "Movie?"

She nodded. "And television. Did you ever see a show called 'Young Blood'?"

"No, can't say as I have. Your husband was in it?"

"Yes." Betsy could hardly believe that even an isolated Rocky Mountain rancher could have completely escaped the "Young Blood" phenomenon. In one way, it was a relief to think he had, although it made her explanations more difficult. "You don't watch much television," she ventured.

He slanted her a quick, somehow hostile, glance. "I lack both the time and the inclination."

She sighed. "Evan was on that show. Then he made a movie."

"Well, I'll be a . . . You married a movie star?"

She tried to ignore the disapproval in his voice. "I married my childhood sweetheart," she corrected. "His big break came afterward."

"I see." He sounded grim; gone was the camaraderie they'd shared on their earlier passage through the mountains.

She found she didn't want to let it go that easily. "I don't think you do understand. Evan wasn't a movie star to me. He was my husband and I loved him." She stared through the car window, barely seeing the views that had made her gasp with appreciation only a few hours earlier. "When he died—"

"How?" Ben interjected. "How did he die? He must have been young, if the two of you grew up together."

"He was twenty-four. We were the same age. He died—" she swallowed hard "—in a scuba-diving accident." Her lips felt numb. She wasn't used to talking about this; she'd barely let herself think about it.

"So that's why you came to Colorado," Ben said slowly, as if he'd just figured it out, "to get away from the memories."

"Not exactly." How much did she want to tell him? The closeness she'd felt toward him was a thing of the past, anyway, now that he knew about Evan. She'd found that most men had one of two reactions to the widow of a celebrity: either they came on too strong to prove themselves as desirable as some Hollywood pretty boy, or they backed off completely, unwilling to risk their egos in competition with a celebrity, even a dead one.

She didn't think Ben had anything to prove, and his ego certainly seemed intact. Nevertheless, there'd already been a definite cooling in his attitude toward her.

She was surprised to realize that she didn't want to let their previous closeness go without trying. "I'm going to tell you something hardly anyone knows, because it doesn't make me look very good," she said after a moment. "I was thinking about leaving California even before I heard about Cupid, because of something that turned out to be a...a misunderstanding with one of Evan's fans."

"That's why you came so close to losing it back there?"

"Yes. But at the time...well, I even went to the police. I'm sure they wouldn't have taken it seriously had Evan not been who he was. The police were actually quite nice to me. They assigned one of their top men to the case."

"And he found...?"

"Nothing."

"Were you satisfied with that? Maybe..."

She shook her head. "Detective Mackenzie was great, one of the best." She didn't want to admit that the detective had eventually suggested she'd let her imagination run away with her. "But then a few days later I found out my mother might have come from Cupid, and here I am." She gave a nervous little laugh. "It seemed like a good idea at the time."

"Did that sort of thing—" he jerked his head toward the west, where Aspen lay behind the wall of mountains "—happen a lot in California?"

"All the time. I shouldn't have been so unprepared today, but I thought things would be different in Colorado."

"Aspen isn't Colorado," he said flatly. "*Cupid* is Colorado. Nobody in Cupid will stand around staring at you, even if they *have* heard of your husband."

"That's what I'm hoping," she admitted. "That's one of the reasons I'm going back to Cupid, at least for a while."

He didn't answer. Before, he'd have had something to say, something indicating approval. Before, he'd been interested in what she did. That, apparently, was over.

Slumping into the corner of her seat, she turned her face toward the window and closed her eyes, remembering....

HER MOTHER had glared at the two young people standing before her hand in hand. "You will *not* marry the day after graduation. You will marry when hell freezes over! I absolutely forbid it!"

Trembling before the predictable wrath, Betsy glanced at Evan for support. He met her mother's furious gaze with a calm self-possession Betsy could only envy.

"Mrs. Campbell," he said, "I don't think you understand. Betsy and I love each other and we're going to be together, with or without your blessing. We hoped you might see it our way—"

Joanne's laughter cut like a blade. At forty, she was thin and tanned and at the peak of her beauty, dripping diamonds and sarcasm with equal disregard. "How dare you come in here and make such an outrageous statement. You're nothing but a...a hoodlum!"

This opinion was scarcely new to Betsy. Her mother had maintained all along that Evan came from the wrong side of the tracks, which he did, and that he was standing between Betsy and a future of unlimited potential, which was debatable.

But she'd also said he'd never amount to anything. There, Betsy knew with absolute certainty, her mother's judgment was in error. Evan was so handsome, so talented, so wonderful, that it would only be a matter of time before he had the world at his feet.

"Mother, please, we don't want to go behind your back but—"

"Don't even *think* about it." Joanne's jaw hardened. "I am the only family you have in this world, Elizabeth, and I didn't devote my entire life to you just to see you throw everything away on the first boy who looks at you."

Joanne turned on Evan, a new and dangerous gleam in her eye. "Elizabeth, wait outside in the hall," she commanded. "I want to talk to this boy alone."

"No!" Betsy's hand spasmed around his. She couldn't let him face the dragon alone.

Evan calmed her with a smile. "It's all right," he murmured. "I'll just see what she wants. There's nothing she can do to hurt me—as long as you love me."

And she had, so very much. Pacing the wide marble hall, she thought about Evan, who was, quite simply, her champion. She adored him, believed in him when his own family scoffed at his acting aspirations. They just didn't appreciate or understand him, but she did.

It seemed like forever before the wide double doors banged open and Evan strode out, his young face suffused with fury.

She flew to him. "What is it? What—?"

"Later," he said. "I'll tell you later. Let's get out of here."

JOANNE HAD TRIED to buy him off. He told Betsy about it as they drove down the curving driveway and past the scrolled gates opening onto the street. She wished she could be shocked, but it was the logical next step for her mother to take.

She said as much.

Evan looked sad. "Logical for her," he agreed. "But the logical next step for us is something completely different."

"I don't understand."

"Yes, you do." He smiled at her, a dear sweet smile that melted her bones. "She'll come around, sweetheart, but it'll take time."

"I'm so tired of waiting."

"I know, and so am I. But when she has time to think about it, she may be at least a little impressed that I wouldn't take her money."

Betsy groaned. "You don't know her like I do. She'll never come around, Evan."

She only dimly realized he'd stopped the car. He turned toward her, his face earnest.

"She's right about one thing, Betsy. We're only eighteen. We've got lots of time. If we wait a few months, even a year, we'll still have our whole lives before us."

She shook her head furiously. "Anything can happen in a year."

"Such as?"

"You could find someone else."

He laughed.

"You could get run over by a truck."

"Sweetheart, I'm going to live forever."

She felt like crying. "But we've waited so long already!"

He smiled, a slow unfolding of sunny assurance that would someday light up screens large and small all across America. But on that particular day, his smile was for her alone. "Betsy, darling, sweetheart, we're both through waiting for *that.*"

And following his gaze, she saw that they had stopped in the parking lot of the Bide-a-Wee Motel.

UNTIL THAT NIGHT just a few days before their high school graduation, Evan and Betsy hadn't consummated their relationship. They had waited out of respect for each other and for the institution of marriage; they had waited because they loved each other so much they wanted to prove that what they felt was more than merely physical; and they waited because no one else they knew *was.*

That night in a seedy motel in West Hollywood, the waiting ended in a burst of sweetness that bound them together more tightly than any ceremonial words could ever do. When Betsy returned home the next day, her mother took one look and knew.

"How could you?" Joanne raged. "Fast-talking, good-looking men are all alike. If there's one thing I wanted to teach my daughter, it's that you can't trust any of them."

"Are you talking about Evan now...or my father?" Betsy asked softly.

Joanne didn't flinch from a subject they'd never discussed. "Both. I'll concede Evan's charming and attractive, but he's never going to have two coins to rub together. An actor—don't make me laugh." Her eyes flashed. "As for your father, if there's anything worse than being an actor, it's being a musician."

"Evan's different."

"So was your father, in the beginning. I'm speaking from bitter experience, Elizabeth. Go for the security. Always go for the security. And whatever you do, don't squander your youth on good sex."

To this day, Betsy remembered how shocked she'd been that her mother would say such a thing to her, but Joanne wasn't finished.

"Postpone the wedding," she'd bargained, "and I'll even send you to that ridiculous trade school you're so hot for."

Betsy didn't tell her mother that she and Evan had already agreed to postpone their wedding, which was how she became a student at the International Institute of the Culinary Arts of America. She was in class eleven months later when her mother had a burst brain aneurysm. Joanne was in a coma before Betsy and her stepfather could reach the hospital, dead by the time Evan arrived two hours later.

The day after the funeral, Betsy and Evan were married. Two days later, they moved to New York City.

New York was...New York. Betsy waited tables. Evan waited tables and went on auditions. She didn't mind. In fact, she rather liked getting out into the real world. It was hard work, but it wouldn't be forever, just something to bring in a few dollars while Evan looked for his big break. Not once did her confidence waver; she knew he'd be a star. His first agent called him "sexy-sensitive," and he was, in reality, as well as type. But for six months, nothing happened—no acting jobs whatsoever, not even a commercial.

They didn't get discouraged. They were young and in love. They were poor, but so were their friends, mostly other actors. Betsy didn't care, so long as they were together. Only in retrospect did she realize that even then, Evan was protecting her from the harsher realities of their lives, including the seriousness of their financial situation.

But life, as she'd discovered by then, is funny. When Evan got his break, it came not from New York but from the state they'd fled for greater opportunity. During a busy lunch hour at the café where they both worked, one of Evan's customers, a rather bellicose and inebriated individual, took offense when a man at the next table cast him an annoyed look. He threw the contents of his wineglass at the fellow and an altercation ensued, punches thrown. Evan stepped in to mediate.

But then the drunk attacked him. The incident ended with Evan fired and tossed out on his ear. His outraged wife quit in loyal protest and followed him through the door, where they stood on the sidewalk holding hands and staring into each other's equally dismayed eyes.

In retrospect, it made a funny and wonderful story to tell the press. For the man who'd been the drunken bully's first victim followed them outside and uttered those immortal words: "You handle yourself pretty well, kid. You wouldn't happen to be an actor, would you?"

A TELEVISION PRODUCER. The man had been an honest-to-gosh television producer!

Betsy smiled even now at the memory. Evan had been on his way. He landed a part in a new television series, "Young Blood," and they moved back to California, all in the space of a few months. The show was a spontaneous hit, and the first—and biggest—star to emerge was Evan.

The rest, as they say, was history. Since Betsy had no longer needed to work to make ends meet, she'd returned to her studies at the IICAA. Even if she never worked as a cook, chef or baker, she'd reasoned, she could cook for the man she loved.

By the time Lisa Marie was born four years ago, Evan had been making big money, and the Ross family lived in a beautiful estate in Laurel Canyon, surrounded by everything money could buy. Evan was getting nibbles from the movies and fighting off teenage fans. So there Betsy was, married to this big star who was still the boy she'd gone to school with, her best friend.

Evan had just completed his second movie role when paradise was lost. He'd taken up a number of dangerous sports, including skydiving; he'd laughed when Betsy urged him to be careful. Later, she would suspect that he'd needed the rush of excitement to remind him that he was a person first and a movie-and-television idol second. Whatever drove him, killed him.

She was numb for a long time afterward, which was just as well, because she might not have been able to stand losing her husband and her best friend both at once. A few months after the funeral, Betsy and Lisa Marie moved out of their isolated canyon home and into a very nice, very sterile, high rise on the beach. There Betsy devoted her time to her child, as much from her own needs as Lisa's. Friends drifted away and loneliness moved in to stay.

Chase Britton was one of the friends who'd remained loyal, offering quiet support to the young widow—until constant battles with his ex-wife got the better of him. He sold his L.A. restaurant and returned to Aspen, his hometown, leaving Betsy a warm invitation to visit. He'd even offered her a job, if she ever decided to put her training and talents to work.

Not that I ever would, Betsy had thought at the time, but it'd been nice of him to ask.

Then on a day not long ago, her stepfather had delivered the fateful box of letters. After reading them, Betsy had taken down the big atlas and fumbled through its pages until she found Cupid, Colorado....

BEN DROVE with only half his attention on the treacherous mountain road, watching her surreptitiously, waiting...wondering. He suspected she'd forgotten he was even in the car, so deep in thought did she appear. Her face was a blank canvas, and he could only wonder what memories she might be reliving.

Not that it mattered in the long run. Her background was even more privileged than he could've imagined. He'd been an idiot to act on the attraction he felt for her, even to that slight extent on top of the pass. Now he realized that succumbing to the temptation to put his arms around her was among the worst mistakes he could have made. She was the widow of some big-shot movie star, a hothouse flower not hardy enough to thrive in Ben's world. He should be grateful he'd found out before he got in any deeper.

He should be grateful . . .

Damn it, he was already in deeper than he liked. He'd held her in his arms, teased her, let his imagination run away from him. Now he knew he'd been wasting his time; he had nothing to offer a woman like this.

Ben didn't know squat about movies or the lifestyles of the rich and famous, and he cared even less. All he knew was cows and horses, life-styles of the tough and bullheaded.

He was what he was and he'd be damned if he'd try to put a fresh coat of paint on himself to please some woman. So why did this knowledge stick in his craw?

Because he didn't like being patronized, he decided. Didn't like it one damned bit. He grunted for emphasis.

She straightened, blinking as if he'd just awakened her. "I'm sorry?"

"Huh?"

"You said something?"

"Not a damned thing." *Look at her, giving me the works with those big baby blues.* He clamped his teeth together and kept on driving. They'd reached the southern outskirts of Cupid. As he approached the Y in the road, a small gray animal darted from the trees and directly across the road in front of him. Swearing, he whipped the wheel to the left and missed the little critter by a whisker.

"What was it?" Betsy asked. "A coyote?"

"A fox," Ben said shortly.

"It looked like a coyote to me," she said absently, gazing out the window as he took the right fork of the Y and drove down Main Street. "I guess nothing's what it seems anymore."

I'll say, Ben thought. Turning left at First, he drove into the parking lot of the Rusty Spur and killed the engine. Then he pulled the key from the ignition and dropped it into her lap. She gave him a startled glance, but he wasn't in the mood for it. He opened the driver's door. "It's been . . . different."

"Wait!"

He wished he hadn't noticed how hurt she looked by his abrupt manner. "What for?"

"Can't you at least let me explain?"

"Explain what? Hey, now that I know—"

"You don't know anything—not about me." She lifted her chin defensively. "I'd hoped we could be friends."

"Seems unlikely."

"It's that or nothing, Ben." She glanced down at her wedding ring. "I'm not ready for anything else, and I honestly doubt I ever will be."

His lip curled. "Get a grip, Betsy. You're not ready for anything else with one of us *commoners.*"

She gasped and leaned forward, her fists pressed into the plush bucket seat he'd just vacated. "That's an awful thing to say to me." Her cheeks were pink, but the self-controlled tenor of her voice remained constant.

"You think so?" He looked into her face, and his resolve to be the one who walked away first weakened, then disappeared completely. "Oh, what the hell. I'll never rest until I know." Catching her chin with one hand, he leaned down and crushed her mouth with his.

It was a fast, hard, hot kiss, both too much and too little to please him. He knew he'd caught her completely off guard, but perhaps her mouth would have been that soft, anyway, would have willingly surrendered to his aggressive demand.

He lifted his head, breathing hard. "Relax," he drawled, staring insolently into her astonished face. "That was just a test." He released her and straightened. "See you around, Elizabeth Ross."

He felt her gaze following him to the front door of the café. The place was closed for the day, and inside, Joey and Lisa sat at a table, coloring books and crayons spread before them. Ben picked up the startled boy and carried him toward the back door.

"I'm takin' Joey home now," he called to Nancy. "Thanks for watchin' him."

At the pickup, he deposited the boy on the bench seat, then climbed in and started the engine.

"You and Lisa have a good time?" he asked gruffly, throwing the truck into gear and pulling out onto the road. He avoided looking at the BMW as he passed it and had to stifle the desire to curse the truck's sluggish performance. Damned BMW had ruined him.

Joey merely nodded, his thumb already firmly anchored in his mouth.

"DAMN IT, BEN, if you think I'm going to do all the work around here while you chase after some—"

"I said I was sorry." Ben tossed his hat toward the coat rack and faced his angry brother. Jason was madder than hell and Ben was in no position to blame him.

"Sorry and fifty cents'll buy me a cup of coffee at the Rusty Spur," Jason roared, "assuming I ever have enough time to go into town again!"

"Hell, go now," Ben invited. He was so disgusted with himself that he didn't even want to argue. Tugging off his denim jacket, he added it to the already overloaded coat rack. "Go tomorrow. Stay for a week. See if I give a good—"

"Uh-oh, she's caught on to you already," Jason sniped. "Showed you the road, did she? Bright girl."

"Shut your—"

Julie piped up. "We know you were with Nancy's niece. I had lunch at the Spur and Nancy told me."

"Trouble in paradise?" Jason cooed.

They weren't going to leave him alone, Ben realized. He'd made a horse's ass out of himself that first day, and now he'd compounded his stupidity. They weren't going to leave him alone until they dug out every last detail.

"No trouble," he said, struggling to keep his temper in check. "I drove her to Aspen, drove her back, left her at the café and came on home. End of story."

"End of relationship?" Julie shot him a probing glance.

"No relationship to end." Ben tried not to grit his teeth too noticeably. "She's a good-looking woman, but we don't have a damned thing in common and never will."

"Oh, come on." Julie raised her brows. "You're a man and she's a woman. That's usually about all it takes."

"Not this time."

Ben headed for the kitchen, but Jason stepped into his path.

"Now you've gone and made us curious," his younger brother drawled. "Did you get your face slapped or what?"

Ben made a growling sound deep in his throat. Ignoring Jason, he turned to Julie. "You ever hear of an actor named Evan Ross?" he demanded.

She looked puzzled. "Yeah, sure. Hasn't everybody? Unfortunately he died not long ago in a..." Her eyes went wide and transparent with shock. "You don't mean ... !"

Ben nodded. "Betsy was married to this Evan Ross. But did she see fit to mention this to me? Hell, no. I probably still wouldn't know if she hadn't been cornered by some of his fans."

Julie's mouth hung open; she looked stunned. "Betsy was married to that *hunk?* Ben, he was wonderful! Gorgeous, charming, a great actor..."

Just what he wanted to hear, Ben thought grimly. Another woman telling him how wonderful Evan Ross was. "Yeah, that's pretty much what *she* said." He knew he sounded like a sorehead, but who wouldn't?

Jason licked his lips. "Hot stuff from Hollywood, huh? Maybe I should go into town one of these days and..."

"You do and I'll..." Ben stared his brother down with that unspecified threat. Then he uncurled his fists and stomped into the kitchen.

CHAPTER SEVEN

"SO HOW'D IT GO in Aspen?" Nancy looked up from the pan she was scouring. Cora had gone home, leaving Nancy with cleanup chores.

Betsy reached for an apron and tied it around her waist. "Chase offered me the job, but I turned it down, at least for now. I'll be staying here for a while."

With a broad grin, Nancy said, "You don't look very happy about it."

"Something else happened..." Betsy glanced around. "I saw Lisa out front. I hope she didn't give you any trouble." Grabbing a dish towel, she began drying the pans piled high in the rack while trying to ignore the knot in her stomach.

"Not a lick. Joey, either. He's a good little kid, too. Kinda pathetic, though."

"Pathetic?"

"Well, his mother—" Nancy stopped abruptly. "I'm sorry, that's something you'll have to hear from Ben."

Betsy felt a shaft of resentment. Apparently she wasn't the only one with secrets. "Speaking of

Ben—'' she put the dry pan on a counter and picked up the next ''—he's annoyed with me.''

"I figured, the way he grabbed Joey and took off.''

"It was my fault," Betsy said quickly. "I should've told him about Evan."

"Your husband? Honey, Ben knew you were married."

"Yes, but he didn't know Evan was an actor, and famous."

"No kidding." Nancy sounded surprised.

"I wasn't trying to keep secrets or anything," Betsy said. "How do you say, 'My husband was one of the hottest young actors in America' without sounding like you're bragging or exaggerating?"

"*Was* your husband one of the hottest young actors in America?"

Betsy nodded. "I never enjoyed his celebrity, but it's even worse now that some kind of cult seems to have sprung up around him."

"Sometimes that happens when famous people die so young," Nancy said with quick sympathy.

"I suppose. But I hate being recognized, and that's what happened today in Aspen. Ben bailed me out, but he was pretty irate about it afterward."

"He'll get over it. He always does."

That was supposed to make it all right? Betsy wondered. She'd never met anyone so ready to fly off the handle, but she couldn't even plead ignorance—he'd done it the day they'd met, with his sister.

Nancy looked thoughtful. "Evan Ross," she said with dawning comprehension.

"Yes. He was on television, and he made a couple of movies."

"Evan Ross! Good heavens, you were married to Evan Ross? I saw that movie of his—the one about the hit man with amnesia. John dragged me off to Denver special to see it. Cute boy, as I recall."

"That was Evan all right."

"And you say Ben was bent all out of shape when he found out?" Nancy frowned. "He does have a hot temper."

"I don't suppose I can blame him entirely," Betsy said, *for that, anyway.* Maybe she *had* given him the wrong signals on top of that mountain pass. Maybe he thought she was coming on to him. Oh, Lord. "I certainly don't want to cling to any of that 'wife of the movie star' baggage. I wanted people to get to know me before making that connection, but now...if word of this gets out, I'm afraid—"

"*If* it gets out?" Nancy arched her brows. "It *is* out. Those Camerons are a tight bunch, and you can bet Ben's told them—and they'll be talking about it to everyone they meet. This is a small town, sugar, and it's got a grapevine you won't believe. We look after our own, though, so you don't need to worry too much."

"I don't think I understand."

"Around here, folks won't talk and whisper behind your back, but they might walk right up and say, 'I hear you were married to a big Hollywood star. Is that true?'"

"What happens when I say yes?"

"Depends on who's doing the asking. But nobody's gonna invade your privacy. If you don't want to talk, that's your privilege. But if you'd care for a word of advice..."

"Please."

"Don't keep it all locked up inside. There's no need to go into intimate details, but you don't have to tense up, either. If you build a fence, people'll think you got something to hide, human nature being what it is. If anybody pushes too hard, look 'em right in the eye and tell 'em to back off!"

Betsy smiled politely, but she couldn't imagine telling anyone to back off under any circumstances.

"WELL, HEL-LO THERE. You must be the little lady who's got my big brother in an uproar."

Startled, Betsy looked up from the apple pie she'd been cutting and into a pair of gray eyes—but not Ben's. The face, although ruggedly handsome, was too young, the smile too cocky. This man was a younger version of Ben, a good copy but not the original. Nevertheless, she returned his infectious smile. "And who might your big brother be, cowboy?"

He hauled back on his counter stool in an exaggerated display of astonishment. "Ben Cameron, that's who. You got so many local boys in a lather you can't keep 'em straight?"

"It's my pies," she confided, although she had been the target of considerable male interest since she'd arrived in Cupid. "The way to a man's heart is through his stomach." She slid the tip of the pie server into the pan and extracted a big wedge overflowing with juicy apples, which she deposited on a plate. "Care for a slice while it's still hot from the oven?"

"You talked me into it. And a cup of coffee if you don't mind." He settled back on his stool and licked his lips. "I'm Jason Cameron, by the way."

She pushed the plate of pie across the counter, watching his face light up when the aroma of apples and cinnamon hit him. "I knew that," she admitted. "I'm Betsy Ross."

"Well, I know *that*." His admiring gaze swept over her.

Grinning, she retrieved the coffeepot, righted his cup and poured. "So where's big brother today?" she asked a mite too casually.

"He better be workin'." Jason shoveled a big bite into his mouth and chewed blissfully. "Okay, who made this pie?" he demanded when his mouth was again empty. "This is the best pie I've tasted since Miss Marie died."

Miss Marie. Betsy had heard Ben refer to her grandmother with that same combination of familiarity and respect. She enjoyed hearing it. "I'm the official baker around here these days," she said with understated pride. "Bread, pie, cake, you name— Why, what's the matter?"

Jason looked incredulous. "You? I thought you were just a little piece of Hollywood fluff."

"Gosh, I wonder where you got an idea like that?" Annoyed, Betsy turned away. Ben had no right to characterize her that way. He didn't know her well enough.

"Jason Cameron," exclaimed a familiar female voice, "what are *you* doing here?"

"What's it look like? I'm eatin' a piece of pie. What are *you* doing here?"

"I came to see my *friend*. Yoo-hoo, Betsy! Is this big jerk bothering you? If he is..."

Betsy picked up the coffeepot again and returned to the counter, where Julie had claimed the stool next to her twin's. People in this town drank coffee from dawn to dusk, Nancy had warned. Never approach anyone without coffeepot in hand.

Betsy poured without asking. "How's it going, Julie?"

Julie shot an I-told-you-so glance at Jason before responding to Betsy with a dazzling smile. "Fine. Just thought I'd drop by to be friendly. I didn't expect to find *him* here."

"Public restaurant." Jason chugalugged the last of his coffee and stood up. He winked at Betsy. "I'll see you around—and don't believe a word old Jewel here says about me. I'm a prince."

He sauntered out of the café, an attractive boy, no doubt about it. But if he intended to hit on her, he'd be in for a rude awakening, Betsy thought.

"Ignore him," Julie commanded airily. "I do."

"I don't know," Betsy said innocently. "He's a cute kid." And a lot easier to figure out than his brother.

Julie, who was the same age and vulnerable to the "kid" comment, grimaced. "If you say so. But I didn't come here to talk about my brother. I came to see you." She glanced around the café, nearly empty at midmorning. "Any chance you could take a break?"

Nancy, entering from the kitchen with Lisa Marie in tow, spoke up. "You bet there is. That girl's been workin' since before six this morning. You two find a place to relax and I'll bring over a couple of those light rolls she took out of the oven a little while ago."

When they were seated in a booth, Julie reached for a golden brown roll and slathered on the butter. She took a bite, and her velvet brown eyes closed ecstatically. "Wow, this is great! Where did you learn to bake bread like this?"

Betsy shrugged. "That particular recipe came from one of my mother's cooks. But I also studied at a culinary institute in California for a while."

"Why?"

"Why not? I've always loved to cook—or, actually, bake."

"To each his own." Julie popped the final crumb into her mouth. "I, on the other hand, like to eat, but I am no kind of cook."

"I'm sure you have other talents and interests," Betsy said staunchly.

Julie grimaced. "Several. My biggest interest is getting out of this hick town."

"You don't like Cupid?" Perhaps it was different if you'd grown up here; it certainly had been for Betsy's mother. But to Betsy, this little town seemed like a dream come true.

"What's to like?" Julie's mouth turned down at the corners. "It seems all I've ever wanted to do was get away. Let me amend that, get away and *stay* away. Somehow I just keep coming back." She brightened. "But when Scott and I get married, he's promised we'll live in Denver."

"Is that why you're marrying him?" It just popped out, quickly followed by an alarmed, "Oh, dear, forgive me. But the way you talk about leaving..."

Julie scowled. "I guess it's a natural mistake, considering that you're well aware of Ben's opinion," she conceded. "I happen to be madly in love with Scott and him with me. We're blissfully happy."

Betsy didn't think Julie looked blissfully happy when she said it. Nevertheless, she responded enthusiastically, "That's wonderful!"

Julie picked up her coffee cup. "What about you? "Am I blissfully happy?"

"No, although I hope you are," Julie grinned. "What I meant to ask was, are you planning to live here?"

"For a while, anyway."

"You picked Cupid over California—over Hollywood, Disneyland, the wonderful world of movies and fun in the sun?"

Betsy nodded.

"So which one of us is nuts?" Julie demanded incredulously. She hesitated, sighed, fiddled with a bread crumb, looked up suddenly. "Betsy, at the risk of being horribly nosy, is it true that you were married to Evan Ross, the movie star?"

Here it comes. Betsy nodded.

"Wow!" Julie's face glowed with excitement. "What was it like to live with a star? Was he as nice offscreen as he seemed to be on? Was he that handsome, or was it all makeup and camera angles? How did it feel to be the envy of every woman in America under the age of thirty-five? What did you do when women..."

The questions tumbled out, one on top of the other. Remembering Nancy's advice, Betsy tried to be as forthcoming as possible. Fortunately that wasn't too hard, because Julie was interested in the superficial things. Or so Betsy thought, until Julie sprang the biggie.

"Will you give me an interview for the *Cupid Chronicles?* Please, pretty please? You can trust me, I'm really accurate, and in the long run it'll save you from having to answer the same questions over and over. Please, Betsy? I might even be able to get something on the wire. This could be my big break."

At the first mention of a newspaper interview, Betsy's stomach clenched and her palms turned cold and damp. It was one thing to talk about Evan to a friend—a potential friend, even—and quite another to bare her heart and soul for the gratification of strangers. All she wanted was to live her own life, be her own private person. That didn't seem like so much to ask.

Julie apparently saw refusal written on Betsy's face for she sighed. "Why not?" she asked plaintively. "It'd be a friendly interview. Don't you trust me?"

"Trust has nothing to do with it."

"What, then?"

Betsy shook her head. "I'm sorry, Julie, I truly am, but the last thing I want to do is call attention to myself. I hope you understand. But even if you don't, I'll never give you or anybody else an interview."

"I *don't* understand." Julie slid from the booth and stood up. "But what the heck," she added philosophically. "It's your life and you're entitled to do what you want with it." A broad smile blossomed with unexpected sincerity. "I hope we're still friends."

"Of course." Deep relief funneled through Betsy.

"I'd like you to meet Scott one of these days, too." Julie's mouth turned down at the corners. "As soon as he gets back from Grand Junction."

Betsy would like to meet Julie's fiancé, the man Ben detested. There was always the possibility that she'd like him. "I'll look forward to it," she said.

"Good." Julie glanced down at her wristwatch. "Wow, I've got to get back to the paper. Gene'll kill me for being gone this long as it is—and coming back without the story?" She rolled her eyes.

"Tell him it's my fault," Betsy suggested to assuage her guilt.

"Don't worry," Julie said, "it is and I will!" With an airy wave, she headed for the door.

"And tell Ben I said hello," Betsy called after Ben's sister. She hoped Julie hadn't caught the wistful note in her voice. Truth was, she'd like to have Ben for a friend and saw no reason it couldn't happen, despite what he'd said.

Despite what he'd done...

AFTER THE CAFÉ closed midafternoon, Betsy and Lisa Marie strolled down Main Street to the bank a block away to make the Spur deposit. Their plan was to meet Nancy in an hour or so at Marie Thayer's old cottage on Lovers' Lane, where Betsy would get her first real look at what she felt confident would be her new home.

Following a morning thunderstorm, the day had turned warm and golden. Everyone Betsy passed greeted her with smiles and often with words, many calling her by name. It was a complete mystery to her, this small-town friendliness, but also gratifying.

At the bank, she fell into line behind the only other customer, a woman she'd served at the Spur. "Hello, Mrs. Kunkle," she said. "Beautiful day, isn't it?"

Lisa echoed, "Hello, Mrs. Kunkle."

"Hello, yourselves!" Folding a deposit slip, Annabelle Kunkle smiled at mother and daughter. "My goodness, how pretty you look today, Lisa Marie. Is that a new dress?"

Mrs. Kunkle moved aside so that Betsy could lay the small canvas bag of cash and checks before the teller. Behind her, she could hear the doctor's wife talking to Lisa, asking about her pink dress and black patent shoes.

The clerk, a bespectacled young man, finished counting the money, checked the deposit slip and nodded. "Right the first time, Betsy. Looks like business is picking up at your aunt's café."

She didn't have a clue who the clerk was, but he obviously knew all about her, so she nodded. "That's what she says. I—"

Lisa's sudden squeal sent shivers down her back, and she whirled. Just inside the ornate door to the bank stood Ben Cameron, just as big and tall and good-looking as she remembered. Joey stood beside his father, a hopeful smile on his face.

Betsy needed time to catch her breath, so she took first things first. "Lisa Marie! I've told you not to shriek like that. It scares me to death!"

"But, Mama, Joey's here!" Lisa rushed to the little boy and threw her arms around him. "Did you come to play?"

Joey, looking both pleased and flustered by her enthusiasm, glanced up questioningly at his father.

While his father looked at Betsy, but not questioningly. In fact, she couldn't discern a single emotion he might be feeling, so controlled was his expression.

"Hello, Betsy."

"Hello, Ben." She accepted the deposit slip offered by the interested young teller and turned back to Ben. She swallowed hard. "I'm glad to see you. I wonder if we could talk about what hap—"

"Not now." His glance flicked over her as if she was a stranger. "I'm in kind of a hurry."

"Then by all means, don't let me keep you." She felt resentful color flood her cheeks. "Come, Lisa Marie."

"But Mama—"

"*Now,* Lisa Marie. Aunt Nancy's waiting for us."
Head high, Betsy led her reluctant daughter out of the
bank and turned left on Second Street. Damn that Ben
Cameron! He not only had a temper, he was downright rude, and she was well rid of him.

And she felt just awful about it.

BEN SAW BETSY and Lisa walking along Lovers' Lane
and pulled to the curb beside them. So much for his
vow to avoid the movie star's widow.

It was a vow he'd been serious about keeping, too.
But it'd been easier to make than to keep. Seeing her
in the bank had shot all his careful reasoning to hell
and gone.

Besides, he could hardly be blamed for being a tad
curious about what she'd wanted to say to him. "Hey,
Betsy!" he yelled through the open window.

She glanced in his direction, tightened her grip on
Lisa's hand and walked faster. Grinning, Ben and the
pickup kept pace. "Don't be so touchy," he suggested. "You said you wanted to talk."

"Touchy!" She whirled on him, fire in her eyes.
"You don't have time, remember?"

"I decided to make time. Whatever you want to say
to me, Betsy, I'm ready to listen."

Actually he figured he knew what she wanted to say
to him. If she had any gumption at all, she'd tell him
to go straight to hell.

He'd not exactly covered himself with glory on the
Aspen trip. Once he'd calmed down, he'd ticked off
his transgressions: he'd assumed a helluva lot at the

top of Independence Pass, playing her like a violin; he'd been jealous of Chase Britton, when he didn't have any right to be; he'd been surly and unreasonable about rescuing her from her late husband's fans—hell, about her late husband; and then there'd been that kiss . . .

So Ben was prepared to take his medicine. "Speak to me, Betsy!" he roared.

Betsy tossed her blond curls. "Go away!" She wouldn't even look at the truck inching along beside her. Cutting sharply to the left, she marched right up to Miss Marie's little cottage.

Ben pulled into the driveway behind Nancy's minivan just as Betsy's aunt came out of the house. She waved.

"Just what we'll need on moving day," she called to him. "A guy with a strong back and a weak mind. Come on in here, Ben Cameron."

Betsy stopped in front of her aunt, and Ben saw her shoulders heave in a great sigh. Then she turned, her mouth set in a determined line, and marched up to the pickup.

"Cover your ears, Joey," Ben muttered, watching her approach with considerable satisfaction. This time she was going to really let him have it, after which they could get back on their former friendly footing.

Betsy took a deep breath. "I apologize," she said. "It was entirely my fault, and you had every right to—"

Ben didn't hear the rest of her speech because he was backing out of the driveway over his son's objec-

tions and heading back to the ranch in a worse mood
than the one he'd left in. Now why the hell had she
gone and ruined everything?

NANCY USHERED Betsy and Lisa inside. "This is the
answer to your housing crunch," she announced. "It's
furnished, too. Place is nothing fancy, but it's clean
and snug and filled with happy memories."

The house seemed to reach out and draw Betsy into
its embrace. It was perfect and she already loved everything about it, from the old-fashioned entry to the
screened porch in back.

"Where's my room?" Lisa asked. "Is it pink? I like
pink. Is there room for Teddy? Maybe Joey'll come
back to visit me someday..."

While Lisa continued with her monologue, Betsy
looked around. The rooms were tiny and dark, but at
the same time, somehow welcoming. The living room
lay to the right of the entry, and she realized her
grandmother had sat in that very overstuffed chair,
piled logs in that small stone fireplace. And there was
the dining room, barely large enough to hold the oak
table and four chairs; the kitchen, possibly the biggest room in the house, with a table and chairs, old
refrigerator and gas cookstove, cabinets with peeling
white paint showing blue beneath.

Nancy led the way into a short hall. "There's just
one bathroom and it's small," she warned. "There's
also only one actual bedroom, although a little sitting
room opens off it, which I think would do very well
for Lisa Marie."

Betsy stopped short, staring at the bed with its wrought-iron frame, its mattress covered by a patchwork quilt of many fabrics and colors. Leaning down, she trailed her fingers over the multitude of quilting and embroidery stitches. "Did your...my... grandmother make this quilt?"

"Oh, sure." Nancy hustled across the room to the open arch connecting it with the sitting room. "These are all her things. I didn't have the heart to get rid of them, and heaven knows, I don't have room for all this stuff."

Betsy had room, in her heart and in her home.

"The bathroom's right here." Nancy indicated a square extension into one corner of the bedroom. "The only entry is through the hall—funny how they used to make these old houses." She led the way, opening the door and stepping aside.

Betsy walked in and felt a burst of pleasure. The tub was the old-fashioned claw-footed kind, with high rolled edges and ornate fixtures.

"This is wonderful!" Betsy gave her aunt a grateful glance. "We'd *love* to live here, wouldn't we, Lisa? When can we move in?"

"Whenever you say." Kneeling, Nancy put her hands on Lisa's shoulders. "You like this little house, don't you, sweetheart?"

"Oh, yes!" Lisa declared. "Teddy does, too, but he wants Jocy to come play with us. He can, can't he, Mama?"

"That's entirely up to Joey's father." Betsy tried not to grit her teeth. What on earth had set the man off this time? "Shall we go out back and see what kind of yard we've got? Maybe there'll be room for a swing set."

Lisa darted down the narrow hall, Betsy and Nancy following more slowly. Betsy was delighted by what she found: a small fenced yard, the forest so close evergreen branches actually hung over the fence at the corners. And green. Everything was so green. She'd heard someone at the café remark that this had been a wet spring.

Movement among the trees beyond the picket fence caught her attention. "Lisa. Lisa, look!" She spoke with soft urgency.

Lisa turned, her gaze following her mother's pointing finger. When she saw the deer, a wondrous smile dimpled her cheeks.

Deer in the backyard, Betsy thought. Amazing!

THEY MOVED IN the next morning, and it seemed everyone in town dropped by to see how it was going and offer assistance. Nancy was busy at the Rusty Spur and therefore not available to make introductions, but that didn't seem to faze anyone. They'd knock on the frame of the open front door, then walk right in with a hand or a casserole stuck out and an explanation on their lips:

"Your grandpa used to sneak me penny candy when I was just a kid—you know, the kind that costs four bits now..."; "Used to have breakfast every day at your grandma's café..."; "Went to school with your mama...''; "Can we help you? Anything, just name it...."

Surprised and pleased, Betsy offered refreshments, welcomed willing hands to move what little furniture and boxes she had. Midafternoon found her at last alone, hanging clothes on wire hangers dropped off by the wife of the local dry cleaner, when yet another knock announced more callers.

To her pleasure, she found Joey on her front step, along with his aunt Julie and two other women.

Julie indicated her companions. "Betsy, I'd like you to meet my grandmother, Etta May Cameron, and my sister, Maggie Colby. Gram and Maggie, this is—"

"We know who this is." The old woman thrust out her hand. "Call me Grandma, Betsy. Everybody does."

Her grip nearly crushed Betsy's fingers. Alert eyes as gray as Ben's and Jason's gleamed in a lightly lined face. Grandma Cameron was the very picture of the Western woman in jeans, plaid shirt, Stetson hat and boots.

Betsy was impressed. "Come in and have some tea," she invited. "Lisa's out back, Joey. I think I have a few cookies if you'd..." But he was gone, darting down the hallway and out of sight. "Apparently not," she added with a smile.

"Us, either." Grandma Cameron planted her fists on her hips. "We come to help, not hinder. While we got you settled in snug as a bug, I thought I might fill you in about your grandfolks. We was of an age, you know—friends forever." Her eyes sparkled with self-deprecating humor. "That is, if you've a mind to listen to an old woman ramble on."

Betsy returned the smile, knowing she was going to like Ben's grandmother—and wondering what he might have told this outspoken old lady about her.

If he cared enough to say anything at all.

CHAPTER EIGHT

BETSY SETTLED QUICKLY into her new home and her new routine, which in the absence of any kind of social life centered around her child, her new family and her new job. The Rusty Spur was practically its own universe, she soon discovered, because everybody came there—everybody except Ben Cameron and, curiously enough, Julie's fiancé, Scott Hale.

Some people came for food, some came for the bottomless cup of coffee, and some just to sit and talk by the hour. Betsy's arrival seemed to add a new enticement—and it wasn't just her baking, either.

Local cowboys and townsmen alike now came to check out the "new girl" and often to flirt. The female population came, too, but they were more interested in the widow of the movie star. As Nancy had predicted, they weren't obnoxious about it, and after satisfying their curiosity, seemed ready to accept Betsy at face value.

Within days, she felt like an old-timer. She'd disposed of everything except personal mementos before leaving California, and now she was comfortably settled in her grandmother's house with her own few things around her. She'd set up the sewing machine in the corner of her bedroom, and her special baking pans and cooking utensils were all put away neatly in the kitchen.

Lisa was thriving, which was the most important thing to Betsy. The little girl loved the baby-sitter recommended by Nancy, and her only disappointment seemed to be Joey's continuing absence. It became almost a ritual between her and Julie; Lisa would look piteously into the face of Joey's aunt and inquire plaintively, "Won't Joey *ever* come to see me again?"

No matter how often it happened, Julie still seemed uncomfortable when she made excuses. Betsy recognized the real problem, though: Ben was avoiding her, and the children suffered for it.

As time went by, she found Ben and Joey on her mind more and more. And the other Camerons, too. Betsy had come to like Julie very much, also Maggie, the older sister. Julie was vivacious and friendly, as was her twin, Jason; Maggie was thoughtful and reserved, much more like the absent Ben. Grandma Cameron, in Nancy's words, was a pistol: a plainspoken woman with a heart of gold. She'd told so many stories about Owen and Marie Thayer that they'd come alive to their entranced granddaughter.

Preparing now for the noon rush at the Rusty Spur, Betsy paused in wiping down the counter. Leaning on her elbows, she rested her chin on her palms and gazed through the big plate-glass window at the gorgeous day. The air here, unlike what she'd breathed in California, practically sparkled. As warm as it had been lately, the thought of her recent arrival in a snow-storm seemed downright silly.

A chuckle roused her from her reverie.

"Looks like somebody's got a bad case of spring fever," Nancy guessed. "What you need is a nice young man to take your mind off your problems."

Betsy straightened. "I don't have any troubles," she denied, grabbing up her rag and setting to work on the counter with a vengeance. "I certainly don't need a man." Struck by a new thought, she halted her frenzied activity to look at her aunt thoughtfully. "But I do need, I don't know, a project of some sort. I have too much free time."

Nancy slid a tray of silverware into place. "I still think I'm right. You haven't had a date since you hit Cupid. At your age, that's unnatural."

Betsy laughed. "Now how can you be so sure I haven't had a date?"

"Did I mention the grapevine in this town?"

Betsy chuckled. Of course, and she'd seen enough to believe it. She'd been asked out any number of times but hadn't been tempted—well, maybe a tiny bit by Ben Cameron. Fortunately for her resolve, the man was a perfect mystery to her. How did you deal with a person who wouldn't even accept an apology without losing his cool?

But once Ben's image flashed across her conscious-ness, she found it impossible to dispel. She was still thinking about him when Julie barreled in, out of breath and frowning. Julie never walked anywhere;

she ran. Everything about her seemed to operate in fast forward.

"Quick!" she cried. "I need a hamburger, hold the onions, and coffee. Gotta eat fast so I can get to a noon interview."

Nancy headed for the kitchen. "Comin' right up."

Betsy poured the coffee. "You sure seem excited about this interview," she observed. "Who's it with?"

"It's not the interview that's got me excited. That's with the principal at Cupid Elementary—piece of cake." She gulped down a slug of coffee. "I'm just running late, that's all. Scott came by and everything's a big mess." She dumped about a quarter cup of sugar into her mug. "He's pushing me to set the date."

"Pushing? You mean you've changed your mind about getting married?"

"Certainly not!" Julie looked insulted. "But I refuse to set the date until I know I can be ready in time."

"Is that a problem?"

"It is if everything's going to be perfect—and everything *is* going to be perfect." Julie looked grimly determined. "I only plan to do this once."

"Perfect is asking for a lot," Betsy suggested gently.

"Why? I'll bet *your* wedding was perfect."

"No, Julie, my *marriage* was perfect. My wedding was . . . something else."

"C'mon, big movie star . . ."

"Evan was an unemployed actor when we got married, and it was just a few days after my mother's funeral, so we weren't in a very festive mood. We went to city hall and stood in line with a bunch of strangers. We had no flowers, no cake, no wedding dresses, no nothin'—except the two of us, promising to love each other forever." Emotion, quick and unexpected, almost choked her. "And we did," she managed to add, "at least as long as Evan was allowed."

"I'm sorry." Julie patted Betsy's hand awkwardly. "I must sound like a spoiled brat."

Betsy pushed back her precious memories. "Of course not. I guess most women dream about their wedding day. But maybe you shouldn't get too hung up on perfection, Julie. That can lead to big disappointments."

"I suppose."

Obviously she didn't believe it. "So what's the problem specifically?"

"I can't find a wedding gown."

"Are we talking formal white gown, veil, train, the whole enchilada?"

Julie nodded. "It's got to be the most beautiful gown in the world—and not cost me an arm and a leg. Everything else—flowers, food, cake and so forth—I'm willing to compromise on, but not the dress. Still, I can't put Scott off forever. There's one dress..." She sighed. "Well, I may have to settle for something less than perfection."

Julie looked so young and anxious Betsy's heart went out to her. "What are you looking for?"

Julie groaned. "The closest thing I've found is in a pattern book. It's a reproduction of an Edwardian wedding gown and it's gorgeous, but it's also covered with lace and tucks and ruffles. Unfortunately I don't sew a lick, and Maggie doesn't sew *that* well, even if she had the time, which she doesn't, what with Chuck—" She shrugged. "I've been to Denver twice, trying stuff on. The closest thing I found costs $2400, can you believe it? At that price, it should be made of solid silver or something."

"Wedding gowns can be very expensive," Betsy agreed, her mind busy. Should she volunteer to make the dress? She was looking for a project to occupy the long, occasionally lonely evenings. This was something she could do at home at her own pace. It wouldn't even cut into her time with Lisa Marie.

Nancy called for pickup, and Betsy accepted the hamburger on the pass-through shelf, placing it before Julie. Moving the plastic mustard and catsup bottles within easy reach, she said with exaggerated casualness, "Maybe I can help you."

Julie swallowed a bite of hamburger and licked her lips. "Help me with what?" She brightened. "I get it—the wedding cake. Of course!" She bounced on her stool. "I should have thought of that myself. You bake fabulous cakes. Would you?"

"Sure, but I was thinking about something else." Betsy shifted uneasily. Maybe she was being too quick to plunge in, but she did like Julie and the Camerons—even the one who was angry with her. Besides, it would take longer to *make* a gown than to have one fitted, which might give Julie and Ben more time to work out their differences.

"What, then?" Julie frowned.

The bell over the door announced another customer. Betsy edged away. "It was probably a silly idea. I'll be glad to do a cake for you. We'll let it go at that."

But Julie obviously wasn't prepared to do that. She waited until Betsy had taken Newt Turner's order before pouncing. "Tell me what you meant before. I have a feeling it was something I want to hear."

The combination of hope and doubt on Julie's face was Betsy's undoing. "I just thought that if you'd show me the pattern you like, maybe I...*maybe* I could help out. Oh, what the heck. If you want me to, Julie, I'll make your wedding gown."

Julie jumped off her stool. "Do you mean it? That's the nicest thing anyone ever offered to do for me."

"I haven't done it yet," Betsy said hastily. "Maybe you shouldn't take a chance. I mean, you don't even know if I'm any good."

"I have complete and total faith."

"I've never made a wedding gown," Betsy argued against herself. "I have made evening clothes, and I'd think that would be pretty much the same. And you have to realize, it'd take some time. A wedding gown would require meticulous workmanship, a lot of hand detailing. You'd probably not be able to get married until...oh, at least September."

Julie was unfazed by this news. "Don't try to talk either one of us out of this!" she exclaimed. "You've saved my life, Betsy! Someday I'll repay you, I swear it. Next time you need a favor, you can count on me."

"But—"

Julie glanced at her wristwatch. "Gotta go do that interview. Look, let's talk again tomorrow. Ohhh, I'm so excited! Thank you, thank you, thank you! How could my brother be dumb enough to let you get away from him?"

"Huh?"

But Julie raced from the café, her exuberance going a long way toward erasing any lingering doubts in Betsy's mind—about the gown, anyway, if not about Julie's big brother. What had she meant by that last comment? Maybe she hadn't meant anything...

Fresh doubts assailed her. Although she was confident she had the skills to make the gown, she was less than certain about getting so intimately involved in someone else's business, especially someone she barely knew.

"WHO THE HELL does Betsy Ross think she is?"

Grandma Cameron gave Ben a disapproving glance before turning back to the griddle full of pancakes. "Julie knew you'd react like this," she said calmly. "That's why she asked me to tell you—and three days after the fact, at that."

Ben stomped up and down the kitchen, shooting baleful glances his grandmother's way. He'd been up since four trying to save two more late calves and had lost them both. Hours past breakfast time, he still hadn't had a bite to eat, and his stomach was growling as loud as he was.

He stopped short, his boot heels noisy on the hardwood floor. "The last thing we need is somebody encouraging Julie to marry that rattlesnake."

"Betsy isn't encouraging anything." Granny flipped the last of a tall stack onto a plate, added a tangle of bacon strips and slapped the whole thing down on the table. "It's a nice gesture on Betsy's part, that's all. I don't think she's even met Scott."

Ben glared down at the pile of food. But hungry as he was, tired and dirty and unshaven as he was, he had something important to do before letting a hot meal calm him down. Spinning around, he headed for the door.

"Darn you, Ben Cameron, you come back here," Granny scolded. "You can't go into town lookin' like that."

"Says who?"

"Me, that's who." She followed him into the living room. "Don't do it, boy. That girl hasn't done a thing to you. You've got no right to—"

The rest was lost in the slam of the front door.

THE LUNCH RUSH at the Rusty Spur was just picking up steam when Ben Cameron barged through the front door. Betsy, in the process of refilling coffee cups at the Liars' Table, saw who it was and a smile blossomed on her lips—a smile that quickly faded.

He looked awful: tired, rumpled, red-eyed and mad as hell. Pausing, he glanced around impatiently.

She'd been about to greet him, thinking—hoping—he wouldn't be angry at her about Julie's gown. His wrathful expression stopped her cold.

"Betsy! There you are."

She flinched at his tone. "Here, Ben."

He bared his teeth in something less friendly than a smile. "We need to talk."

She lifted the coffeepot. "All right, just as soon as I finish—"

"Now!" He held open the front door as if he expected her to meekly walk away from her job.

She shook her head. "I can't go with you now. We're really busy here. I'll come as soon as I—"

"Look, I've got something to say and you can hear it here or out there, but I'm damned well going to say it."

Betsy poured coffee with hands that shook, intensely aware they had the attention of everyone at the big round table. "I have work to do, Ben. If you don't mind waiting..."

He took a menacing stride toward her, and she saw the hard expression on his unshaven face. "Have it your way," he said. "I want to know why the hell you're taking sides in something that's strictly family business."

Betsy gasped and coffee splashed over the rim of a cup. "I wouldn't do that!"

"The hell you wouldn't! You already did."

She looked around frantically for something to mop up the spill, finally reaching for the napkin dispenser.

"I...I don't know what you're talking about," she declared, ashamed of the way her voice trembled.

He took another step, and Marshal Dwight Dweakins, who occupied the chair directly in his path, swung around ready to confront the angry rancher if need be.

"Then Julie must be a liar," Ben said, including Dwight in his condemning glance. "She said you're going to make her wedding dress. Is that or is that not true?"

Betsy almost slumped with relief. "Of course it's true. But I wasn't interfering. She said she was having trouble finding—"

"You know I don't want her to marry that...that guy."

"Yes, but—"

"You sat right here in the Rusty Spur and heard us go round and round about it."

"Yes, but—"

"And afterward, I explained my reservations to you, chapter and verse."

Betsy nodded, resigned to her fate.

"And still you've got the gall to stand there and—"

The marshal shifted his bulk in his chair. "Ben, why don't you shut up and let the girl get a word in edgewise?"

"Why? She knew how I felt and she deliberately interfered—"

"I *didn't!*" Fighting panic, Betsy squared her shoulders in a show of defiance she was far from feeling. "I wasn't taking sides, Ben, I was just trying to help. Julie said—"

He made a scornful sound. "Julie's a kid. She's either high as a kite or down in the dumps."

"Maybe so, but I had no ulterior motives, I swear it. It just happens sewing's one of the things I'm g-good at and—"

"Give it a rest." His mouth curved down. "You're good at moving in and taking over."

"Then I apologize." She could hardly force herself to say the words.

"What do you mean, you apologize? You admit I'm right?" He looked astounded.

"You're *not* right, but I can't stand this . . . this shouting and public display."

"I really hate that." Ben looked around the room as if he expected support. "I hate a phony apology worse than—"

"It isn't phony! I'm apologizing for interfering, not for deliberately going against . . ." She paused for breath, feeling the build-up of pressure in her throat. The angry rumble of the lunch crowd did nothing to reassure her. This was what she got for shoving her nose into other people's business. This was what she got for trying to go against her own nature and fit in with people she didn't understand.

Suddenly Aspen looked awfully good. Chase would never take her to task this way, in public or in private. No civilized person would. She wanted to defend herself but didn't know how; worst of all, she couldn't even be sure that Ben wasn't right. What did she know about the way members of real families interacted with each other? Maybe a family was an island unto itself...

"Go on." Crossing his arms, Ben rocked back on his boot heels. "I'm still waiting for you to say something that'll make sense."

Every eye in the place turned toward her. She thrust out her jaw in an attempt to stop it from trembling. "Ben Cameron," she cried in a voice that quivered, "you're the most unpredictable man I've ever met in my life. I'll say it again—I'm sorry! *Now leave me alone!*" Whirling, she ran into the kitchen, yanking off her apron as she went, and raced out the back door.

FOR A MOMENT, there was a stunned silence in the Rusty Spur, broken by Nancy's emergence from the kitchen. "I just saw Betsy run out. What's going on here?" She looked around in bewilderment.

Marshal Deakins stood up, his narrow gaze on Ben. "That temper's gonna get you in a heap of trouble one of these days, cowboy."

Ben bristled. "What's that supposed to mean?"

Annabelle Kunkle slid from the booth where she'd been lunching with friends. "If you don't know, Ben Cameron, then shame on you." Her face beneath the carefully coiffed gray hair brimmed with outrage. "I may just have to mention this to your grandma next time I see her."

Nancy stepped up nose to nose with the startled rancher. "What did you do to my niece?" she demanded. "So help me, Ben, if you've hurt her..."

"I never laid a finger on her," Ben protested. "I gave her every chance to come up with a logical explanation. The way you people are acting—"

"Oh, we ain't actin'," Johnny King snarled. He'd recently started working part-time across the street at the service station, and gainful employment hadn't done much for his personality.

Annabelle chimed in self-righteously. "Why don't you pick on someone your own size?"

Ben retreated a step. He was always ready for a fight, but something told him he had no chance of winning this one. He frowned. "What're you people sayin'? That I was too rough on her?"

The angry chorus of assent that greeted that innocent remark swept away any lingering doubts; as far as this community was concerned, Ben Cameron had put his boot in it, big time.

BETSY RAN ALL THE WAY home to her grandmother's house. Thank heaven Lisa hadn't been at the café to see that awful confrontation, she thought wildly as she slammed through the front door. Lisa was at the park with the baby-sitter, which was just as well. Betsy felt awful; the last thing she wanted to do was put on an act for her daughter.

In the tiny bathroom, she splashed cold water on her face and drew several deep breaths, trying to calm herself. What had she done that was so terribly wrong? If Ben couldn't see that all she wanted was to help...

Feeling a bit calmer, she walked out into the back-yard. It was a beautiful sunny day, although the grass was still soggy from an early-morning hailstorm. Dejected, she sat down on one of the swings on the set she'd bought for Lisa. Closing her eyes, she leaned forward and rested her face in her hands.

"THEY SAID I CAME DOWN pretty hard on you. If I did—"

Hell, she didn't even let him get the words out of his mouth before she jumped up from the swing and started backing away.

"How did you get in here?" she demanded, looking around as if expecting to find a secret passageway or something.

Her eyes were red, but at least she wasn't crying, he thought with relief. "The front door was standing wide open."

"Well..." She just sort of sputtered into silence and stood there gazing at him as if he were a wolf and she a fluffy little lamb.

"Look," he said, "I'm getting desperate—about Julie, I mean. I made the mistake of telling Hale to back off—"

"Oh, I get it. That must be why he's leaning on her to set the date."

"He is? That son of a..." Ben clenched his teeth and his fists. "Everybody in the family's talked to her."

"Talked to her or yelled at her?"

"Jason yelled, I guess, but Maggie and Granny went a little easier. Now you come along and make it simple for her."

"No, Ben, that's not how it is at all!" She looked at him incredulously. "Do you think I can just glance at a pattern for a formal wedding gown and produce the finished project the next day? It's going to take me *ages*."

"Aw, hell." All the fire went out of him. "You mean this is a ploy to *delay* the wedding?"

She groaned. "You just don't get it, do you? Of course it's no ploy. I like and respect Julie too much to do a thing like that. I plan to make her the greatest wedding gown a girl ever had. To do that, I'll have to work *very* slowly and *very* carefully. If while I'm doing that, she has a chance to decide she's making a mistake... well, that's all right, too."

Ben wanted to kick himself. "I guess I misjudged you," he ventured. "I didn't realize you were on my side."

"I'm *not* on your side. I'm on Julie's side. For all I know, Scott Hale's the greatest guy in the world, despite the apparently all-but-unanimous disapproval of the Cameron clan. I haven't met this man yet, but I'm going to. And when I do, I won't let your opinion influence me one way or the other."

Ben took his lumps because he deserved them, but he still had a problem. "Then why did you apologize back there?" He jerked his chin in the direction of the café. "Why didn't you tell me what I could do with my—"

"Because I don't operate that way!" She wrung her hands together as if she was at her wit's end trying to make him understand. "I've been a peacemaker all my life. I hate tension and fighting and... and general unhappiness. That's why I apologized."

"You shouldn't have," he said shortly. "When you're right, you've got to stand up for yourself. People respect strength."

"Meaning, *you* respect strength."

"Sure. Don't you?"

"I respect people who don't fly off the handle at the least little thing."

He laughed. "Kinda puts me in a bind to hear that. Okay, Betsy Ross, I apologize. Does that satisfy you? I was wrong and I apologize. Can we go on from here?"

She looked at him as if she couldn't believe what she was hearing and seeing. "No, Ben Cameron, we can't. You're... too hard on my nerves." She turned her back, presenting stiff shoulders to him. "You were right when you said we could never be friends. Please close the front door on your way out."

HE'D NO MORE THAN GONE when Nancy came rushing out into the backyard. "I met Ben on my way in," she said. "Did he apologize?"

Betsy shrugged. "For all the good it'll do."

"I read him the riot act, for all the good *that*'ll do— me and everyone else who was there."

"Let it go, Aunt Nancy. I'm a big girl. It's time I learned to take care of myself, I guess."

"At least you're not packing to leave. I was kind of afraid..."

"Believe me, I thought about it. I have to wonder if maybe I don't really belong here, after all."

"Hogwash." Nancy's lips thinned. "Those Cameron boys may act like wild men, but they don't mean anything by it."

"It really doesn't matter." Betsy twisted the diamond ring on her finger. "Ben Cameron is bossy and bad-tempered, but the worst thing is, he's completely unpredictable, at least to me. There's no chance we'll ever be friends after this."

"I'm sorry to hear that," Nancy said slowly. "But I'm glad you're not going to take off on me. You're sure?"

"I'm sure."

"Good." Nancy turned toward the back door. "I really have to get back to the Spur."

When Betsy said she should head back there, too, Nancy insisted she stay put and take whatever time she needed to recover. "The lunch crowd's thinning, I've got the two girls in to help, and we'll manage fine." She paused. "You'll be all right?"

Betsy nodded. "Thanks, Aunt Nancy."

After Nancy had gone, Betsy sat in the backyard for a long time, thinking. New grass sprouted beneath her feet; perennials poked through in the flower beds. Beyond the fence and across the clearing, she could see movement inside the fringe of trees but didn't know what animal lured there. It could be anything; the area abounded with wild animals.

Rising, she gave the swing an extra push before wandering over to the gate in the picket fence. Now that she'd found a place where she could belong, she wouldn't let anybody or anything make her leave—not before she was darned good and ready.

A door slammed inside, and she heard the sound of running feet just before Lisa burst through the back door, the baby-sitter right behind her.

"Mama, Mama, you're home early! Can you play with me now?"

Betsy swooped her daughter up into her arms. "Sure can, sugar."

Home. This really was her home and no overbearing rancher was going to run her off.

CHAPTER NINE

JULIE DROPPED BY Betsy's little house on her way home from work the next day, speaking woefully about the scene in the café. "I suppose this means you take back your offer to make my dress," she concluded.

Betsy had worried that question to distraction and felt there was only one thing she could do—but not for the reason Julie would suppose. "I'm afraid so," she said regretfully. "Ben was right about one thing—I did contribute to a rift in your family, however inadvertently. I'm truly sorry. I hope you understand."

"I understand all right. I understand that my brother's a *jerk* and it's time somebody told him so."

"Please don't," Betsy said, "not on my account, anyway. I won't be the cause of any more trouble in your family."

She meant it with all her heart and soul, for no one had more respect for family unity than Betsy Ross, even when the family involved wasn't her own.

JULIE'S VISIT was on a Thursday; the next day, Betsy had another guest after she'd gone home from the café in midafternoon. She was checking cake layers in the

oven—another five minutes and they'd be perfect—
when she heard a knock on the door.

"I'll get it, Mama," Lisa called from the living
room.

"Lisa, don't." Betsy heard the front door open.
Wiping her hands on her apron, she hurried into the
other room, less than pleased. Lisa knew better than
to answer doors, but she'd gotten complacent about
the rules since they'd moved to the country.

Ben Cameron stood framed in the open doorway,
Joey beside him. Betsy had never seen such a shame-
faced expression on Ben's face. She met his sheepish
gaze, waiting for an explanation.

Lisa tugged at her sleeve. "Mama, Mama, Joey's
here! Can he play? Can he come into the backyard?"

Joey pulled his thumb out of his mouth. "We
brought you somethin', Lisa."

"A present!" Lisa clapped her hands and jumped
up and down in excitement.

Betsy had spent many hours contemplating this
meeting. She'd decided to remain cool and aloof, no
matter what the provocation, but there hadn't been
any provocation as yet and she already felt anything
but cool and aloof. In fact, if she didn't know better,
she'd think she was actually glad to see him.

Ben looked awkward, standing there with both
hands behind his back. "I've been thinking," he ventured in a gruff voice.

"Really?" She refused to give him the slightest en-
couragement, although she suspected her voice was

somewhat more tart than appropriate from someone who no longer cared.

"Oh, hell." He looked disgusted. "You don't intend to make it easy, do you."

"Should I?"

"You got a point there." He stepped inside, trying to maneuver his hands around in front without dropping whatever it was he held. "I brought a peace offering."

What he'd brought was a puppy. Lisa's joyous shriek terrified the poor little thing; it whimpered and tried to claw its way up Ben's chest. He managed to control the pup long enough to set it on the floor, where he held it with one big hand when it would have darted away.

Then it was too late, for Lisa pounced. "It's beautiful," she declared, crouching and grabbing the puppy. She hauled it against her chest in a fearsome hug. "Oh, Mama, did you ever *see* a more bee-*ooo*tiful dog?"

Betsy figured she *could*—in any dog pound in America. The puppy was a mongrel of indeterminate origins, its nondescript brown fur sticking out in all directions while its tail twitched from side to side. It struggled with all its might, but not to get away; instead, it lunged for Lisa, bathing her face with its tongue. Joey hunkered down beside the newly introduced pair, beaming.

Betsy groaned. "Now look what you've done," she accused Ben. "I'll never get that...that *thing* away from her."

He looked hurt. "Why would you want to? Every kid needs a dog. Besides, you need a watchdog."

"Says who?"

His frown vanished. "I get it. I'll bet you never had a pet when you were growing up in La-la Land, right? No dogs allowed where streets are paved with gold."

"It's not that." Betsy bit her lip. Every kid might not *need* a dog, but Lisa certainly wanted one. He was right on the other count, however. They could definitely use a watchdog on general principles—although looking at this nominee for the job raised serious doubts as to its suitability for the job.

But there was another problem: she just didn't feel up to any additional responsibility, especially a little dog.

Joey looked at her, his expression hopeful. "I picked this dog out all by myself," he said proudly. "It was the prettiest one of all Daisy's puppies. You like it, don't you?"

That did it; Betsy knelt, reaching out to scratch the little mutt behind one floppy ear. She smiled at Joey and he hung his head in pleased confusion. "It's a very nice dog," she declared. "Lisa Marie and I appreciate you thinking of us, Joey."

Grinning, Joey sidled up to her. She slipped an arm around his slender body, giving him a kiss above his left eye.

Lisa stood up, holding the pup around the chest while the rest of him dangled like a rag doll. "C'mon, Joey," she commanded, "let's take Erica out back to play, okay?"

Ben glanced at Betsy. "That okay with you? If you want me to take the mutt away, say so now, before she gets too attached to it."

"She's *already* too attached." Betsy gave a long-suffering sigh. "And since Joey picked that puppy out special, I suppose I am, too. Maybe we do need a dog around here."

"A dog named Erica," Lisa put in.

"Better make that Eric," Ben advised, straight-faced.

Lisa laughed. With the dog beneath one arm, she wrapped the other around Ben's leg. "You're funny, Mr. Cameron. Eric isn't a girl's name!"

"My point exactly."

The two kids looked puzzled momentarily, then, giggling, carried the puppy into the backyard, leaving Ben and Betsy alone. The satisfied gleam in his eyes signaled the abrupt departure of all humility.

"You won't be sorry," he told her confidently. "It's important for kids to grow up around animals."

He was so irrepressible that she felt herself weakening toward him. "That's beside the point, wouldn't you agree? There was no way I could disappoint those two." The timer in the kitchen went off. "Cakes in the oven," she explained. "Make yourself comfortable and I'll be right back."

His idea of comfortable was to follow her into the kitchen and perch on a chair while she bustled about taking the cakes out of the oven, flipping them from their pans and onto baking racks to cool. When she turned to him at last, he was sniffing the air appreciatively.

"Sure smells good," he hinted broadly.

"If they were frosted, I'd give you a slice, but..." She shrugged.

"I wouldn't mind a chunk bare."

"You're kidding."

He shook his head. "Hot cake right out of the oven with a glass of cold milk is my idea of good eats. But if you have other plans for that cake..."

She didn't have other plans. She needed a fancy frosted layer cake like she needed—like she needed a dog.

So she cut a big wedge out of one golden layer and served it to him with a tall glass of milk. He ate with such obvious relish she found herself feeling just the tiniest little bit friendlier toward him. If there was one thing in this world she missed, it was watching a man enjoy the bounty of her kitchen.

He finished his snack, and awkwardness settled around them like fog. After a minute of strained silence, Ben stood up, giving her a defensive glance.

"Before I call Joey in, I wonder..."

Her scalp prickled with tension. "Yes?"

"We're having a little birthday party tomorrow for Grandma."

Betsy brightened. "That's wonderful. How old will she be?"

Ben shrugged. "Who knows? She won't say, but she's got to be close to eighty. Anyway, I, uh, was

wondering if you'd like to come to the party. Lisa
Marie, too, of course.''

"Oh, I don't think that's a good—"

"It'd mean a lot to Joey," he added hastily.

"That's not fair!" She bit her lip, refusing to look
at him. "Why are you doing this? We've agreed we
can't be friends."

"Who did?"

"We did! When we got back from Aspen, you told
me we'd never be friends. I...I hoped you were wrong,
but after the way you yelled at me the other day in the
Spur—"

"You call that yelling?" His eyebrows soared.
"That was nothing more than a noisy conversation."

"It was yelling," she insisted, "and a little of it went
a long way." When he started to interrupt again, she
held up her hand. "Please, let me finish," she requested with dignity. "When you followed me here, I
told you, right out there in that backyard—" she
pointed "—that I agreed with you we'd never be
friends."

"Oh. Is *that* what you were trying to say?" He
looked astonished. "Well, forget it. I didn't agree with
you when you agreed with me. In fact, I've changed
my mind about everything."

"What are you *talking* about?"

"Everything. The ruckus at the Rusty Spur, the
misunderstanding about the trip to Aspen. All that
Hollywood-star stuff caught me by surprise, that's all.
I'm having a tough time figuring you out, Betsy.

You're—" he grinned and gave her back her own word for him "—unpredictable."

"*I'm...*" Fumbling mindlessly for his cake plate, her clumsy hands sent it wobbling on the edge of the table. She gasped and made a grab for it.

He was faster, snatching the plate from midair. Then he stepped to the counter and put it safely down. The action brought him very close to Betsy, almost touching her. In fact, if he lifted his arms—as he was doing now—she'd be within the loose circle of his embrace, just as she'd been that day on top of the pass.

Only then her back had been toward him, and now she was looking right into his face. Holding her breath against a panic attack, she stared. He made a low satisfied sound deep in his throat and tightened one arm around her waist. Pulling her against him, he held her there, tipping her chin up with his free hand.

"Before was just a teaser," he murmured. "Let's see what it's like to really..." Bending his head, he claimed her mouth with his

She shocked herself by letting it happen, and then it was too late, because she got all tangled up in sensations she hadn't felt in a very long time. She didn't have a lot of experience with this sort of thing—making out in the kitchen—and found herself responding to his kiss with a pent-up emotion she didn't even recognize.

Evan had been gentle, accommodating, never demanding, and that was her standard of comparison. Evan had always started slowly, advanced by careful degrees with her complete acquiescence, stopping at any point at which he sensed the slightest reluctance on her part.

Not Ben Cameron, who kissed her as if he knew damned well that reluctance was the last thing on her mind. He wanted; he assumed she wanted, too. Cupping the back of her head, he deepened the kiss, thrusting his tongue into her mouth, which had become soft, welcoming—

Suddenly, with a strangled cry, she shoved him away. She felt surrounded, absorbed, swept away, even now that they were no longer touching. Pressing her hand to her throbbing lips, she stared at him, aghast. It took a couple of tries to get her voice to work again, and then she cried, "What makes you think you can come in here and—"

"Don't play games, Betsy." He didn't seem at all annoyed, just a bit perplexed. "We both know—"

"I don't know anything." Her mouth throbbed, her breasts tingled, she felt hot and cold—all at the same time. Her body still felt the imprint of his at every point where they'd touched.

"Okay, sure." He moved a few steps away as if realizing how much his nearness intimidated her. "We'll pretend it never happened if that'll make you happy— which it won't. So, will you come to Grandma's party? It's no biggy, just the family for cake and ice cream."

She found herself staring at his mouth and licked her own lips in reaction. "It...doesn't seem like a very good idea."

"Why not?" He cocked his head, tendons standing out on his strong brown throat. "Grandma likes you, Betsy. All the Camerons like you."

"Even you?" Oh, why had she asked that stupid question?

His grin melted her bones. "Especially me, as if you needed to ask."

"F-forget I did! I like your family, too, but—"

"It's me, then." He looked almost playfully mournful, as if he was fishing for a compliment and didn't care if she knew it.

"No. Yes!" He was confusing her; she no longer knew what she was saying. "Look," she said desperately, "we can't be friends and we sure can't be *more* than friends, which doesn't leave us with a lot of options."

"No?"

"No!"

"Is it something I said?"

She couldn't help laughing at his tone. "Not really. In fact, it's not even personal." That startled him, but she rushed on. "I had a good marriage, Ben. From what I've seen, that puts me way ahead of most people. But I don't ever expect to be that lucky again and I won't settle for less, if that makes any sense."

"Not a lot."

"Then I'll say it right out. I don't sleep around and I'm not interested in marriage. If friendship's not a viable alternative—" she shrugged, for there it was "—nothing's left."

He looked suddenly very serious, creases deepening in his lean cheeks. "That about puts us at an impasse."

"I'm afraid so. I'm sorry."

The back door banged open and the two children stampeded into the kitchen with Erica yipping at their heels. Joey jumped up and down, as excited as Lisa Marie this time, so excited he could hardly talk.

"Daddy, Daddy," he cried, "Lisa says she'll come to Grandma's birthday party and she'll bring Erica! Daddy, can she ride my pony? Can she see the calves? Can she..."

In his enthusiasm, the little boy reached out and touched his father's hand.

Betsy saw the shock on Ben's face, and then the fierce love and protectiveness as his hand closed over the smaller one of his son.

Lisa threw her arms around her mother's waist and hugged with all her might. "Joey says he'll teach me to be a cowgirl, Mama! Can we, can we go? Please? Can we?"

Betsy's gaze met Ben's above the children's heads. She didn't want to go, but her reasons were purely selfish. She nodded slowly. "We'll go," she said to Ben, adding as a face-saving measure, "if I can make the birthday cake."

"You don't have to do that." He sounded just as formal and reserved as she. "You're a guest."

"It would give me great pleasure."

"Okay, if you're sure. One more thing..."

"Yes?"

"If I do anything you don't like—let's make that *when* I do something you don't like—it'd help if you'd speak up so we can talk about it."

It sounded reasonable when put that way, yet she knew it wasn't reasonable at all. What he really meant was that she should give as good as she got, and that she doubted she could ever do.

A tug on her hand spared her from answering. Lisa looked up with a frown of disapproval.

"You cut that cake without any frosting," the little girl accused. "Can Joey and me have some, then?"

"Please, Mrs. Ross?" Joey added his entreaties. "I'm hungry!"

"And I wouldn't mind just one more little sliver," Ben put in with a grin.

It was as if they'd never had a cross word. Betsy stewed while she cut the cake layer, as if they'd never shared whatever it was they'd just shared.

BEN PICKED THEM UP at the cottage after the Rusty Spur closed the next day. Lisa and Erica came running out to meet him. He set about loading the dog into the bed of the pickup, securing the animal carefully with a rope so he couldn't fall or jump out.

By the time that was accomplished, Betsy had joined them. With Lisa in the middle on the bench seat, Betsy squeezed in next to the passenger door with the cake cradled carefully on her lap.

It had been a long time since she'd put so much effort into a baking project, and she'd enjoyed it enormously. Finding out Grandma's favorite flavor had been easy. As Julie said, "Anything, so long as it's chocolate."

Chocolate, it most definitely was: three kinds, in fact, combined in a high-rising three-layer extravaganza. Betsy had used a chocolate mousse for the filling, and for the frosting... ah, that was the pièce de résistance.

The cake was wrapped in a thin sheet of melted and tempered chocolate, its top covered with chocolate ruffles in an overlapping rose-petal design. Betsy had always excelled at working with chocolate, which required infinite patience and precision. In the center of the giant "flower," she'd placed one white birthday candle, appropriate for a lady of a certain age.

Relaxed and happy, she enjoyed the ride, exclaiming about the view at every bend in the road. Ben played tour guide, pointing out the sights with such decorum she suspected he, too, might be uneasy at this, their first meeting following the kitchen encounter.

Betsy herself had dealt with it by *refusing* to deal with it. She'd decided that from now on, "pleasant but impersonal" would be her watchword. Fortunately that was easy enough to maintain traveling through the beauty of a Rocky Mountain springtime.

She wasn't prepared for her first sight of the ranch compound, its red roofs set off by the green mountainside. As they drove across the bridge over a fast-moving little creek, she breathed an impressed, "Wow! I never dreamed it would be so... so elaborate."

"I don't think 'elaborate' is quite the word." Ben drove into the ranch compound, between corrals on the right and outbuildings on the left. "This is strictly a working ranch. Everything you see has some utilitarian purpose." He indicated a large brick structure. "That's the bunkhouse." He pointed to each building as they passed. "Calving sheds are over there, and that's the barn . . ."

None of it seemed utilitarian to Betsy; it all seemed wildly romantic. But as Camerons poured out of the huge two-story house with its wraparound porch and rushed to greet the new arrivals, she found herself too overwhelmed by their number to think about anything else.

GRANDMA CAMERON poured lemonade and offered it to the newcomers. "Sure are tickled you could join us for my birthday party," she said to Betsy. "A little bird told me you'd be bringin' something mighty special." She gestured at the cake box.

Betsy set it on the party table. "I couldn't imagine what I might get you for your birthday, so I told Ben I wouldn't come if he didn't let me make your cake," she said. "This is one of my favorite recipes." While she spoke, she unfastened the latches on the cover. "I hope you like it, too."

She lifted the high-domed cover, and there sat her masterpiece on a crystal-and-silver plate in all its improbable chocolate glory. The gasp arising from the assembled Camerons was more than enough reward for her labors.

"Good grief, what *is* that?" Awe filled Jason's voice.

Julie pretended a sophistication she didn't possess. "What's the matter, you never saw a cake before?"

"That is undoubtedly the most extraordinary piece of edible art I've ever encountered." Maggie walked around the table to view the cake from every angle. "Betsy, you're an artist."

Ben and Grandma crowded forward for a better look, then made a path for Chuck, who'd been a shock to Betsy. She'd had no idea that Maggie's husband was confined to a wheelchair. Everyone seemed to take it for granted, so she supposed whatever put him there must have happened a long time ago. Now he grinned at her.

"Boy, oh boy," he said, rubbing his hands together. "You can make all *my* birthday cakes from now on."

She smiled back. "It's a deal." She meant it, too. "When is your—"

"Hold it! She can't waste time making birthday cakes when she's got a wedding dress to sew." Julie grabbed Betsy's hands and spoke imploringly. "Now that you and Ben have made up, you'll make my gown, won't you?"

Betsy glanced at Ben, uncomfortable that his family thought there'd been anything between them to be "made up." But he ignored the question in her eyes. "Julie," she began, "Ben—"

"Has changed his mind!" Julie cut in anxiously. "Haven't you, big brother?" She flashed her dimples at the brother in question.

"Yeah, sure." Ben sucked in a breath that strained the pearl snaps on his shirt. "But if you don't have time to do it, Betsy, I'll understand—*we'll* understand. Right, Julie?"

He was giving her a way out, Betsy realized; was he being polite or did he want her to take it? That question must have been plain in her eyes because he went on.

"Really, it's up to you. Where she gets the dress isn't going to be the determining factor in whether or not she marries that guy."

"If you really mean that," Betsy said slowly, "then of course, I'll be happy to make the gown. I really hated to break my promise in the first place."

"Hallelujah!" Julie looked ecstatic.

Betsy laughed nervously, unsure whether she'd done the right thing or the wrong. "Do you have the pattern? I'd better take a closer look at it before we start making serious plans."

"It's upstairs."

"I'm going with you," Maggie announced. "Somebody needs to provide a voice of reason, and that always seems to fall to me."

Grandma watched the three young women go, a nostalgic smile on her face. "That child's got a good heart," she said to no one in particular. "I wouldn't like to see it broken."

IT WAS THE MOST laid-back party Betsy had ever attended. No one seemed in any special hurry to get down to presents or food or anything else in particular. Instead, they talked, drank lemonade, moved in and out of smaller groups, played with the children, put Jason's new CD on the player...

Joey and Lisa had gone outside right away, since Granny didn't allow dogs in her house, not even canines as special and superior as Erica. Every ten minutes they felt obliged to stick their heads into the living room to inquire whether or not it was finally time for *someone* to saddle the pony.

Ben and Jason, the sole candidates for someone, finally took the hint, and both of them departed for the barn. Betsy, who'd never been around horses of any size and never wanted to be, wasn't sure she could stand to watch her daughter's first riding lesson.

Opting to stay inside with Granny when Julie and Maggie went outside to watch, she asked plaintively, "Are you sure she'll be safe?"

"Sure as I can be," Grandma said enigmatically. "Sometimes we're as safe as we think we are, Betsy."

That bit of philosophy wasn't terribly comforting, but Betsy bit her tongue and tried not to think about her daughter on a horse. Only when she thought of Ben did the worry start to pass. If there was ever a man to have by your side in times of potential danger, he was the one. He wouldn't let anything happen to Lisa.

The brothers eventually grew weary of hoisting kids up and down, so they tied the patient little pony to the porch railing where Joey and Lisa could crawl off and on to their hearts' content. Which they proceeded to do with much glee.

When Ben and Jason entered the house, they saw Betsy and Grandma quietly talking off in one corner. Jason gestured across the room. "Whattaya figure those two are up to?"

Ben shrugged.

Jason's brows arched and his mouth curved in a devilish grin. "I'm real glad you talked Betsy into comin' out today."

Ben felt his hackles rising. "How so?"

"I like her, that's all."

"What's that supposed to mean?" Ben didn't care for the way his little brother was looking at Betsy.

Jason screwed up his face in mock confusion. "I like her, that's all. She's great lookin', she's a great cook, she's great fun—at least when she's not being yelled at."

His laughter grated on Ben's ears, and then Jason added, "'Course, I'd never yell at her myself, although I understand you kinda went out on a limb in that department. I like to think I'm smart enough to learn by your lousy example." He winked in a conspiratorial manner. "You know what they say about catching flies with honey."

At that point, all Ben's frustrations, and they were legion, surged to the fore. Without stopping to think, he hauled back and rammed his fist into his brother's face. Jason dropped like a stone and lay there, stunned.

But only for a moment. Roaring a challenge, he staggered to his feet and stood there, wavering and shaking his head to clear it.

Betsy looked up just in time to see Ben's blow. When the younger man hit the floor, she jumped to her feet with a cry of alarm. Had Ben lost his mind? At that moment, the front door opened to admit Lisa and Joey, Maggie and Julie behind them.

Julie sized up the situation quickly. Planting her hands on her hips, she glowered at her brothers. "What's going on here? Grandma, make them stop! This is supposed to be a birthday party."

Grandma didn't have a chance, for Jason had come roaring back. Head down, he butted Ben in the chest, grabbed him around the waist and wrestled him to the floor. Fists flew, punctuated by an occasional grunt as they thrashed around in a frenzy of punches and counterpunches.

Lisa Marie stared at the men, her blue eyes wide. "Mama, Mama!" She flew across the room. "Uncle Jason is killing Joey's daddy!"

It was all Betsy could do to remain calm. "No, sweetheart," she soothed, "they're just…" Just what? Ruining a birthday celebration, frightening women and children?

Only she was the only woman and Lisa the only child who seemed even slightly alarmed. Maggie had settled on the arm of Chuck's chair, and they both watched with a kind of detached interest. Julie stamped her foot and shouted imprecations of the "Were you born in a barn?" variety, while Grandma regarded her grandsons with what looked like resignation.

Ben surged to his feet. ''You better learn to watch your mouth little brother, if you know what's good for you!''

Jason jumped up, too. "Make me, big bro—"

Ben proceeded to do that very thing. Grabbing his brother by the scruff of the neck and the waist of his jeans, Ben hurled him across the room, effectively ending the fight.

And the party, for when Jason went down, the cake table went with him.

CHAPTER TEN

JASON HIT THE FLOOR amidst crashing dishes, splattering cake and splintering table. Betsy clutched her daughter and stared at the mess in horrified disbelief. Jason must be, if not dead, at least seriously injured. She'd never witnessed a physical altercation before—she didn't even want to call it a fight—and was stunned into speechlessness by the violence.

Then Ben made it worse. Stalking across the floor, he stood over his victim with fists clenched like some victorious Neanderthal. "Had enough?" he demanded.

Betsy gave a little gasp of dismay. She couldn't believe he'd say such a thing to a man who was flat on his back, especially a brother.

"Not hardly!" Jason blinked twice and sat up. Moving gingerly, he tested his shoulders, his arms, his legs, looking for injury. Apparently finding nothing serious, he stood up, not easy to do in the midst of glass shards and wooden splinters and slippery chocolate.

"Didn't hurt *me* much," he announced, as arrogant and hard-eyed as his brother, "but we played hell with that cake."

He lifted an arm for their inspection. Chocolate smeared his long-sleeved shirt from elbow to cuff, and when he turned to check, his backside, as well.

Ben gave a disgusted grunt. "Damn you, Jason. You ruined the birthday cake."

"I was tryin' to ruin *you,* if that's any consolation."

Grandma stamped one booted foot. "Stop it, both of you! You act like you ain't got the brain of a gnat between you."

Betsy patted Lisa distractedly and spoke to Julie. "Does this mean the party's over?"

Julie looked startled. "Not necessarily. Sometimes we bust up two, three cakes without ruining the fun. But I don't know, that was a pretty fancy creation."

Ben looked penitent. "Aw, Betsy, I'm sorry. We didn't mean to ruin the cake."

Maggie leapt into the controversy. "You two bone-heads don't have the first idea how long it takes to make a cake like that. It'd serve you both right if Betsy never speaks to either one of you again."

Jason paused in his fumbling attempts to scrape birthday cake off his backside. "He said we were sorry," he muttered.

"You don't act sorry!" Julie yelled at her twin. "Look, you've scared Lisa."

Lisa was watching the adults bicker, her mesmerized gaze going from one speaker to another. Realizing she was the center of attention, she burst into tears and buried her face against her mother's side.

Betsy could hardly speak, she was so upset—and she especially couldn't speak about what was really bothering her, since she was the only one apparently concerned about the fight. "We'd better clean up that mess," she suggested in a tight voice. "It can't be doing that hardwood floor any good."

Ben rubbed his bruised knuckles. "If Jason wasn't so clumsy, the cake wouldn't—"

"Don't try to blame it on me!" Jason shouted. "You're the one—"

Grandma had had enough. "Will you two quit brawling like a couple of little boys? Jason, get out of here and clean that chocolate off."

"Aw, Granny, I don't wanna miss the party." Lifting a hand, Jason licked at the brown smear on the side of his hand. "Hey, this is good!"

Ben noted Betsy's rigid expression and made one last stab at reconciliation. "Betsy, I apologized about the cake. What do you want from me?"

His insensitivity was the last straw. "The cake? The cake?" She clenched her fists and glared at him. "What kind of shallow simpleton do you think I am? *I don't care about the stupid cake!*"

She couldn't believe he'd made her lose her temper, but the man was positively uncivilized. Dropping to her knees, she began scooping cake onto a sliver of the shattered plate, keeping her head down in hopes no one would see the tears in her eyes.

"You sure care about *something,*" Ben muttered.

"You big galoot!" Granny knelt beside Betsy, resting a hand on her shoulder. "You two boys spend so much time scrapping with each other that we've all gotten used to it, but it's no way to act around company."

"But—"

"But me no buts, Benjamin Cameron. You and your brother can just take it on outside and beat each other to death, if that's what'll make you happy."

"Oh, for the love of—"

"Git!"

Ben and Jason looked disconsolate walking out the front door and leaving a trail of chocolate crumbs behind them. After a brief hesitation, Joey started after them.

"C'mon, Lisa," he invited. "Maybe they'll untie ol' Poco and we can ride around the house!"

"Oh, boy!" Trauma forgotten, Lisa ran after him.

For a moment Betsy stared at the front door and then she began to laugh. Sitting back on bent knees, she shook her head helplessly and laughed, trying to find some meaning in what had just happened.

Granny grinned. "Laughin's always better than cryin'," she said with approval. "But we're all real sorry about your cake. It looked mighty good."

Betsy brushed at damp cheeks. "I can make another one," she choked out. "It really *isn't* the cake that upset me, it was the fight." She cleared her throat and shook her head, trying to settle down. "Did I understand you to say they do that often?"

Maggie and Julie knelt on the other side of the mess. "Often enough," Julie said. "You okay now, Betsy?"

"I'm fine, really. I'm just not used to seeing two men try to kill each other."

"Is that what you thought?" Julie sounded astounded that Betsy could draw such a conclusion. "Gosh, kiddo, boys'll be boys. Didn't anyone ever tell you that?"

"Not a soul. What does it mean?"

Maggie sighed. "In this case, it means that Ben and Jason have been scrapping with each other all their lives. Especially the last few years. Ben says the day Jason can whip him is the day little brother can head out on the circuit, with his blessings."

"What circuit?"

"Boy, you *are* a foreigner!" Julie said incredulously. "The rodeo circuit. Jason thinks professional rodeo is just waiting for him to show up and teach 'em how it's done. Ben thinks there's too much work needs doin' at home, and rodeo is just Jason's version of running away from his responsibilities."

"But Jason's only a boy!" Betsy objected. "I suppose Ben never ran away from anything."

"Once." All the lightness was gone from Granny's tone and she sounded dead serious. "He'll pay for it the rest of his life."

Julie quickly switched the subject back to Jason. "Anyway, Jason never misses a chance to start something with Ben, and that's why."

"But it wasn't Jason who started the fight today," Betsy said.

Julie frowned. "You must be mistaken."

Betsy shook her head with certainty. "Ben struck the first blow. Poor Jason was simply defending himself."

"Poor Jason?" Both his sisters seemed to find great humor in that characterization.

Betsy just smiled and shrugged. She'd called it like she saw it.

Granny looked thoughtful. "If that's true—and I'm not saying it's not, but if it is—it's a first. Ben's got a temper, but I've never known him to strike the first blow."

Julie piped up. "Whatever Jason said or did must have been *awful*."

Nothing could be awful enough to precipitate a fight in the middle of a birthday party, Betsy told herself while they cleaned the mess and mopped the floor. But she might as well quash any lingering curiosity on that subject, because it really didn't matter. The mere fact that Ben could act like a savage was all she needed to know.

She should never have let him worm his way back into her good graces. The Camerons were a volatile family, and she had no business getting mixed up with them.

But she *was* mixed up with them, at least for a little while. She'd promised to make Julie's wedding gown—again—and she couldn't back out a second time.

"So, will we need to go to Denver to get the fabric for your gown?" she asked when order had been restored.

That new topic pleased Julie enormously. "You'll go with me? Oh, Betsy, that's wonderful! I can't tell you what this means to me. Can you get away this Saturday? We can shop, do lunch, have a great time. I'll come pick you up—you'll baby-sit, won't you, Maggie? We can drop Lisa Marie off here to play with Joey..."

And so it was decided, as the four women sat around the kitchen table, sharing coffee and conversation and three-day-old muffins Julie pulled out of the bread box.

IF IT WASN'T the cake, what the hell was it? Ben puzzled the question over in his mind and found no ready answer. Betsy had seemed a little cowed by the crowd at first, but he'd thought she'd settled down and started to actually enjoy herself.

The front door opened and Betsy and Julie came outside. Ben, leading the pony with Lisa on board, stopped so abruptly that Joey walked up his heels. Absently Ben picked the boy up and set him behind the saddle.

Julie shaded her eyes with a hand. "Where's Erica? Betsy needs to get on home."

Both children set up a howl of protest, but Betsy waved them silent. "I'm sure that poor little pony can use a rest," she argued. "Now it's time to find Erica, okay?"

Ben resisted the urge to grin. Betsy didn't know squat about animals, including domestic ones. That "poor little pony" was fat and lazy and a long way from earning his keep. But when the kids slid down, Ben made no protest, just led Poco back to the easy life in the near pasture.

When he returned, Betsy and Julie had Erica cornered near the porch. Just as Julie reached for the pup's collar, Joey and Lisa rushed up to "help." Seeing his chance, Erica darted between Joey's legs and raced for the barn, ears, tail and tongue flopping. The noisy posse took off after him.

The shaggy brown pup was having a high old time of it, easily avoiding their increasingly ineffectual efforts.

It did Ben good to see Joey so relaxed and happy. Sitting on the front steps, Ben waited for the inevitable capture of the canine wonder. It came in about ten minutes with Julie carrying the pup toward the pickup truck.

Betsy and the two children appeared around the corner of the barn, flushed and laughing. They were far enough away that Ben couldn't hear what was said, but suddenly they stopped. Betsy dropped to her knees and pulled the two kids into her embrace, giving each a kiss. For a moment they simply huddled there, wrapped in each other's arms.

Watching the little scene, Ben felt a surprising stab of envy. They looked so right together, but where Joey was concerned, Ben was usually left out in the cold.

He sighed. Joey wasn't only becoming attached to Lisa but to Betsy, as well. And why not? The boy missed his own mother, and there wasn't a damned thing his father could do about that.

Except . . .

No, damn it! Betsy would never fit in here, not in a million years. It'd be a mistake to let the boy hope.

Still, there was no reason Ben shouldn't take one more crack at mending the rift between Betsy and himself, and if it didn't work, to hell with it. He met Julie at the tailgate of the truck.

"Let me do that." He took the pup from her.

"*Now* he offers." Julie rubbed dirt off her hands onto her denim-covered thighs.

Betsy and the kids arrived while Ben worked to secure the wriggling dog. When that chore was completed to his satisfaction, he jumped down beside them.

"Betsy. . ." he began.

She looked at him calmly, as if he was a stranger. On her own, Julie drew the children a short distance away.

"I really am sorry about the cake."

"I don't want to hear another word about that cake." Her eyes flashed briefly and she added, "Are you sorry you hit your brother?"

"Oh, for—! My brother doesn't need you to fight his battles for him."

"That's not what I'm— Oh, forget it. I have to get home." She turned her back on him.

"Now what're you mad about?"

"If you don't know, I'm not going to tell you!"

"Why do women always say that when they don't have a leg to stand on? I may not be Mr. Cool, but at least I'm no quitter." That last was said with malice aforethought.

"Meaning I am?" She glared at him over her shoulder.

"What do you call this?" He gestured at the pickup. "You *could* hang around to talk about this, instead of running out. If that's not cowardice—"

"Goodbye, Ben." She was calm again, as calm as if she'd flipped a switch turning off strong, and therefore troubling, emotions.

"What do you mean, goodbye? I'll drive you just as soon as I get cleaned up a little."

Julie turned with a sheepish grin, dangling the keys from her fingers. "I told her I'd do the honors. I knew you'd be busy."

"Damn it, Julie!"

Betsy smiled sweetly. "I've already said my goodbyes to everyone else. Thanks for inviting me, Ben. It's been . . . an education."

He watched them load up and drive away, and then he watched them out of sight. Beside him, Joey sighed.

"Have a good time, son?" Ben turned toward the house, Joey beside him.

"Yes, but . . ."

"Yes, but what?"

"I didn't get any of Grammy's birthday cake, and Lisa's mama made it *special!*"

The boy spoke so plaintively that Ben had to grin. "Life's full of little disappointments," he counseled, dropping a light hand on his son's shoulder as he said the same words his own father had said to him so very long ago. "You gotta learn to take it like a man."

"Is Lisa's mama mad at you, Daddy?"

"Maybe...a little."

"What'd you do wrong?" the boy asked, genuinely puzzled.

"Not a doggoned thing," Ben said.

"Then why...?"

"She's a female, Joey. They don't need reasons."

More together than they'd been in a long time, they entered the house.

AT BETSY'S REQUEST, Julie dropped them off at Nancy's. "Then I'll pick you up next Saturday for our trip to Denver," Julie promised.

"No need. I can drive."

"This is my party and I'll do the driving," Julie declared. She added with a grin, "Besides, I've heard about you and mountains."

"Okay, you can do the driving but not next Saturday. The Saturday after that, if it's all right with Nancy."

"Oh." Julie looked briefly disappointed. "Okay, if that's better for you."

"It is," Betsy said firmly, but she was lying. She had no plans for next Saturday, but she was putting off the shopping expedition out of deference to Ben, and in so doing, she'd created a one-week delay in the wedding preparations. Although why she should do such a thing for him was a mystery to her. And Scott Hale was probably a very nice man.

If Ben disliked him, he seemed almost certain to be.

Nancy opened the front door with a big smile. "So how're things at the Straight Arrow? You have a good time?"

Lisa nodded. "Oh, yes, Aunt Nancy! We had a wonderful time, didn't we, Mama? Me 'n' Joey—"

"Joey and I, sweetie."

"Joey and I rode the pony, and Daddy and Uncle Jason—"

"Daddy!" Betsy felt as if someone had stabbed her in the heart.

Lisa looked momentarily confused. "Joey's daddy, I mean, and Uncle Jason—they smashed Mama's special birthday cake and Grammy gave them what-for."

Nancy's quick glance assessed Betsy's discomfort. "I'll bet she did."

"Then I got to pet the calves and chase the chickens, but they don't like being petted." Lisa looked around. "Where's Chester? He likes to be petted."

The little girl scampered away in search of the cat. Nancy slipped an arm around Betsy's shoulders. "My goodness, it sounds like you've had quite a day. Come on into the kitchen and tell me all about it over a glass of iced tea."

"You're sure we're not intruding?" Although she knew what Nancy's answer would be, Betsy still felt awkward about barging in unannounced—but felt awfully good, knowing she could.

Together they walked down the hallway.

BACK AT THE RANCH, Julie tracked Ben down and confronted him. "Betsy says you started that fight, and I want to know why."

Ben just looked at her with chilly eyes. "That's none of your business."

"Look, if you ever expect to get back on Betsy's good side—"

"Her *good* side? You gotta be kidding! I wouldn't touch her good side with a ten-foot pole."

He stomped out of the room. After a moment's thought, Julie went in search of Jason. She found him in the horse barn, brushing down his buckskin gelding.

"Okay, wise guy, what'd you say to Ben to make him take the first swing?" she demanded.

Jason gave her a sour look and took another long swipe down the horse's back with the currycomb. "That guy's got no sense of humor."

"Depends on the subject."

"The subject was *her*. You'd think they were married, or at least engaged, the way he acts."

"I see." At least, she was beginning to. "What did you say exactly?"

He pushed back his Stetson, leaned against the horse's broad flank and frowned. "Damned if I know. Something about...her looks, I think." His brow cleared. "But it was no insult, I'm sure of that. Hell, if he's not interested, I'm more than ready to..."

If he's not interested? Men could be so stupid sometimes.

WHEN RUNOFF from a long cold winter hit Horse-thief Creek, the banks of the little stream first bulged, then spilled over into irrigation ditches. The water brought new life to meadows yellow with the stubble of last summer's grass, which had become last winter's hay.

Looked good, Ben thought with satisfaction, crossing one hand over the other on the horn of his big Western saddle. The Camerons irrigated more than 1200 acres here and on a second ranch higher in the mountains. The grass would be four or five feet tall by August, with each acre producing enough to carry a cow through another winter. What hay they couldn't raise, they bought, so the state of the hay fields in May and June said a lot about profits for the next year.

Ben had been so busy lately that this was his first opportunity to get out and really look around. While his back was turned, spring had come in with a vengeance. May was feeling a lot like June.

June. Julie had wanted to get married in June. He hadn't heard anything more about that damned dress, but Betsy was probably finished with it by now; how hard could it be?

Not that anybody was talking to *him* about Betsy, weddings, or much of anything else, and he'd be damned if he'd ask. Elizabeth Ross was out of his mind and out of his life.

Lifting the reins, he headed for the house. He'd been out since early morning, just looking around and enjoying the day. Now all of a sudden, the sunshine seemed less warm and the air not nearly so soft. To hell with it. Maybe he'd drop by the Hideout later, have a few beers, flirt with the women.

By the time he reached the ranch compound, he'd made up his mind. He'd even let Jason come along if the kid'd promise to act like a grown-up for once in—

His hand tightened spasmodically on the reins, and the well-trained cowpony sat back on his haunches. Ben stared at the two kids chasing Granny's cat through the flower beds. What in hell was Lisa Marie Ross doing at the Straight Arrow?

But what he really wondered was whether Betsy was here.

Banging the surprised horse with his heels, Ben rode up to the ranch house at a gallop, and the horse obediently skidded to a stop in front of the hitching rack. Ben swung out of the saddle, tossed the reins over the bar and turned to meet the kids racing up to him.

Which surprised him, really. Joey was still more likely to run the other way. And he knew Lisa liked him, but he still wasn't prepared for her to run right up and throw her arms about his waist in a big hug.

"Joey's daddy, Joey's daddy!" she cried. "You've come back!"

"Huh?" Ben looked over her head at Joey, who had stopped a few feet away. The boy looked mystified, but he'd go along with anything where Lisa was concerned. "What're you doing here, Lisa?"

"Playing with Joey." Planting her little fists on her hips, she stamped one pink boot, which set the fringe to dancing. "Joey, come hug your daddy, please."

Now she'd gone too far, Ben thought—and did a double take when Joey shyly obeyed. The press of his son's arms was brief but certainly welcome.

Lisa gave Ben a sunny smile, and he found himself grinning back at the daughter of the woman he'd vowed to avoid like a rattlesnake. "Uh..." He hesitated; she waited, her head cocked to one side like an inquisitive bird. "Uh... is your mother inside by any chance?"

"Nope. She went to Denver with Aunt Julie." The little girl whirled around. "Joey, now we gotta hide before the wolfs catch us!"

"Huh?" Joey glanced down, saw his sheep dog, Killer, sitting there with tongue lolling out, glanced to the right where Erica battled the frayed end of a rope tied to a corral post. "Oh, yeah—wolfs. Let's go!"

Watching them, Ben felt his resentment soften. Maybe he'd misjudged—

No, damn it! He wasn't going to get sucked back in by a little girl with the power to bestow a gift Ben had almost given up on—a hug from his own son.

BETSY AND JULIE picked up one tired and happy child that evening when they returned from their successful shopping expedition. Lisa had had a wonderful day with Joey. They'd played with the dogs and Granny's cat, had ridden the pony, made a batch of sugar cookies with Maggie and generally run wild. Betsy supposed that was all right—once in a while, anyway.

In a large, carefully wrapped package in the trunk were hundreds of dollars' worth of white silk broadcloth and lace, interfacing and buttons and thread and hooks, all proudly paid for by Julie. Betsy had her work cut out for her, but she looked forward to the challenge. The gown would be breathtakingly lovely, she was sure of it.

Betsy hadn't seen Ben since the birthday party, although she'd seen every other member of the Cameron family and was on excellent terms with them— even Jason. He'd come into the café and she'd tried to give him the cold shoulder, but found his sheepish apology impossible to resist.

Ben was made of sterner stuff obviously. He'd made no attempt to see her or communicate with her in any way, which suited her just fine. Although she'd calmed down, she was still of the opinion he'd been in the wrong.

Unfortunately Julie had spent a good part of their driving time talking about her oldest brother. Betsy had dreaded a chance meeting with him, but he'd been gone when they'd dropped Lisa off with Maggie.

So Betsy had all day to dread a chance meeting with him on their return. She wasn't a bit disappointed when someone said that Ben was out checking fence. She had no idea what he might be checking fence *for*, but was relieved she wouldn't have to face him.

When the time came to go, neither Erica nor Killer could be found. It took some doing to convince Lisa that her pet had probably followed Joey's dog for a romp in the fields and forests. Only when Julie and Maggie promised to see the pup safely returned was

Lisa willing to climb into the back seat of Julie's car for the ride home.

They entered Cupid just in time to see what Julie took to be the vehicle of her intended. She twisted the steering wheel of her old rattletrap, her hands apparently following her eyes. "That's Scott's car! He must've got back from Cheyenne a day early. Let's follow. I can't believe you haven't met him yet, Betsy."

She kept up a running commentary as they followed the silver Cadillac down Main, separated by a couple of cars that had pulled out onto First Street.

"That's him...that's not him...yes, it is, I'm sure of it." Julie followed the Cadillac south at the fork of the road. "He's heading for the Hideout."

"I can't take Lisa into a bar," Betsy said indignantly as they pulled into the Hideout parking lot.

Julie laughed. "It's what you'd call a *family* bar during the day—only gets rowdy at night. They serve food, even have a kiddy menu. You'll see, it'll be fine."

With little choice in the matter, Betsy unbuckled her seat belt and helped Lisa out. The little girl was tired but happy, and unusually docile.

Betsy had to admit she'd been curious about the Hideout, a weathered log building with a tall false front. The parking lot always seemed to be filled with dusty pickup trucks, so it must have something going for it. Pushing open the double doors, they entered.

And came face-to-face with a buffalo—a full-size stuffed buffalo, mounted on a platform facing the door. Lisa was enchanted, rushing to pet the creature on one moth-eaten shoulder while Betsy examined their surroundings.

The Hideout looked like something out of an old cowboy movie. Mining and cowboy paraphernalia, maps, stuffed birds and animals covered its rough plank walls. A large dance floor took up the entire middle third of the cavernous room, with an enormous and ornate bar to the left. An assortment of old one-of-a-kind furniture ringed the dance floor. Six booths lined the wall opposite the bar, and a bandstand occupied the far end of the room. Absolutely nothing matched, yet everything went together to create a curiously appealing rustic atmosphere.

Country-and-western music throbbed over a loudspeaker, and a half-dozen or so couples two-stepped around the floor, completing a picture as foreign to Betsy as a Bedouin tent in the desert.

Julie pointed. "There he is! C'mon, gang."

At their advance, Scott Hale looked up from his spot at the far end of a fairly crowded bar. His blond hair gleamed, and a big smile split his smoothly handsome face. "Hi, sweetheart," he greeted, drawing Julie into his arms for a kiss.

Betsy waited, already smiling. What did Ben have against this guy? she wondered. He was adorable. She kept right on thinking that until Scott, still holding Julie in his arms, caught Betsy's glance—and winked.

Betsy quickly discovered that she didn't like Scott Hale any more than Ben did. Nevertheless, she was soon wedged into the big corner booth with Lisa and the happy couple. At least Lisa was enjoying herself.

She'd never been in a place like this, and she loved watching the dancers almost as much as she'd enjoyed petting the buffalo.

While they waited for the hamburgers they'd ordered, Julie gave Betsy a big smile. "So, did I tell the truth? Is he a doll or what?" She snuggled closer to Scott.

Scott's grin was not the least bit self-conscious. "C'mon, baby, you're embarrassing the lady," he protested with false modesty. "She used to be married to a movie star, for Pete's sake, running around with that Hollywood gang—"

"You've got me all wrong," Betsy protested. "I never ran around with any Hollywood—"

"—hobnobbing with big shots," Scott talked right over her, his gaze roaming restlessly around the room. "Hey, there's a friend of mine. Beau, over here!"

Beau, the big, slow-moving cowboy who was a regular at the Rusty Spur, ambled over. "Howdy, Betsy," he said, "Julie. Yo, Scott, what's happenin'?"

"Sit down, sit down," Scott invited expansively. "Betsy here was just about to tell us about her life in Hollywood."

"Julie!" Betsy's expression said, *Save me!*

Julie did, sort of. "Leave Betsy alone," she ordered her fiancé. "Let's dance while we wait for our food."

Which cut Betsy's problems directly in half, for Beau said, "Hollywood? You used to live in Hollywood?"

Betsy couldn't imagine anyone in town who didn't know about her Hollywood connection by now. If she'd stumbled on one, she wasn't interested in clarifying things. "Let's don't talk about that," she said. "Let's talk about you. Have you lived in Cupid long?" She reached for her wineglass.

Beau guffawed. "Not long, just my whole life. Hey, there's Johnny King! Johnny, over here!"

Johnny slipped into the booth without waiting to be asked and deposited his beer, in a long-necked bottle, in front of him. Lisa looked at him a little fearfully, then moved over to sit closer to her mother.

"Well, well, well," he drawled, staring. "Fancy meetin' you here, Betsy, and all alone. I heard you was taken."

His expression made her flesh crawl; his words made her wish fervently that she was, as he put it, taken. If she had been, she wouldn't have had to put up with the likes of him.

Before she could set him straight, a familiar voice sent shivers down her spine.

"You heard right, King. Get your butt outta that booth and your face outta my sight, because I'm not feelin' long on patience tonight."

Ben.

And one quick glance told her what he thought about finding her and her innocent child in a booth with two men at the local honky-tonk.

CHAPTER ELEVEN

"GOODIE!" LISA EXCLAIMED brightly. "Joey's daddy and Uncle Jason!"

Jason, standing slightly behind his grim-faced brother, smiled. "How y'doin', ladies?"

Ben said nothing, nor did he glance at the little girl; all his attention was on her mother. He'd dropped by for a beer and a little social activity, and this was what he'd found: Betsy in a booth with two of the lowest lowlifes in town.

His gaze locked with hers. "Come on," he ordered brusquely, "we're getting out of here."

Betsy didn't argue, just turned to Beau, wanting him to move so she could get out; grumbling, he stood up and she scooted out of the booth, dragging Lisa after her.

Taking Betsy's arm possessively, Ben glared at Johnny and Beau. "You two boys ever take a notion to get...friendly with this lady again," he said softly, "I suggest you think twice. Because next time, I will surely rip your gizzards out and feed 'em to the buzzards."

Beau's mouth worked, but no words came out.

Johnny tried bravado. "Hell, Ben, we were just keepin' her company for you. No need to get all touchy."

"You been told."

Betsy stared at him wide-eyed, but whether she was shocked or scared or relieved, he hadn't a clue.

Lisa tugged on his sleeve. "Joey's daddy, what about my hamburger?"

"Beau and Johnny can eat it—and pay for it," Ben said. "Let's go." He held out his hand.

Lisa took it.

JASON WATCHED THEM leave, his brow wrinkled in thought. He hadn't seen Ben this worked up over a woman since... Crystal. Somebody grabbed his elbow and yanked. Jason turned, ready to put a fist in Johnny King's face just on general principles. The two had gone to school together and hadn't liked each other then, either.

But it wasn't Johnny. It was Julie and her sleaze of a boyfriend.

"Was that Betsy and Ben I just saw leaving?" Julie demanded. "What happened?"

"Hi, sis. Didn't see you here."

"We were dancing. Are you going to tell me what happened?"

Jason shrugged. A flash of yellow caught his eye, and he recognized Bernadine Rentfrow sashaying up to the bar. Bernadine was just about as hot to trot as any female in town, and Jason did like to trot. He tried to shake off Julie's hand, but she tightened her grip.

"Nothing happened," he protested. "Ben was ticked off to find Betsy and Lisa here with Beau and Johnny."

"Betsy wasn't with Beau and Johnny."

"We saw her, Julie." Bernadine was giving him the eye, and Jason was getting impatient.

"She was here with me!" Julie planted her hands on her hips and glared at him. "She didn't even want to come, but I insisted because I wanted her to meet Scott."

Finally forced to acknowledge a man for whom he felt nothing but disdain, Jason said, "Yeah, Scott. How's it goin'."

Scott frowned. "It *was* goin' fine." He glanced at his intended. "Do you think we oughtta go after her? She came with you, so maybe you oughtta make sure nothing's wrong."

Julie considered. "Maybe...not," she decided. "I'll check in with her later. I think Ben can handle the situation. Wouldn't you agree, Jason?"

Jason nodded enthusiastically. He would have agreed to anything in his haste to answer Bernadine's heavy-lidded summons. But in this case, he happened to mean it.

BEN DROVE Betsy and Lisa home, and not a word was said inside the cab of his pickup. Mad and getting madder, he laid rubber turning into her driveway.

She didn't ask him in, just opened the truck door and climbed out, taking Lisa with her.

He watched her walk to the door and fit the key into the lock. He ought to leave, just drive away, but he'd be damned if he'd let her off that easily. Climbing out of the truck, he slammed the door for emphasis and followed her into the house.

Without a word, she led Lisa Marie to the kitchen, seated her at the table and set about making a peanut-butter sandwich. Pouring a glass of milk, she put that on the table, too.

"There, honey," she said calmly. "You eat your supper while Mama has a few words with Mr. Cameron."

Lisa nodded and reached for her sandwich.

Without a word to Ben, Betsy led the way into the backyard. He followed, beginning to feel a little sheepish about his anger.

She turned slowly and he braced himself for anything. Gathering dusk cast shadows but little illumination on her face.

She spoke. "You had no right to do that."

So calm, so cool. A muscle in his jaw ridged with his effort to match her self-possession. "Maybe not, but when you see an accident about to happen, you have to do what you can to prevent it."

"Really." She turned and walked a few steps away.

"You don't know those two guys."

"Of course I do. They're customers at the café."

"They're pond scum—at least Johnny King is. Beau . . . Beau just tends to do what he's told."

"That's not the issue." She turned to face him. "You can't tell me what to do or who to do it with. I'm an adult, in case you haven't noticed."

In case he hadn't noticed? He'd noticed too much. Like now, her breasts lifting beneath crimson silk with every breath she drew, and her khaki-colored slacks clinging to round hips and sleek thighs. He could remember how that adult body had felt pressed to his, how those ripe lips had tasted...

She was still talking. He tried to concentrate on her words and not on the growing ache in his gut.

"And I'm perfectly capable of managing my own life."

She was talking to him as if he was some stranger who'd wandered in off the street. It ticked him off big time.

He reached for her, his hands closing around her rigid arms just above the elbow. She gasped but didn't try to pull away, just stared at him. He felt a tautness in her that hadn't been apparent in her voice or her words; the balance of power was shifting. As long as she could hold him at bay, she was in control.

Once he touched her, *he* was in control—or maybe not. At the moment he didn't feel in control of anything, least of all himself. But neither was she.

Neither was she—for she'd begun to tremble. "Ben," she whispered, no longer cool, no longer collected. "I—"

"Shut up," he said in a voice so rough he hardly recognized it, "and kiss me."

She caught her breath and those luscious lips parted. Taking advantage, he slid one arm around her waist and yanked her hard against him. Before she could resist, his mouth covered hers urgently.

Her wholehearted participation shocked him, for with a sigh, she slipped her arms around his waist and raised to meet him.

He kissed her as if he'd never get enough, and in truth, he wasn't sure he ever would. Betsy Ross was under his skin, and he didn't seem able to stay away from her no matter how hard he tried. The chemistry between them was inexplicable, but so damned powerful.

When he'd seen her in the Hideout with those two deadbeats, he'd been struck by such a surge of possessiveness he'd been forced to act. Now he wanted to possess her in deed, as well as in thought. He reached for her breast.

She moaned and leaned into his kneading hand. Beneath the silk, her flesh rose soft but resilient into his palm. Her nipple hardened, peaking between his thumb and forefinger, and she pressed herself more tightly against his thigh.

They'd gone too far too fast. He tore his mouth away and raised his head, gasping, grappling with himself for control.

Suddenly some sixth sense sent alarm shooting through his body, freezing him in the act of unbuttoning her blouse. He heard a scratching, followed by a low, vibrating, purring sound. It acted like a bucket of cold water hurled over his burning body.

"Betsy!" He caught her arms and stood her a few inches away, enough to break the blissful contact.

Slowly her eyelids drifted up, and he saw confusion replace the dreamy languor. She straightened, quivering. "What?"

"Do you feed Erica in the backyard?"

"Erica?"

He heard it in her outraged exclamation: *You're asking about the dog at a time like this?*

"Please, sweetheart, it's important. Do you?"

She shook off his light hold as if it offended her, as indeed it probably did at this point. "What if I do?"

Her voice held a little breathy note that told him she had no more been able to turn off her passion than he had. He wanted to groan in his frustration but forced himself to move, to urge her toward the house.

"I think we've got company," he said softly.

"What?" She glanced around as if expecting to find an audience. "Where?"

"Not that kind of audience. You feed the dog in the far corner of the yard under the tree, don't you."

"Sometimes. Why do you ask? What's going on?"

She let him guide her toward the door with one hand at the small of her back. Beneath his palm, she felt fluid and boneless, the way she'd felt in his arms.

"There's something back there eating the dog food."

She gasped. "What?"

"I can't be sure. I think it might be a cat."

"A wildcat?"

"Or it could be a raccoon, or even a fox. It's a little early in the season for bears."

They'd reached the door and she was through it in a flash. He followed more slowly, well aware that although his mind had cleared, the turbulence in his flesh had not.

BEN WAS OUTSIDE with a flashlight checking for unwanted visitors when Julie and Jason arrived, Scott opting to remain at the Hideout. Jason went straight out to join Ben, while Betsy finished tucking Lisa into bed before returning to the kitchen.

At which point Julie demanded, "What's the matter? You look, I don't know, upset."

"I'm fine," Betsy said too quickly. She wasn't fine; she was trembling with the aftershocks of her encounter with Ben. Even now, she couldn't believe that he'd swept away all her reservations in a single moment.

What would've happened if they hadn't been interrupted? She shivered.

The back door opened and Ben walked into the room, Jason right behind. "We can't make out what the hell it was, but dog food's scattered all over," Ben said in disgust. "I should've warned you not to leave anything edible outside. That's never a good idea in these mountains, but the way your yard backs up to the trees makes it even more important to be careful."

"All right. I . . . don't know much about animals, wild or otherwise." *Or about men, either—wild or otherwise.*

"I know," he said. "It's my fault. I should've warned you."

"You're not my keeper." She strove to keep her tone level. "I can look out for myself."

"Yeah, right."

Julie watched, her avid gaze swinging from one to the other. She smiled at no one in particular. "Well, I'll bring in the stuff we bought today in Denver, Betsy. Then I guess I'd better get going. C'mon, Jason."

"I'll ride with Ben." Jason was looking at Betsy when he said it, his eyes thoughtful.

"You'll ride with me!" Julie gave him a shove.

"I'm leaving now, too," Ben put in.

"No need to rush," Julie said quickly. "Take your time."

Ben's lips thinned. "I'm going *now*, Betsy . . ."

"Yes?" *Why didn't they just go, all of them?* She desperately needed time to think about everything.

"I'm sorry if I was out of line, dragging you out of the Hideout like that."

"You misunderstood, Ben. I was there with Julie and Scott, not those other two."

"Whatever. I'm still sorry." He walked to the front door and everyone followed. With his hand on the knob, he turned and said quickly, "And I'm also sorry about the damned birthday cake!"

Before Betsy could respond, he was gone.

Which was just as well, because she wasn't sure whether she wanted to kick him or kiss him.

LATER SHE SAT at her window staring up at stars so near she might almost have plucked a brilliant handful. Turning, she reached for her hairbrush. As she ran the bristles through her short curly hair, she asked herself, very calmly and very rationally, what she was going to do about Ben.

She barely knew him, yet in some ways she felt as if she'd known him always. She'd been drawn to him from the first, the prototype of a cowboy against which all others must come up short. But she'd refused to consider the sexual attraction that hummed between them until he'd forced her to confront it.

How could he affect her so? In her entire life, she'd never loved any man, emotionally or physically, except Evan. She had never dreamed she could, never really wanted to, not even after his death.

Now she found herself restlessly tossing the brush aside and pacing the length of the small bedroom, only to pace back again. She'd never felt such sexual tension, not even with Evan. The difference, she supposed, was that now she knew too well what she was missing.

She wanted Ben so badly her teeth ached.

This was not good. She had no intention of embarking upon either a cheap love affair or a second-rate marriage. She'd spend the rest of her life alone before she'd do that.

But first she had to get through this interminable night....

Betsy began work on Julie's wedding gown the next day, knowing that if she didn't keep busy, her thoughts would drive her crazy. She threw herself into the project with a vengeance—and waited to hear from Ben.

And waited.

Maggie brought Erica home, to Lisa's relief, and then Julie dropped by to check on the progress of her gown. Between sewing at night and working at the café during the day, Betsy was always busy—but not too busy to miss Ben, and to wonder what he was doing, and if he ever thought of her.

She didn't have much free time now that she'd started on the gown. Even working with a commercial pattern, this was going to be quite a project. When she told Julie so, the bride-to-be was philosophical.

"I'd rather have you take your time and end up with the most fabulous dress in the history of the civilized world than settle for anything less than perfection," Julie said earnestly.

Betsy had hoped for that answer, especially now that she'd met Scott. "All right. But I won't take any shortcuts," she warned. "Classic sewing techniques tend to be tedious and time-consuming because so many of the little details are done by hand, but the result should be worth it." She gave Julie an oblique glance. "Since you're willing to be patient, you might also want me to make your petticoat and a camisole to go underneath. That would add to the authenticity."

"Betsy, you're wonderful!" Julie jumped up from her perch on a stool to give Betsy a warm hug. "You're sure you don't mind?"

"Mind? I'm enjoying it," Betsy said firmly, and it was true.

SHE THOUGHT THINGS were going well at the café, too, until a few days later. She'd forgotten a quart of milk she'd intended to take home earlier and stopped by in late afternoon to pick it up. She found Nancy at a table, poring over the books.

"I'm surprised you're still here," Betsy began, stopping short at the furtive expression on her aunt's face as she slammed the books closed. "What in the world is wrong, Aunt Nancy?"

Nancy seemed about to deny that anything was wrong, then sighed. "I should've told you before," she said, "but I was excited when you arrived, and I did so want you to stay."

"Told me what?" Betsy sat down in a chair opposite Nancy's and looked with dismay at the ledgers spread across the table, a queasy feeling rising in her stomach. If there was one thing she wasn't good at, it was numbers.

"Don't look so alarmed." Nancy managed a rueful laugh. "The Rusty Spur is in a kind of . . . well, in a financial hole."

Betsy frowned. "But I thought business was booming."

"It is, thanks to the best baker in the Rockies." Nancy had regained her composure. "The problem is, when I took over, the café was *already* in the hole. Unbeknownst to me, Mom was losing money steadily. She just wasn't any kind of businesswoman, and I didn't realize it until she was gone." Nancy shook her head wearily. "I guess we just tend to expect our mothers to know what they're doing."

That remark struck a chord with Betsy, since she'd once thought the same herself. "How bad is it?" she asked with dread.

"On a scale of one to ten?" Nancy laughed. "I'd say about a seven, with ten being the worst. I've been shorting the business to pay off a lot of Mom's old debts. Now I don't have anything left for improvements, and that's what we need if we're going to keep this place afloat."

"I wonder..."

Nancy looked up. "What?"

"The things I bake seem popular. If we could just add a bakery..."

Their glances met, and Nancy nodded. "I thought of that, too. If we could add a full bakery, do special cakes and sell bread by the loaf and offer pies and cookies..."

"It would also draw people into the café," Betsy offered eagerly. "I'd love to do it!" The enthusiasm slipped away as quickly as it had come. "But if we don't have the money..."

"Maybe I can get a bank loan," Nancy ventured.

"Do you think you could?"

"No. Well, maybe. John would sign with me."

"So would I, for all the good it'd do. Let's think about this for a while. Maybe there's another way."

Actually, Betsy knew there was another way. She looked down at the diamond engagement ring, the one that had come *after* the wedding band because there hadn't been any money before. Then she looked away.

She wasn't ready to do that yet.

"How many times do I have to tell you not to park there!"

Ben's roar nearly caused Julie to drive over Granny's flower bed. Trembling with resentment, she rolled down the window of her old car. "Don't you yell at me, Ben Cameron!"

"Then move it!"

She did, grumbling under her breath and wondering what had come over her big brother *this* time. Once inside, she hurried straight to the kitchen where Granny was preparing chicken for dinner.

Grabbing a carrot stick out of the saucepan, Julie plunked herself down in a chair. "What," she demanded, "is the matter with Ben?"

"It's that girl." Granny swatted at the hand reaching for a second carrot and moved the pan onto the stove.

"Well, yeah, I know he's interested in her, but I can't believe any woman could turn a reasonably stable guy like Ben into a raving maniac."

Granny laughed. "Sweetie," she said fondly, "grow up! A girl who's about to get married oughtta know about the birds and the bees."

"I know all that stuff," Julie said airily. "Are you telling me that Ben's gone all lovesick on us?"

And then she remembered what she'd seen that night a couple of weeks ago, when she and Jason had barged in at Betsy's house. She remembered the slightly unfocused look in Ben's eyes, and the shallow breathing and the tautness of his features.

And Betsy, trembling and tense.

Granny slung a cast-iron skillet onto the stove. "He needs a wife," she said bluntly, "and Joey sure as the world needs a mother. It's plain as the nose on your face. And what's he doin'? Is he rushin' off to town every night to court that girl? No! He's stompin' around here makin' our lives miserable—and we don't deserve it!"

Julie couldn't agree more.

She found Ben in the horse barn mucking out stalls, a job he loathed. He'd stripped off his shirt and had already managed to work up a sweat, his skin rippling and shining with the smooth movement of powerful muscles. He worked with a concentration and a ferocity that, from her newly enlightened position, Julie understood perfectly.

"Ben," she said. "It's June. You know what happens in June, right? Everybody pairs off two by two, starting with the birds and the bees. So why are you all alone and knee-deep in horseshit? Don't you think it's time you did something about Betsy Ross, even if you do it wrong?"

After a first shocked glance, Ben threw down his pitchfork and sucked in a breath that made his broad chest swell. "You know, Jewel," he said, "for once, you may be right."

JUST THE DECISION to see Betsy again lightened Ben's spirits. He hadn't realized how wrapped up in her he'd become until Julie did her clumsy matchmaking. Even Jason didn't balk when Ben announced his intention to go into town the next morning. In fact, he thought he heard Jason mutter something on the order of "High time!"

Joey was happy, too. He'd missed Lisa Marie; steeped in his own misery, Ben hadn't realized how much. Now the boy bounced on his side of the seat, even darting an occasional grin at his father. Once at the café, Joey ran on in to find out if this was one of Lisa's café days. Betsy, pouring coffee at the Liars' Table, looked up and smiled. She put the pot down, knelt and let the boy run into her arms, her own closing about him in a big hug. Shocked, Ben watched his son lay his cheek on her shoulder. Over the boy's head, Ben's gaze met hers. He saw no recrimination in her clear blue eyes, only the welcome he'd yearned for.

Lisa Marie raced up, took one look at her mother hugging Joey and turned to Ben. "Joey's daddy!" she shrieked, throwing herself at him. Catching him around the waist, she pressed her cheek to his side.

Betsy untangled herself and stood up. One hand resting lightly on Joey's shoulder, she approached Ben almost shyly. "Would you like a table? Help yourself."

He nodded.

"Coffee?"

He nodded again, still standing there just looking at her, at her fresh high color, the delicate pink tint of lips that tasted like strawberry wine— Damn! Enough of that. He sat down hard on the nearest chair, Joey and Lisa on either side of him.

Betsy retrieved the coffeepot from the Liars' Table and poured for Ben. "Can I get you anything else?"

He looked her right in the eye. "You," he said, softly but with emphasis. He saw the flash of confusion in her face, followed by the rising color brought on by understanding.

"Uh..." She licked her lips. "Lisa, would you like to show Joey your new coloring books?"

"C'mon, Joey. I got Cinderella and Snow White and..."

He followed happily. "You got any boy stuff? Like The Crusher or Mick the Monster or..."

Betsy sank into the chair across from Ben. "What was it you wanted?"

"You," he said again, "on a picnic with me. And Joey and Lisa Marie, of course."

She heaved a sigh that must have been relief, although it also might have been disappointment. "Oh. When?"

"Saturday?" He was perfectly willing to accommodate her, any day, any time.

"Could we make it Sunday? Nancy needs me here on Saturdays till at least two."

"No problem." His heart pounded; they were going to get another chance.

"On the clear understanding..."

His heart did a flip-flop, then settled back into its former mad rhythm.

"On the clear understanding that I still have grave reservations about you. Us...me."

He nodded. "I do, too."

"I wasn't mad about the birthday cake. I was mad about the *fight*. I'm not used to people resorting to physical violence. I'm not used to people who yell and argue and...and carry on."

"The fight?" He was mystified. "But we're always—"

She cut him off. "I know. Julie told me. It's no big thing to you and your family, but to me, it's...the end of the world."

"I see." He didn't. "Okay, fair's fair. You were honest with me and I'll be honest with you. I wasn't mad at you the day we went to Aspen. I was jealous. Jealous of him, the big movie star you loved—probably still love, for all I know."

She looked down at that damned big ring. "I do still love him. I want to be very clear about that. But there's no reason you and I can't be..." She frowned. "We've ruled out so much I'm not quite sure what's left."

"Let's start over by ruling everything back in. Start from scratch and see what happens."

She nodded. "Maybe that's best. If we can just be honest, respect each other's point of view..."

"Respect is good," he agreed. "So tell me honestly—why are you going on this picnic with me Saturday—I mean, Sunday?"

She stood up. "Lots of reasons," she said airily. "Because it sounds like fun. Because our kids are crazy about each other." She put her hands on the table and leaned forward as if about to confide the secrets of the universe. "And because you're just too damned sexy to turn down!"

Picking up the coffeepot, she sashayed off while Ben stared after her in stunned silence. He didn't know which shocked him most: that she'd used a swearword or called him sexy.

CHAPTER TWELVE

BEN WAS MORE than willing to pick them up Sunday morning, but Betsy declined, remembering the last time, when she'd ended up riding home with Julie. Although confident no such thing would happen again, she insisted on driving herself and Lisa Marie to the ranch. Why take chances?

Today would be a test. If they could get through an entire social event together and still be on speaking terms, there just might be a chance for this relationship—whatever it was.

Betsy couldn't vouch for Ben, but she was determined to make it work on some yet-to-be defined level. No one was more shocked than she, therefore, when she almost blew it within the first ten minutes of her arrival at the Straight Arrow.

The meeting and the greeting went without a hitch. The weather was delightful, temperatures rising into the seventies with a cloudless blue sky.

Then Ben led the horses out of the corral.

Betsy watched with dismay. "*That's* why you told me to wear jeans!" she accused.

"Well, sure." He looked genuinely puzzled. He also looked genuinely wonderful, tall and lean and in his element. He handled the horses with the same casual ease with which she handled a rolling pin.

She edged away. "I'm afraid of horses."

"You're what?" He stared at her; he might as well have said, *Lady, are you crazy?*

"I've never been around them," she hedged, backing farther. She swallowed hard. "They're even bigger than they look in the movies," she added faintly.

At that unfortunate moment, Lisa raced around the barn with Joey right behind her. "Horses!" she shouted, stopping so abruptly that the little boy ran into her. She hardly seemed to notice. "Are we riding horses to this picnic? Hooray! Hooray for Joey's daddy!"

"Hooray!" Joey joined in, jumping around in circles. "Hooray for Daddy!"

Ben looked so dumbfounded that for a minute, Betsy forgot to argue. When she remembered, she said, "Look, I'm a city girl. Can't we just drive?"

He gave her for a long assessing look, his mouth thinning to a hard line. Then he said, "No."

"What do you mean, no?"

"I mean, where we're going, cars can't get. And before you point out the obvious—yes, there are a lot of nice places we could get to by car, but that wouldn't be doing you any favors, sweetheart. Didn't anyone ever teach you we need to face up to our fears?"

She didn't like hearing him call her sweetheart, nor did she care for the tingle shooting up her spine. "But I don't know how to ride," she wailed. "Honestly I don't. I've never been on a horse in my life."

"No problem. I've taught lots of tenderfeet."

He said it with a confidence that made her feel even more unreasonable. She looked at the horses and they were just as big as ever. She swallowed hard. "But why? Why go to all that trouble?" she asked plaintively.

"Because I want to share this with you," he said. "Because anyone who doesn't ride is missing out on something special, and I ... don't want that to happen to you."

She felt a piercing sweetness at his words, spoken with simple sincerity. But even if she tried, she felt sure she'd disappoint him. She didn't think she could learn to ride a horse, even with his help. Desperately she cast about for a way out. "Wh-what if I ... just can't do it? I don't know anything about animals. You know that."

He looked her up and down, from the tips of her Hollywood cowboy boots to the top of her new Colorado Stetson. "I know it'd be a shame not to try," he said at last. "Animals are important on a ranch, all kinds of animals, but especially horses. Riding is and always has been a good part of what I do for a living."

Some things can't be compromised; maybe we are too different, after all.

Neither of them said the words, but that knowledge hung heavy in the air between them.

Betsy nodded slowly. She would try. For all their sakes, she would try.

HORSES, BETSY QUICKLY learned, were big but not necessarily mean. By the time the little party rode out of the ranch yard an hour later, she felt . . . maybe not like an old cowhand but fairly secure in the saddle of a beautiful black mare. Ben rode a tall reddish horse he called a sorrel, with Lisa Marie in front of him in the saddle and his arm securely around her middle. Joey looked confident straddling Poco's broad back.

Since the mare seemed to know what she was doing, Betsy tried to relax and enjoy the scenery. Ben set an easy ambling pace down the dirt road toward Cupid for twenty minutes or so before turning his little band of intrepid riders southwest onto a broad trail into the trees.

He kept a close watch on Betsy, whose mount followed a step or two behind his own big sorrel. "You're doin' great," he said with warm approval. "You underestimate yourself, Betsy."

She gave him a skeptical glance. "Maybe, but I think of it as knowing my limitations."

"Sometimes we have to push past limitations."

"I suppose." She wasn't convinced, but arguing was futile. "Oh, look! There's a bluebird!"

"Robber jay," he corrected, adding quickly, "Same difference, unless you're an ornithologist."

Betsy laughed, suddenly feeling very good indeed. Her muscles ached for action and her head was light with the intoxication of clear and fragrant mountain air. She was glad to be here . . . with Ben.

The picnic site was located in an aspen forest, beside a meandering mountain stream that tumbled cold and crystal clear over a rocky bed. Heavy granite boulders dotted the banks and littered the hill leading down to the water's edge. The tender leaves of aspen quivered in the gentle breeze.

The beauty of her surroundings took Betsy's breath away. It had been worth the two-hour ride to get here, even though muscles already growing stiff warned her she'd pay for it tomorrow.

Joey dismounted without assistance. Ben stepped down and put Lisa on her feet, then turned to Betsy and held up his arms. A slight smile curved his lips.

Lifting one leg over the saddle horn, she slid off, supremely confident that he would catch her. He did, and proceeded to lower her with infinite slowness, letting her body slide down his in intimate detail.

Her feet touched the ground at last, and she found herself sandwiched between Ben and her horse. She put her hands on his biceps, but could neither step back nor push him away. Breathlessly she met his gaze, steady and relentless.

"The children . . ."

He flexed his muscles against her. "The children," he agreed, stepping back. "But hell, it was just too good a chance to pass up."

She couldn't disagree with that.

While Joey and Lisa explored, Ben hobbled the horses and Betsy spread their blanket-tablecloth on a two-foot-high bank near a curve in the shallow stream. She'd coaxed Sam into letting her bring the picnic lunch and had given the menu considerable thought. She'd settled on roasted chicken, freshly baked bread,

crudités with cottage-cheese dip, fruit and Floren-
tines—crisp orange-and-almond cookies glazed with
bittersweet chocolate. A thermos of lemonade completed the repast.

Ben was lavish with his praise of the simple meal.
The children were too excited to eat more than a few
bites before they were up and running again.

Betsy watched with increasing anxiety as Lisa and
Joey ventured out on a boulder extending into the
water. When she couldn't take it any longer, she called
out sharply. "Lisa Marie, I wish you'd stay away from
the rocks. The soles of your boots are slick and I'm
afraid you'll fall."

Lisa frowned. "No, Mama, look! I'm taking off my
boots!" Sitting down, she proceeded to do just that.
She was quickly joined by Joey, who also removed his
boots and socks.

"Don't, Lisa—"

"Let it go, Betsy."

She glanced at Ben. "But—"

"What's the worst that can happen?"

"She could fall, she could step on something sharp,
she could hurt herself—"

"And she could learn from her mistakes. There's a
reason they say experience is the best teacher."

"She's just a little girl."

"Someday she'll be a big girl. When she is, we want
her to know how to take care of herself."

We. His use of the word threw her off stride; he
sounded as if he intended to be around to take part in
Lisa's growth and well-being. "Well...okay." She bit

her lip and gave in in the interests of peace, hoping she wouldn't regret it.

WHEN THE REMNANTS of the meal were cleared away, Ben and Betsy sat side by side on the blanket, talking quietly about inconsequential things while they watched their children frolic in the sunshine. Ben couldn't remember ever feeling so comfortable with a woman.

The kids ran up after a time, flushed and sweaty and asking for the last of the lemonade. Betsy put her foot down. "You're both getting too excited," she declared. "I want you to lie down right here and close your eyes for just five minutes while I tell you a story."

"Aw, do we have to?" Lisa asked cheerfully, flopping down and closing her eyes.

"Yeah, do we have to?" Joey parroted her complaint and her actions without noticeable distress.

So Betsy told the story "Goldilocks and the Three Bears" while Ben saw to the horses. "Once upon a time . . ." Her clear voice floated to him as he stood at the edge of the stream, watching the horses drink.

Once upon a time, Ben Cameron had done something that he must now try to explain to Elizabeth Ross.

He hoped she would understand. *He* sure as hell didn't.

By the time he'd moved the horses to a new spot to graze farther away, the kids were asleep and Betsy had only gotten to the part where Goldilocks messes up everybody's bed. Watching her smooth the blanket beneath Joey's cheek, Ben felt an overwhelming rush of protectiveness.

Something about Betsy had brought out the protector in him from the beginning, but this feeling was more intense than anything he'd experienced before. It scared him, made him want to pull back and play it safe. Then she looked up at him with a question in those guileless blue eyes, and he knew he couldn't do that, not with her.

He held out his hand and she placed hers in it, let him draw her to her feet and lead her away. Walking beside him toward the fringe of aspen, she gave him a questioning glance.

He hoped his smile was reassuring, but it felt wooden. "There's something I need to explain," he said.

"Oh?" She took a few more steps. "Something... bad?"

He shrugged. "Damned if I know." He stopped short and swung around to face her. "I've put it off, but... it's time I told you about Joey."

He saw the surprise on her face, but then she nodded. "You're right, it *is* time."

"A FEW YEARS AGO I got tangled up with a local girl..."

Betsy, who had taken a seat on the trunk of a fallen tree, looked up at him. Sunlight filtered through the leaves, making a lacy pattern on her face. "And her name was Crystal," she said.

Ben felt as if she'd punched him in the gut; he felt sick. "How did you...? Who told you?"

"You did."

"Like hell!" He'd never told anybody. A lot of people knew because they'd been there at the time, but he'd *never* talked about Crystal before.

Betsy could have drawn out the suspense, but she didn't. "You told me that day in Aspen. When you rescued me from those women, you said I was your wife, Crystal." She laughed ruefully. "I wasn't likely to forget."

When she hadn't mentioned it, he'd thought she *had* forgotten or else had missed his blunder entirely. Now he saw his mistake. He hadn't known her very well then. If he had, he'd have realized it was not her way to confront him directly with personal questions. Even now, she waited for him to go on at his own pace.

Get it over with, he thought. "Her name was Crystal Ramsey. We went to school together."

She'd been a wild young thing.

Maybe that was what had appealed to him most. As her contemporaries used to say admiringly, Crystal had guts she hadn't even used yet. She also had red hair and green eyes and a body that wouldn't quit. She'd played the field quite a bit during high school, but Ben hadn't been one of those early conquests. They'd been casual friends, nothing more; someone to share a soda with, even a beer behind the ball-field bleachers once or twice.

Eventually she'd gone to work at the Hideout. Ben saw her occasionally, swishing her hips at the boys and flipping that fiery hair around like a red flag in front of a pasture full of bulls. He'd admired her from a distance, admired her spirit as much as her more obvious assets. Then one day she sat down on his lap, grabbed him by the ears and said, "Cowboy, I've been wantin' to do this my whole life!" and kissed him.

All of a sudden everything changed. No longer was she "good old Crystal." Ben fell. Hard. She did, too— at least temporarily.

"A few years ago we got... involved," he said.

Yeah, they'd gotten involved. For a while there, they were the hottest couple going in Cupid. Crystal never hid anything, never held anything back. They couldn't be in the same room without her putting her hands all over him; she was more than bold; she was fiercely aggressive. There wasn't much of anything he wouldn't have done for her, except the one thing she asked.

Crystal wanted to move to Denver. When she told him, Ben knew their relationship was in a heap of trouble, since he wasn't about to move anywhere, and especially not to Denver. He hated Denver and its poisonous yellow air.

"Eventually I asked her to marry me."

Since he'd been unable to stand the thought of losing her, marriage had been his trump card. He'd thought it was going to take the whole pot—for about a week. "I guess I should've known she wasn't the kind of woman who'd be happy as a rancher's wife. I shouldn't've been surprised when she up and left town."

Hell, she hadn't even said goodbye.

Her defection had hurt, but he'd gone on with his life. He dated here and there when he could find the time, remembering Crystal with regret, knowing that if he'd been thinking at all when he'd proposed to her, it hadn't been with his head.

"One day about six months ago, I got a call from a man who said he was in Denver and had something for me from Crystal."

Ben almost hadn't gone to meet him. Finally curiosity had gotten the better of him, and he'd shown up at the specified place, a hotel on the western edge of Denver. There he'd received the shock of his life.

"What he had for me was my son—an almost four-year-old son I never knew anything about."

Ben had felt as if he'd been run over by a truck. The guy, who said his name was Kevin, told Ben that he and Crystal and the boy, Joey, had lived together in Santa Fe until a few weeks ago when she'd been killed in a holdup at the bar where she worked. He liked the boy, Kevin said, but figured the kid was Ben's responsibility now.

He handed Ben a New Mexico birth certificate with the boy's name on it. Ben was getting pretty hot by then, figuring this was some kind of scam. Hell, he'd wanted to marry Crystal. She sure hadn't had to go off alone to have his baby.

Then the guy opened the bedroom door and Ben walked in and saw his son for the first time—and he *was* his son. The little guy lay curled up in a kind of pitiful little ball on the very edge of the bed, damp black hair matted to his head. His cheeks were streaked with tear tracks, as if he'd cried himself to sleep, and one thumb was thrust between his lips.

Ben couldn't breathe; this was his boy. He wanted to grab him up and hug him and tell him everything would be all right now—but of course he didn't.

He was afraid. Ben Cameron, who feared nothing, was afraid. He told himself it was because he didn't know anything about kids, didn't know how to approach them or what to say.

That fear sent him back into the other room, where he thanked Kevin for bringing the boy to him and offered to pay the hotel bill and any other expenses. Kevin got pretty hot about that, telling Ben where he could get off. Then he left.

Ben didn't know what to do, so he just sort of sat there in a cold sweat waiting for the boy to wake up, trying to get hold of himself. He'd always wanted a son—hell, what man didn't? But he'd never dreamed he'd get one this way.

After a while, the boy stumbled out of the bedroom, rubbing his eyes. He was wearing jeans and a raggedy striped T-shirt that didn't look any too clean; neither did he, for that matter. His big toe stuck out of tattered sneakers and his hair wasn't on familiar terms with a barber.

"Wh where's Kev?" the boy asked, his eyes round and scared.

"Gone," Ben said, "but you don't need him anymore. I'm your daddy and I've come to take you home."

Joey had started to cry then, taking jerky glances around as if he thought he might find an escape route. Ben walked over and tried to put his hand on the boy's shoulder, but the kid shied away. So Ben had just opened the door and herded him through and out to the pickup.

"I put him in the truck and took him home with me."

Joey had quit crying by the time they reached the mountains, but he hadn't had anything to say to Ben on the ride to the Arrow. And that was pretty much the way it had stayed.

"Now you know," Ben finished.

Betsy looked horrified. "Your family must have been even more shocked than you were," she said, voice scratchy.

Ben shrugged as if it hadn't been hell to waltz a strange kid through the front door and announce that this was his and Crystal's son. "Yeah, I guess you could say that, but they were real good about it. Even Grandma didn't miss a beat, although she raked me over the coals when she got me alone."

"Poor little Joey."

"He settled in pretty well," Ben said defensively. "He's warmed up to just about everybody—except me."

Betsy bit her lip. "I have noticed he's a lit-tle . . . restrained around you."

"Restrained. That's a nice way to put it."

He's my boy, Ben often thought, yet I'm his least-favorite person. I love him. I buy him toys, a pony, take him with me every chance I get, try to teach him to be a man, and he just doesn't like me.

"Give him time, Ben. Six months—that's nothing."

BETSY DIDN'T SEE any anguish on his face, but still, she thought she felt it. All through the brief and matter-of-fact recitation, she ached for him. He really loved his son, she thought, perhaps more than he realized.

She got to her feet and laid a hand on Ben's forearm. "Poor Crystal," she said gently. "She must have loved you very much to keep your son."

She felt the flex of muscle beneath the soft cotton fabric of his shirt.

"Loved me?" he said in a cool voice. "She's the one who left."

"Maybe she thought it was better to leave than to stay and ruin both your lives. From what you just told me, that's what would've happened. She wasn't cut out for ranch life, you said so yourself."

"Did I?"

It was like talking to a brick wall, but she persisted, determined to break through to the emotion she felt sure he was concealing. "She must have told Kev how to find you. She sent your son to you, and she didn't have to do that if she didn't love you... love Joey and think this was best for him. Joey's here now. He's yours. You have no reason to reproach yourself."

The breath went out of him as if he'd been holding it forever—and with it, she hoped, past regrets that paralyzed his present and threatened his future. She felt such empathy that, without premeditation, she rose on tiptoe and touched her lips to his.

Holding the initiative without coyness, she covered his cheeks with little kisses. Then she cupped his face with her hands, slanting her lips across his at just the right angle, and kissed him with profound tenderness.

Am I falling in love with this man? she wondered hazily as she explored his mouth and felt his increasing response. *He makes me feel alive again, but is that love... or something else?*

Suddenly Ben lifted his head, and she saw his eyes blaze with the passion she'd ignited.

"Betsy, don't start something you're not prepared to—"

An excited voice piped up, intruding on that intensely private moment. At first Betsy couldn't pull her reeling senses together enough to understand the words.

"Mama, look! It's a teddy bear!"

Betsy turned groggily in Ben's embrace. When the children might have awakened, she had no idea, but now she saw that they were at the edge of the stream, and terror stunned her.

Lisa was reaching out, trying to grab hold of a bear cub, while another cub splashed away through the water. Joey stood beside her, looking confused and more than a little frightened. Somewhere out of sight, the horses stamped and snorted in alarm.

Betsy screamed; she had to go to her child, snatch Lisa from danger, but she couldn't seem to move. She stood paralyzed, knowing what needed to be done but completely incapable of doing it.

Ben's hard hand closed over on her shoulder. "Stay back!" he commanded. "I'll handle this."

Relief and shame engulfed her: relief that he was here to take action, shame that she seemed incapable of doing anything herself. Ben exploded across the rocky ground at full tilt. As if in slow motion, she saw him snatch Lisa up into one arm, grab Joey by the hand and turn away from the water.

At that point, it was hard to tell who was most frightened: the bear cubs bolting across the stream or Lisa, who burst into hysterical screaming. Joey also began to cry, probably more in sympathy than anything else.

At last Betsy moved. She picked her way across the rocky ground and took Lisa from Ben's arms. "Are you all right, baby?" She looked up at Ben with tears in her eyes.

"She's all right," he said shortly, his restless gaze scanning the trees. "Relax."

"Relax!" Relief following so closely on the heels of abject terror turned to fury. "How could you bring us to a place where bears roam around loose? I can't believe you'd have so little regard for our safety."

"Oh, for the love of...!" He made an impatient gesture. "This is a forest in the middle of the Rocky Mountains. Where the hell are wild animals supposed to live? They can't all be sent to zoos."

"Maybe not, but you shamed me into letting Lisa wander all over the place without saying a word about the dangers. If I'd known—"

"Yeah, yeah, I know. You wouldn't have come. You miss out on a helluva lot of life with that attitude, Betsy."

"You're the one with an attitude, Ben Cameron!" Once again he'd managed to make her lose her cool, and she couldn't seem to regain it. "Just because you're always ready for a fight doesn't mean the rest of us are." She patted Lisa's tangled hair and the girl's sobs increased. She twisted around to add her condemning glare to her mother's.

Finally Betsy realized Ben was scanning the area, paying little heed to her complaints. "What are you looking for?" she demanded, filled with fresh anxiety.

"Where you find a bear cub, there's bound to be a sow nearby."

"A sow? What's—" A ferocious roar cut off the question and froze her to the spot.

"*That's* a sow," Ben said grimly, turning to face the mother bear plunging out of the timber not thirty feet away.

CHAPTER THIRTEEN

THE BEAR SURGED UP on its hind legs, snarling and flailing the air with long curved talons. It tossed its head and bared its fangs, flecks of foam flying from its muzzle. All that separated the outraged bear and its human enemies was the narrow stream.

Betsy stood frozen with shock. With a shriek, Joey darted to her side. Betsy set Lisa on her feet and grabbed both children, holding them tight against her.

"Don't anybody move!"

As Ben delivered the command, he stepped in front of Betsy and the children, shielding them from the bear with his body. It was perfectly clear he was ready to do battle for them with his bare hands if necessary.

The bear, a rusty cinnamon color, dropped to all fours. Growling and swaying from side to side, it stood with head down, as if trying to decide whether to attack or retreat.

"Don't move," Ben said again in a low unbelievably controlled voice. "We're okay. Just act calm and don't make any sudden moves. And whatever you do, don't look her in the eye. That tends to tick a bear off, and we sure as hell don't want to do that."

Betsy stared down at the children in her arms, the hair at the nape of her neck prickling with fear. She'd never been so scared in her life. What if the bear charged? What if—

The bear charged.

Betsy screamed and fell back a couple of steps, pulling Lisa and Joey with her. They were going to die; they were going to be mauled and probably eaten by a bear. Everything in her demanded that she whirl and run, pushing the children ahead of her to some perceived safety.

Ben's snapped order steadied her: *"Don't move!"*

The charge lasted only a few steps. The bear halted in midstream, rising again on hind legs to growl ferociously. It looked gigantic, towering there, all teeth and claws and power. Lisa began to cry again. Betsy slid one hand over the girl's mouth, muffling the sound, fearing Lisa's sobs would stir the bear to further aggression.

One of the cubs squealed. Instantly the mother bear swung toward the sound, which fortunately was coming from the far side of the clearing. Breaking into a shuffling trot, she climbed out of the water and crossed the open space at a gallop, following her offspring into the woods.

For a moment, nobody moved; nobody spoke. The horses settled down, the children stopped snuffling, and an electric quiet descended.

Ben's shoulders slumped as if from the release of tension. He turned, his eyes glittering dangerously. "Don't even say it," he snapped, forestalling any comment Betsy might have made. "You three haven't got the sense God gave a goose—you'd've made damn sorry pioneers. If that kid—" his angry glance shot to Lisa "—doesn't know the difference between a stuffed bear and a real one, we're in trouble. And you, Joey, quit your sniveling. You're all right."

At last his furious gaze settled on Betsy. "As for you, I don't need any more lectures about the dangers of wildlife. Wild animals are usually more afraid of us than we are of them. If we just leave them alone, they'll usually..."

Still lecturing, he readied the horses, stowed gear behind the saddles and tossed Joey onto his pony. When he went to lift Lisa into his own saddle, Betsy, who'd gotten on her mare unassisted, said her first words since the encounter with the bear.

"Lisa Marie will ride with me."

For a moment Ben stared at her, then shook his head with clear disgust and muttered, "Talk about the blind leading the blind." But when he tried to hand Lisa up to her mother, the little girl wrapped her arms around his neck and clung for dear life, pressing her face beneath his chin. "Please," she said in a wobbly tone, "I want to ride with Joey's daddy."

Betsy's stomach clenched into a knot, and she stared at her child in disbelief. Ben's arms tightened around the girl and his challenging gaze met Betsy's.

"Well?" he drawled.

Did every word he said have to sound like a challenge? Afraid to test her voice, Betsy merely nodded.

Lifting Lisa onto his saddle, Ben swung up himself and proceeded to lead the unhappy little group back to the ranch.

Betsy could hardly believe it. Lisa had never chosen *anyone* over her mother, not even her father. Now it was almost as if she realized her mother hadn't been equal to the crisis—but Joey's father had.

By the time they rode into the ranch yard, Betsy was a mass of conflicting emotions. Climbing stiffly down from her saddle, she held out her arms for Lisa. Ben relinquished the girl and Betsy stood her on her feet.

But when she tried to lead Lisa to the car, her daughter dug her boot heels into the earth and resisted.

"Come *along*," Betsy insisted, feeling desperate. If she didn't get away from here within the next thirty seconds, she wasn't sure what she might say or do.

"I want to stay and play with Joey," Lisa wailed. "I don't want to go home!"

"Well, I *do*." Betsy pulled her recalcitrant daughter toward the car. "I want you to get in that car and get in *now!*"

Lisa stared at her mother as if she'd gone mad, which from a child's perspective was probably true. Betsy never acted this way—opening the car door, pointing, ordering, "In!"

Lisa looked confused but obeyed, to Betsy's enormous relief.

Jaw tense from the strain of keeping herself together, Betsy turned toward Ben. "I'm sorry," she said helplessly. "I'm just not a country girl and I never will be."

So that was that.

INSTEAD OF GOING HOME, Betsy drove straight to her aunt's house. She and Nancy were becoming closer every day, and it seemed the most natural thing in the world to sit at the comfortable kitchen table and, while Lisa was in another part of the house with John, pour out her woes.

"It just isn't working, Aunt Nancy," she said miserably, staring at her ice tea. "Ben Cameron is insensitive and dictatorial, not to mention bossy and judgmental. And boy, does he have a temper!" She rolled her eyes. "And *nothing* seems to scare him. When I think about the way he faced that bear..." She shuddered.

Nancy looked thoughtful. "Nobody can say the boy doesn't have courage."

"But what could he have done if the bear had charged? We were just lucky," Betsy argued.

"I think Ben might say we make our own luck."

"Then I'm doomed." Betsy looked gloomily through the kitchen window at birds flitting around a feeder. *Wild* birds. "I couldn't have done it," she said suddenly.

Nancy patted her niece's hand. "You didn't have to. Ben was there."

Betsy shook her head furiously. "You don't understand. I froze. I was absolutely paralyzed with fear. I didn't feel capable of moving a muscle."

"Are you doubting your courage, hon?"

"I don't think I have any to doubt." Betsy leaned her forehead on her palms. "Even when I saw Lisa trying to grab that bear cub, I just stood there and screamed. I was worthless—worse than worthless." Tears sprang to her eyes. "I took it out on Ben, but I'm the one I'm mad at. Even for the children, I couldn't—"

At that moment, Lisa trotted into the kitchen pulling John behind her. Both were smiling.

"I been telling Uncle John about that great big horse I rode on with Joey's daddy," Lisa exclaimed. "And I told him about that big mean bear at our picnic."

Laughing, John put it into a new perspective. "Ever since Goldilocks, little girls have been meeting bears in the forest," he teased. "You don't want to meet a bear, don't go where bears live."

Betsy applied the wisdom to herself: *You don't want to get mixed up with a sexy rancher with a short fuse, don't go where ranchers live.*

So she wouldn't.

IN NO TIME AT ALL, Betsy and Lisa felt as if they'd always lived in Grandma Marie's little house. Their routine became established, and it was comfortable for both of them. Betsy worked at the Rusty Spur, going in early each morning for the day's baking. Some days Lisa accompanied her, some days she spent with the baby-sitter recommended by Nancy. But always she pined for Joey, and more than once Betsy caught her daughter talking wistfully to Erica about the ranch and the people there.

Early to bed, early to rise became their way of life. Up at five meant to bed by seven for Lisa, by ten for Betsy. Some evenings the two of them went to Nancy and John's for dinner or just to visit, always taking some special baked offering; most evenings they spent at home alone together, unless one or another friendly neighbor dropped by the little cottage on Lovers' Lane. Betsy wasn't even *tempted* to go out with any of the men who pursued her.

She spent hours each day working on Julie's wedding gown, starting when she finished work in midafternoon. It had taken nearly a week just to prepare the fabric, pin tucks stitched meticulously into yards and yards of silk broadcloth before the pattern pieces could be cut. Lace insertion followed: bands of lace sewn into intricate patterns on sleeves, yoke, bodice, skirt, then the underfabric trimmed away.

It was tedious; it was time-consuming. It was worth it, Julie declared as the gown took shape.

Before such praise, Betsy felt like a rat. She'd planned to go slow and thus delay the wedding for *everybody's* sake: Julie's and Ben's in particular. She liked Julie at lot, and disliked Scott Hale with equal intensity. Ben was right about Scott—and why did she keep thinking about Ben? He was obviously doing his best to avoid her. She'd seen him at a distance a couple of times since the picnic and was sure he'd seen her, too. But each time, he'd turned away as if she didn't even exist.

Two could play that game. The next time she saw him, walking toward her on the sidewalk in front of the bank on Main, she crossed the street without even acknowledging she knew him.

THE COWS HAD BEEN SORTED and moved to the higher summer range; the horses had been sorted and moved to the compound for a variety of purposes, including breaking, training and possible sale. Jason and a couple of cowboys had gone with the cows while Ben stayed home to work the horses. The brothers took turns each summer, since both preferred horse work to cow work.

Or had. After a few days of stomping around at home, Ben abruptly drove up to summer camp and peremptorily threw Jason out. "I'm not fit to be around," Ben admitted grimly. "I don't know what the hell's come over me, but I'm better off here than messin' up everything at home. If I feel better by the Fourth of July, I'll come on in. If not..." He shrugged, as if he didn't give a damn one way or the other.

Jason beat it out of there, happy for the reprieve. At dinner that night, he waited until Joey and Grandma and Chuck left the table before giving Maggie and Julie details of what had happened, concluding, "I sure hope he doesn't run into any trouble up there. He's apt to shoot first and ask questions later."

Julie broke open a spare biscuit and slathered on butter. Joey had churned it that afternoon, shaking cream from their own cows in a mason jar until the pale yellow butter appeared. "I, for one, am glad he's gone," she announced. "He's been acting like a cross old bear."

Maggie nodded. "I tried to talk to him about it, and he nearly bit my head off.

"Me, too." Julie finished her biscuit and licked her fingers. "Poor guy's really fightin' it. She is, too."

"You talked to her about it?"

"Tried. She's not a lot more forthcoming than he is."

Julie and Maggie exchanged knowing glances. "As much as I hate to say this, maybe we should do something," Maggie suggested slowly.

"About what?" Jason reached for the last crumbs of meat loaf on the platter.

"About Ben and Betsy, what else?"

"What about Ben and Betsy? Are they still a couple? I thought the little run-in with the bear spoiled that romance."

"Jason, you are *so* dumb!"

"Shut up, Julie! You're no mental giant yourself, engaged to that—"

"Don't say it!"

"Both of you, pipe down and listen to me."

As the oldest sibling and a schoolteacher to boot, Maggie knew how to make herself heard. She didn't continue until she was sure she had their attention. "Okay, how about this. Let's throw a Fourth of July shindig like we used to. Invite the whole town, barbecue a cow, do a little dancing..."

Jason grimaced. "Oh, yeah, Ben'll for sure want to dance."

"He will if Betsy Ross is here," Julie said silkily.

"How you figure you're gonna get her here? Roped and tied?"

Julie nodded. "If we have to, but I don't think that'll be necessary. Who in their right mind can resist a Cameron barbecue?"

Maggie smiled. "Who indeed?"

WORD OF THE CAMERONS' big Fourth of July bash spread rapidly through Cupid. "You'll go with me and John of course," Nancy informed Betsy.

Who shook her head. "I don't know. I may have other plans."

But then Julie came by with a special invitation, followed by Maggie; even Jason made a point of inviting her. Betsy figured there must be a reason they were all so determined to get her there. Could it be...? Yes, she thought. Ben must want her to come.

Betsy changed her mind a dozen times, then at the last minute decided not to go to the party. Ben hadn't come by, hadn't telephoned, had made no effort to see her or talk to her. She might be ready to resolve what she thought of as the bear issue, but he, apparently, was not.

Since the Camerons' party was open to the entire community and required neither formal acceptance nor regrets, Betsy drove southwest, instead of northwest when she climbed into her car that morning. Heading for Aspen, instead of the Straight Arrow

Ranch, she took Lisa Marie and a Gâteau Saint-Honoré with her.

Chase was delighted to see her, which at least partially made up for the hellish drive over Independence Pass. She knew her unexpected appearance helped him put his own personal problems aside, at least for a while. But later, watching him frolic with Lisa Marie in the swimming pool of his mountainside mansion, she wondered if it made him miss his own daughter that much more. Blair was about ten now, if Betsy remembered correctly. The girl's mother had taken Chase for a bundle during the divorce, but the worst thing she'd done was turn his daughter against him.

Only when she and Lisa were about to leave did Betsy steel herself to speak to Chase about something that had been on her mind a lot lately: her engagement ring. "Would it be hard to sell?" she asked, holding out her left hand to display the beautiful diamond.

Chase whistled low in his throat. "You sure you want to do that, Betsy?"

"No." She sighed. "But I may need some cash quick one of these days."

"Let me help you," he said immediately. "I had no idea—"

"No, no." She shook her head. "It's nothing like that. I mean cash for a business expansion. If Nancy and I could open a bakery at the café, sell bread and decorated cakes and pies and so forth for carryout, as well as to serve our café customers, we think it'd go over big. But Nancy's been paying off debts she inherited with the café when Grandmother died, and Uncle John's on a pension, so they don't have a lot of cash to throw around.''

"Neither do you, I take it."

"No." With Chase, she felt no need to whitewash her financial situation. "I'm living very inexpensively at present, and Aunt Nancy insists I accept a small salary, which is more than she's doing. But for the . . . the—''

"Capital improvements," he supplied with a smile.

She nodded. "That's right—new ovens and so forth. It wouldn't take a fortune, but it's more than I can risk right now. This ring . . ." She looked down at it, flashing blue fire. "It's beautiful, but it's never meant as much to me as my wedding band." A narrow golden band, inexpensive and at the same time priceless with its inscription: "To my darling Betsy, with love forever—Evan"

The diamond had come later. Evan had been so proud and happy when he'd given it to her. In her heart she knew that he'd understand if she decided she needed something else even more. At least, she thought she knew it in her heart; she still wasn't quite ready to slip the ring off her finger.

"If you ever are," Chase said gently, "let me know and I'll handle everything for you."

"Thank you!" She gave him a grateful kiss on the cheek.

"Meanwhile, there's something else I want you to think about," he added.

She nodded, glad to oblige him when he'd come through so brilliantly for her.

"My job offer still stands. Judging by that *gâteau*—" he pointed to his plate, with its crumbs of cream puff pastry and caramel "—I'd be getting the best of the deal. Promise me you'll think about moving here to Aspen. This is where you belong, not roughing it out in the middle of nowhere."

Little did he know; she hadn't even told him about the bear. He knew about the kitten, though—the tiger-striped one mewing piteously at his front door when Betsy and Lisa went to leave. Lisa immediately scooped it up and pressed it to the front of her pink blouse over Chase's objections: the animal could be sick, it could be flea-ridden, it could be—

"Mine," Lisa said, giving him a serene smile. "His name could be Roger."

And so it was.

THINGS WERE NOT GOING too well at the Straight Arrow Ranch. Ben, in Julie's words, was madder than a wet hornet. He'd been lured back for the big Independence Day celebration with broad hints that Betsy would be here—and she wasn't. Not that he'd admit that was why he'd come down the mountain. Stalking through the crowd of revelers, glaring out over the red, white and blue streamers tied to every pillar and post, trying to avoid his son's disappointment, Ben called himself forty kinds of coward for hanging around and hoping.

A little bit of that went a long way. As soon as he could, he slipped away and headed into town. He'd find out why Betsy hadn't come when everybody said she would.

She wasn't home. Furious, he drove away, wondering where the hell she'd gone. Aspen?

And trying to convince himself he didn't give a damn if she *was* in Aspen. It was just the thought of her maneuvering the BMW over Independence Pass that gave him a couple of bad moments.

JULIE'S WEDDING DRESS was progressing nicely—too nicely. It would be done by now if Betsy hadn't been doing everything twice in order to make it "perfect."

As if "perfect" existed, she thought, lifting the gown from the dressmaker's form. The circular sweep of the skirt with its deep bottom ruffle swirled gracefully as she turned, a generous mass of silk and lace.

A bittersweet tide of longing swept over her, and in that moment she missed Evan with an intensity that startled her. She actually hadn't thought about him all that much lately. A twinge of guilt accompanied that realization. She touched the rings on her left hand with her thumb, reassuring herself that they were still there.

Sale of the diamond would truly mark the end of a very important chapter in her life. Should she... should she not. Holding the gown before her, she swept in thoughtful circles around the living room.

Her front door opened and she stopped, surprised, holding the gown like a shield. Ben stood there, Joey at his side. Both stared as if they'd never seen her before.

BETSY WAS even more beautiful and desirable than the last time Ben had seen her—and, with that dreamy expression on her face, even more vulnerable-looking. She affected him way down deep on some gut level that made him want to howl at the moon.

It was time he did something about it. He jerked his head toward the hall leading to the back of the house. "Lisa Marie out there?"

She swallowed hard and nodded, her eyes wide.

"Joey, go outdoors and play with Lisa," Ben ordered.

"Yes, Daddy." Joey gave Betsy a shy smile and darted past.

Still Betsy stood there, waiting without a word. Her arms had dropped until the gown no longer shielded her, and he saw she was wearing a pair of khaki shorts and a yellow knit T-shirt. Her dark blond hair was a tangle of curls, and her face was bare of makeup.

Hell, she didn't need makeup. Ben cleared his throat. He felt adrift, out of his depth, but determined. "I came here to find out why you weren't at the party yesterday."

"Oh. Well . . . I'm sorry. Aunt Nancy told me that with these big community-wide bashes, it wasn't necessary to call. Otherwise, I'd certainly have—"

"I don't care about that anymore." He shook his head sharply. "Seeing you like this, what I'd really like to know about is your marriage."

For a moment she met his glance, and then she nodded. "All right," she said simply. "I'll tell you everything."

THEY SAT on Grandma Marie's overstuffed blue sofa and Betsy told him: how Evan was her best friend and protector, how that never changed from the day they met in elementary school until the day he died. And as she explained, a mind-boggling thought occurred to her.

Her love for Evan, although beautiful and very real, was based on a deep and mutual friendship and respect. She'd always been sure of him, even after he'd achieved stardom and was surrounded and pursued by droves of beautiful women. But she could not honestly say they'd had the kind of irresistible chemistry that drew her to Ben Cameron. She'd known Evan inside and out, but Ben was completely unpredictable, a man about whom she'd never been sure of anything—except that he was as attracted to her as she was to him.

If only Ben was... different from the rough-and-tumble rancher he was. She watched his face closely while she told her story, looking for the same deference and respect Evan would have given her. What she saw was interest but little, if any, sympathy or understanding.

Suddenly Ben leaned forward. "That's enough," he said, lifting one hand to stroke the curve of her throat. "I get it now. He put you on a pedestal."

"No!" she objected. "I'd never want to be on a—"

"Good, because that's not my style." He slid his hand up beneath her jaw and traced the line of her lower lip with his thumb, a slow sensuous glide. He shuddered. "I can't look at you without wanting you, Betsy." Holding her still, he leaned over and kissed her—without a scrap of deference or respect.

But there was fire and passion and a growing familiarity, a quickness of response that went beyond the rational. Betsy found herself pressed back until her head was against the couch. Ben shifted so that his chest pressed hard against her breasts while his tongue invaded her mouth, igniting a sweet fire that demanded they move on to the next level....

He drew back slightly, his breathing harsh and his gaze searing. "I appreciate you telling me about your husband. Maybe... I understand a little better now."

"It was time," she whispered, echoing what he'd said before telling her about Joey's mother. She felt such a melting weakness she made no move to break the contact between them; actually she was tempted to suggest he shut up and kiss her again.

For what seemed like the longest time, he stared at her. Then he grimaced. "I won't let it end between us over a damned *bear.*"

"It's not just the bear, it's the... violence."

"What violence?" He whispered the words in her ear.

"Y-you know. The fight with Jason. The time you yelled at me at the Spur—"

He kissed her ear, setting off a fresh series of shivers. "I'm a man of quick action, Betsy. I don't react any differently than anybody else, I just do it . . . faster." He touched her breast with his palm and she jerked as if from an electric shock. "Take the bear, for instance. If I hadn't been there, you'd have done the same thing."

"Stand up to a bear? I don't think so. I was petrified." He was playing with her nipple through the soft knit, exciting her to the point where she could hardly speak.

"Someday you may have to. Then you'll find out that when the fate of those you love—" He stopped short and looked at her, his shock plain. "I mean, the kids."

Her mind reeled from his kisses, from what he'd almost said. "Even for them, I couldn't resort to...to physical violence. I don't think I'm capable of it. That's why this—" he touched his lips to her eyelids and she moaned "—is impossible."

He cupped her breast in his hand and the nipple sprang to rigid life. He was controlling her with his lips, his hands, the pressure of his body. They were nearly horizontal on the couch now, and she felt weak as water, as aroused as she'd ever been in her life. Each time he touched her, she responded more quickly and more completely. Each time he touched her, she wanted more.

He moved his face so close that their noses nearly touched. When he stared into her eyes, she could only hope he didn't see into her soul, the soul that lusted to know all of him. "This is crazy, Ben," she gasped. "We've just laid out all the reasons we're completely wrong for each other...."

"Says who? Just because we don't see eye-to-eye on—"

"Mama, Mama, come quick!"

"Daddy, it's a great big cat up in a tree and—"

"Let me tell!"

Lisa led the charge into the living room, Joey right behind her. Betsy barely had time to sit up; there was nothing she could do about her burning cheeks or eyes that must be bright with passion. A glance at Ben showed her that he, too, was having trouble presenting an unruffled facade.

Lisa and Joey jumped up and down in excitement while Erica barked somewhere in the background. Roger was nowhere to be seen.

"A great big cat," Lisa elaborated. "It's up in the tree and it wants to eat Roger and Erica, I think."

"It wants to eat me, but I can beat it up!" Joey struck a fighting stance.

Betsy tried to concentrate on what the children were saying, but it took enormous effort. "I'm sure it's only the neighbor's tom," she said.

That invited a storm of protest from both children; this was a great big cat.

Ben used both hands to shove back his hair, a gesture that seemed born of distraction. "They might be right," he said. "Mountain lions wander into towns all over Colorado, even Denver suburbs. I'd better take a look."

"Mountain lions!" Betsy felt faint. Bears in the forest were one thing; that was, after all, where they lived. But this was where *she* lived.

Ben gave her an edgy glance. "Don't get excited. It probably *is* the neighbor's cat." He stood up. "Better safe than sorry. I'll go have a look-see."

With Betsy, Lisa and Joey trailing behind, he checked the area out carefully. He found nothing significant in the tree or on the ground, but he stopped beside the dog's dish near the back step.

"I thought I told you not to leave anything out here for wild animals to eat," he scolded.

"I don't," she protested, stung by his tone.

"Then what's in that bowl?"

"Dog food."

"So what's it doing outside?"

"Erica makes a mess inside," Betsy defended herself. "I thought that if I put the dish close to the house—"

"Bears and wildcats and skunks and raccoons don't know nothin' about your intentions. They'll eat anything they can find, whether it's in a dog's dish or a trash can. They've even been known to bust into kitchens looking for food. I know you're afraid of animals, so—"

"Anybody in their right mind would be afraid of a—"

"Uh-oh." Leaning forward, he caught her chin between his palms and gave her a quick hard kiss on the lips, shocking her to the soles of her feet. A glance at Lisa and Joey showed them to be unperturbed.

Ben winked. "Let's make love, not war. Want to go to town Saturday when you're finished work?"

"T-town?"

"Denver. We could take the kids, do whatever you like. Movie, shopping, just walk around Larrimar Square."

Her instinct was to turn him down cold, but she stopped herself. She, too, wanted to give this relationship another chance. She met his challenging look with a challenge of her own, lifted her chin and said, "Yes!"

CHAPTER FOURTEEN

THUS BEGAN their delicate courtship. Ben took to dropping by the Rusty Spur to see Betsy, usually with Joey in tow; he stopped by her little house less often, because he didn't trust himself to be alone with her.

He wanted her physically, even more than he'd wanted Crystal way back when. With Betsy, he wanted more than just a roll in the hay—and she had to want more, too, be ready to accept more, or their budding relationship was doomed. Until he was at least half-way sure they had a future, he'd try to take it slow.

They spent every weekend together, always accompanied by the kids. With a mixture of pleasure and fear, Ben watched Joey's growing dependence on Betsy. The boy turned to her first now. What would it do to Joey if his father and Lisa Marie's mother didn't make a go of it?

For that matter, what would it do to Lisa Marie? As Joey turned to Betsy for a mother's attention, so did Lisa turn to Ben for a father's.

Sometimes Ben thought that for every step forward, they took two steps back. They were so different in their outlooks that it would take a lot of love and compromise to turn that weakness into strength.

But it could be done. He felt it in his gut. If he had to walk a tightrope through a maze to find the right path, that's what he'd do.

The whole town, it seemed, was rooting for them. It was getting downright embarrassing to be stopped on the street and asked about his love life. Especially since it wasn't a question he could properly answer.

She was skittish as a filly when he touched her, and he knew what that meant: it meant she didn't trust herself to say no, and she still thought no was the proper response. He could wait; hell, yes, he could wait. But damn, it was hard. He kept trying, though; there was no quit in him.

Then in August, he and Betsy took the kids to the Garden of the Gods in Colorado Springs. Everything went fine; they admired the fabulous red-rock formations rising sheer on the western side of the city. With the help of another tourist, they even got a photograph of the four of them posing beneath the Balanced Rock.

Betsy was nervous about letting the kids run around like little heathens, but Ben assured her that as long as they didn't try to climb one of the vertical sandstone formations, they'd be fine. They were, too—right up to the moment Lisa Marie tripped and fell off a rock no higher than a table.

The way she carried on, she might as well have fallen off Pikes Peak. Holding her injured wrist with her other hand, she wept copiously. Joey stood up on the same piece of gypsum to see what her problem was and promptly fell off, too.

So while one kid was insisting that her arm was broken, the other bled from both knees. Betsy tried to comfort them, casting accusing glances at Ben, who finally blew sky-high. All the sexual frustration that'd been building reared right up and spit in his eye.

Dampening his neckerchief in the melted ice of the cooler in Betsy's car, he sat Joey down and proceeded to swab off his knees while the boy yelled bloody murder. When he could stand no more, Ben gave Joey a withering glance. "Look," he commanded, pointing. "Look at what you're cryin' about, a big boy like you. A coupla little scratches."

Betsy frowned. "He's just a little boy. How can you—"

"A little boy who quit crying," Ben said. Of course, now with Betsy taking Joey's side, the kid was clouding up again. Ben smeared some antiseptic ointment from the first-aid kit in the car on the injured knees and stood up. "How's Lisa? She gonna live?"

At that point, Lisa let out a shriek that brought hoards of tourists swinging around to see who was abusing children in a city park. Joey, getting in the spirit of the thing, added his cries to hers. Betsy looked ready to burst into tears herself.

WHAT THE HELL am I trying to do? Ben asked himself on the drive back to Cupid—the very long, very cold, very silent drive back to Cupid. *This is never going to work. Betsy's no more suited to be a rancher's wife than Crystal was. Why am I putting myself through this? Good thing we haven't slept together.*

He'd never been so damned frustrated in his life. She had him tied in so many knots he couldn't eat, couldn't sleep, couldn't think about much of anything except making love to her. Maybe it was time to cut his losses. Yeah, that was what he'd do. He'd tell her as soon as they got back. He hoped it wouldn't hurt her too much, but somehow he'd make her see they had no future together.

He pulled up in front of her cottage, and before he could come around to open her door, she jumped out, tugged Lisa out of the back seat and slammed the door. Leaning through the open window, she held out her hand, into which he dropped the car keys.

"Don't call me," she said, "and I won't call you. We'll never be friends or anything else. We tried and it just hasn't worked. I'm sorry, but you can't change my mind."

He watched her until she'd closed her front door behind her, his mouth hanging open in shock. Then he smashed his hand against the steering wheel so hard he cracked his little finger, a fact he didn't discover until three days later when he calmed down enough to go see Doc Kunkle. By then, Joey was fine, Lisa Marie was fine, and he supposed Betsy had always been fine.

Apparently only Ben Cameron had been hurt.

BY THE END OF AUGUST, everybody in Cupid knew about Ben and Betsy's breakup, and the general feeling was one of alarm. Betsy quit going in early at the café to bake; Ben quit communicating in anything other than surly rage. Betsy, never known for her ability to make swift decisions, was now refusing to make any decisions at all. Ben, always known for a quick temper, was now reinforcing that reputation every time he opened his mouth.

Neither was happy and neither would do anything about it. It was getting damned frustrating to those who cared about them.

"I guess it's up to us," Julie told Maggie grimly. It was a Saturday, and the two sisters were changing sheets on the beds at the Straight Arrow. Chuck and Maggie shared the master bedroom on the ground floor, with Grandma in the bedroom across the hall. Ben and Joey shared a bedroom upstairs, with Julie across the hall from them. Jason, who'd moved into the bunkhouse when Joey showed up, changed his *own* sheets—they hoped. Still, they had six beds to handle, which made it a two-woman job.

Maggie responded thoughtfully. "Last time we tried, it was a bust. But if somebody doesn't do something, I don't know what's going to become of Ben."

"Exactly." Julie planted her hands on her hips. "It's been two weeks since they broke up. I don't know about you, but I don't want to spend the rest of my life with a brother constantly on the prod."

Maggie frowned. "What do you mean, the rest of your life? Last I heard, you were getting married this fall."

Julie started guiltily. "I am. Eventually."

She didn't fool her older sister. "Betsy hasn't reneged on your wedding gown again, has she?"

"Oh, no, nothing like that. It's not only finished, it's the most gorgeous thing you've ever seen. Now she's making me some unmentionables to go under it."

Something was wrong. Maggie sensed it, heard it in the chirping quality of her little sister's voice. Like Ben and Jason, Maggie did not favor this marriage; unlike Ben, she was willing to let Julie make her own mistakes.

As she probably should let Ben do, but damn it, Maggie liked Betsy, too. Maggie could see both sides of it. "I don't really know what we *can* do," she remarked.

Julie's smile was smug. "That's the good part. All we have to do is get them together *without* the kids and let nature take its course."

Maggie was amused. "That's all, is it?" She forced the fitted corner of the sheet over the mattress. "And how, pray tell, do we do that?"

"Glad you asked." Julie sat down on the crumple of sheet on her side of the bed. "I've got it all figured out..."

"I'M SORRY," Betsy said, "but I'm not in the mood to go to the Hideout." Holding the can of soup, she reached for a can opener. She, a gourmet cook, was reduced to eating canned soup for dinner.

Julie and Maggie exchanged glances. *They're sorry for me,* Betsy thought with irritation. *They think I can't get a date, so they're taking pity on me. No, thanks!*

"Girls' night out," Maggie said hopefully. "Come on, Betsy. With Lisa Marie at Nancy's for the night ..."

"How'd you know that?" Betsy shot Maggie a surprised look.

"I ... why I ... Didn't you mention it?"

"Oh. Maybe I did. But getting a baby-sitter is never much of a problem, so that's no reason to—"

"Do it for me! I really *need* a distraction."

Maggie and Betsy looked at Julie in surprise. She'd sounded almost desperate.

"What's the matter?" Betsy asked with quick sympathy. "Are you and Scott having problems?"

Julie pulled a cracker from the pack on the kitchen counter near the soup can and began absently crumbling it on the counter. "Well ... yes and no."

Maggie frowned. "Julie, you never said a word to me about this. What is it?"

Julie looked more uncomfortable by the second. "Nothing, really. Well, maybe something." She looked down at the little pile of cracker crumbs. "He's ... pushing me. I'd like to show him I can have a good time without him—or any man, for that matter."

"Pushing you?" Betsy and Maggie zeroed in on the same phrase and repeated it in unison.

"You two can be dumb as rocks sometimes," Julie grumbled. "For sex! He's pushing me for sex. There, are you satisfied?"

"You mean—" Betsy's eyes grew wide "—you're not ... you know."

"That's exactly what I mean—there hasn't been any *you know*." Julie looked defiant and ashamed at the same time.

Maggie frowned. "Can someone explain to me what Julie's sex life—"

"Or lack of same," Julie inserted.

"—has to do with the three of us going to the Hideout for a beer and a little male-bashing?"

"Oh, yeah." Julie blinked. "I was just explaining that tonight's more for me than you, Betsy. You may like sitting here all alone night after night, sewing until your fingers bleed and your eyesight fails—"

"Violins, please."

"Shut up, Maggie." Julie appealed to Betsy. "My treat. I know this will in no way pay you back for what you've done for me—the dress and promising to decorate my cake..."

Maggie was appalled. "You manipulated this poor girl into doing the cake, as well as the dress?"

Julie glared at her sister. "She offered." She turned back to Betsy. "Please come. You'll be letting me say thanks and at the same time helping me get my mind off...you know."

Betsy, whose mind had been firmly on *you know* for weeks, could sympathize. Relinquishing the can opener, she headed for her bedroom to get ready, the Cameron sisters at her heels.

While Betsy brushed her teeth, Maggie confronted her sister. "You didn't tell me you and Scott were having problems," she hissed over the sound of running water in the bathroom.

"Who says we are?" Julie picked up a silver-plated hairbrush. "Boy, does Betsy have beautiful things or what!"

"You said, that's who. Was that just for her benefit, or did you mean it?"

"None of your business." Julie raised her voice. "You about ready, Betsy?"

Betsy appeared in the doorway. "All ready."

She looked beautiful, Maggie thought without a trace of envy. She'd long since accepted the fact that she herself would never be a traffic stopper. But she knew one when she saw one.

Betsy was definitely a traffic stopper. She had eschewed the local uniform of boots and jeans and chosen a white silk shirt and black trousers that fit her perfectly. On her feet were matching black pumps. On her face a subtle makeup that turned her from pretty to drop-dead gorgeous.

Maggie had watched Betsy get ready, fascinated by the process. If she had to guess, Maggie would have said the beautiful woman standing before her was out for bear.

Which, in reference to Betsy, was hysterically funny.

"So what are we waiting for? Look out, Cupid!" Betsy led the way to the front door. "I'll take my own car in case I want to leave before—"

She flung open the front door, putting them face-to-face with the most outrageously handsome man Maggie had ever laid eyes on. She could only stare with her mouth open as Betsy shouted, "Chase!" and flung herself into the arms of this stranger.

Maggie and Julie looked at each other, disconcerted by this hitch in their plans. When Betsy disentangled herself enough to make introductions, their situation became considerably worse.

Chase Britton, Betsy's old friend from California, had dropped by unannounced for a visit. Great.

"But I've come at a bad time," he said, stating the obvious and smiling past Betsy at the sisters. "You're on your way out."

"We're not in any great rush. We were just..." Betsy seemed struck by inspiration. "But you've got to come with us, Chase! We're just going over to the Hideout."

"I think I passed it coming in."

"Yeah," Julie scoffed, "it's an old honky-tonk on the edge of town. You wouldn't be interested, big restaurant mogul like you."

Chase laughed and dimples danced in his lean cheeks. "Betsy's been talking about me, has she?"

Julie shrugged. "My brother Ben..."

"Ahhh." He nodded. "Well, you'll have to come see for yourself someday, because you've got me all wrong. I have a weakness for local color."

He really *was* a great-looking guy with charm to burn. Definitely not the kind of man who should be around Betsy, Maggie thought darkly.

He spoke to Betsy but included them all when he said, "If you're sure you don't mind..."

"Mind! I'm delighted," Betsy declared. "We all are."

"Oh, yeah, delighted," Julie muttered, but only Maggie heard her.

MEANWHILE, BACK AT the ranch, Jason was having a helluva time pulling off his part in his sisters' little scam. The last thing Ben wanted was a night out at the Hideout with the boys; the last thing Jason wanted was the responsibility of delivering such a grouch.

How did women come up with this stuff? Jason wondered, waiting for Ben to join him in the pickup for the ride into town. He wasn't even sure Ben deserved a classy babe like Betsy, anyway.

"Get over and let me drive."

Jason started guiltily but held his ground. "C'mon, Ben, I know how to drive."

"Stuff it, Jason. Either I drive or I don't go."

If Maggie and Julie hadn't ganged up on him and extracted his sacred promise, Jason would have told Ben what he could do with his ultimatums. As it was, Jason slid over.

THE HIDEOUT at seven on a weeknight and the Hideout at nine on a Friday were two distinctly different places, Betsy discovered. The decor was still rustic, but the atmosphere had changed from family to frenzied. Couples packed the dance floor, their movements dictated by the country-and-western band blasting from the stage at the far end of the room. Waiters and waitresses in boots and jeans literally ran between the tables, serving food and drink, mostly the latter.

Chase, Betsy, Maggie and Julie finally found an empty booth. "Wow!" Betsy exclaimed, looking around with interest. "This crowd is really something."

"You bet." Julie spotted someone she knew and waved.

"What's that dance they're doing?"

"That?" Julie looked astounded. "That's a two-step, girl. Folks take their two-steppin' real serious around here."

Chase, seated on the outside, nodded. "It's fun," he said to Betsy. "Shall we give it a go?"

"I'm afraid I don't know how," she demurred.

"I'll teach you."

"How about me?" Julie jumped up. "I'm an old two-stepper from way back." She held out her hand.

After a moment's hesitation, he took it. "Don't go away," he said over his shoulder to Betsy as Julie dragged him toward the dance floor.

The crowd swallowed them up. He eventually returned minus Julie, who'd stopped to chat with friends. Before he could even order a drink, Lorri, Lisa's baby-sitter, approached and asked him to dance.

Betsy had never seen the unflappable Chase Britton flustered, but she saw it now. Too polite to turn the woman down, he followed her onto the dance floor and there he stayed through the next three numbers, passed from partner to partner like a party favor.

Betsy, on the other hand, felt no qualms about turning down would-be dance partners. She was enjoying herself just watching, helped along by the carafe of white wine she shared with Julie and Maggie.

The two-step gave way to line dancing, and Chase finally made his way back to the table. He slumped into his seat, his brow shining with perspiration. "That was a real workout," he groaned.

Maggie, who moments before had been sitting nice and relaxed, stood up abruptly. "Now they got you broke in, it's my turn," she said to Chase, nodding toward eager dancers falling into line.

Chase looked appalled. "Line dancing? I don't think so."

Maggie's brown eyes narrowed. "Come now, you danced with strangers. You mean to tell me you won't dance with the woman who brung ya?"

"You don't need a partner for line dancing."

"I do. I'm shy."

Betsy watched Maggie haul the reluctant Chase onto the dance floor. Alone, she settled back in the booth with a sigh. Where was Ben tonight? Why did she care? As the minutes passed, she found herself becoming more and more anxious. No one stopped to chat; she felt like the invisible woman. She'd even appreciate a kind word from someone she didn't particularly like, someone like Johnny King, but even he gave her a wide berth. What was this, a conspiracy to embarrass her? If she wanted to be alone, she could do that at home.

"Care to dance?"

Ben's compelling voice flowed over her like warm honey. Even before she saw him, she felt the electricity generated by his presence. The very atmosphere of the Hideout changed, became more intimate. When she looked into his eyes, the level of noisy frivolity faded away.

Common sense told her to say no. The last thing she needed was to be held in his arms—or was it the first thing? He took her elbow, and the warmth of his touch traveled up her arm and spread through her cold, lonely body. Lost in a haze, she let him lead her onto the dance floor. Pliantly she went into his arms, settling against his chest with a sigh of relief. The music had magically changed from raucous to romantic. Ben didn't speak, just held her tight. His thighs pressed against hers with every sliding step, his arms bending hers behind her waist in an intimate embrace.

Too soon the dance ended. For a few moments they remained locked in each other's arms. Then Ben straightened to look down into her bemused face.

"Let's go home," he said.

"N-now?"

He smiled. "Don't you think it's time?"

She nodded slowly. "Past time," she whispered, knowing it was true. She loved this man, really loved him. Although a future together was still very much in doubt, she could no longer fool herself into believing that she was capable of simply walking away from him.

"UH...WOULD SOMEBODY like to tell me what's going on here?"

Chase Britton looked around, frowning. Everybody lingered on the dance floor watching Betsy walk out with that cowboy who'd driven her to Aspen the first time. They had their arms around each other and looked as if very soon they'd have more than that around each other.

"Shh!" Maggie darted him an irate glance. "When they're gone—"

The door swung closed behind them and someone in the crowd let out a lusty "Yipp-eee!" Immediately the Hideout buzzed again with noisy confusion.

"I ask again, what's going on?"

Maggie grinned. "Nature's taking its course."

Julie threw an arm around each of them. "Nature, with a little help from her friends," she crowed. "This calls for a real celebration. Wanna dance, Cha—"

"Julie Cameron, what in hell are you doing hugging a strange man?"

It was Scott Hale, and he didn't look happy. *There goes the evening,* Maggie thought glumly.

BEN SLIPPED Betsy's key into the lock, and the door swung open on squeaky hinges. When she would have walked past him, he stopped her with a hand on her arm. She turned, and although it was too dark to see her expression, he felt her tension. He responded by leaning down to slide one arm beneath her knees, the other around her back. Picking her up, he walked inside and kicked the door closed.

"I've missed you," he murmured, nuzzling her cheek. He carried her through the small living room and into the bedroom. In the spill of moonlight from the single window, he stood her on her feet and kissed her.

She opened her mouth to him without hesitation. She was as ready for this as he was, as anxious as he to put an end to their mutual torment. He touched the top button of her silky blouse, she murmured a single word against his lips: *"Yes..."*

Through long, drugging, openmouthed kisses, he fought and fumbled to undress her, hindered by her own attempts to do the same for him. Slowly her gleaming body emerged in the silvery moonlight: ivory breasts springing gloriously from the constraint of her bra, a waist he could almost span with his two hands, rounded hips and buttocks, a flat belly and long elegant legs. Standing in the puddle of clothing at her feet, she reached out to touch his lips with fingers that trembled.

"I've dreamed of this," she whispered.

"It's no dream, sweetheart." His own shirt was open and pushed down around his elbows. He shrugged out of it and reached for her, impatient to feel all that naked beauty pressed against him.

"Wait!" She stopped him with her hands on his shoulders.

What now? Surely there was nothing left to come between them. But incredibly she stepped back, beyond his reach. Disbelieving, he watched her wring her hands as if in some crisis of remorse. Then she drew in a deep breath and straightened. In the shadowy illumination of moonlight, he could see her smile.

She held out one clenched fist. "My rings," she said in a voice taut with emotion. "I've never taken them off, b-but I can't make love with you until I . . ." Her voice trailed away on a breathless note, and she turned her hand palm up, spreading her fingers to show him. Then she turned and dropped the rings onto the bed-side table.

Stepping up behind her, he touched her sleek back, then slipped his arms around her so he could close his hands over the softness of her breasts. Pulling her against him until she fit into the curve of his body, he nipped at her ear, touched and shaken by her gesture.

She let her head fall back against his shoulder, and her hands closed over his, pressing them harder against her breasts. "Please," she murmured, "make me glad I did that."

He turned her in his arms and kissed her, backing her up until her legs hit the edge of the bed. They tumbled down together in a tangle of arms and legs. His mouth settled over the nipple of one straining breast, and she gasped with pleasure. It had been so long, so very long. He nibbled at the tightly puckered bud, then drew it into his mouth and began to suckle. He slid a hand down her belly and between her trembling thighs. Her entire body felt on fire. At that moment, she desired nothing beyond his possession.

She had never been touched as fiercely as he touched her, his impatience just short of rough and a long way from the gentle reverence of her husband. Ben seemed all-powerful, capable of doing anything he pleased with her. It was a relief just to give herself up to his passionate aggression.

Abruptly he rolled between her open thighs and braced above her on powerful arms. His breath rasped in his throat and it took a moment of visible effort before he could speak. Then he said, "I wanted to go real slow our first time, but I can't. I want you too much."

She responded by lifting her hips and grabbing his buttocks to guide him home. He entered her with one swift sure stroke.

Groaning with relief, he held himself still for a moment. She wrapped her legs around him with delicious deliberation, savoring the way he pulsated in the very depths of her. She'd never felt so sexy or so alive.

"C'mon, cowboy," she gasped. "If I recall correctly, there's a little bit more to it than this."

The body above hers shook with silent laughter, sending fresh rivulets of desire radiating through her. Leaning down, he nipped her ear, eliciting a shudder. "Now that you mention it..."

He withdrew slowly, then plunged back hard and sure. "Hang on, sweetheart," he said, his voice ragged. "This is gonna be the ride of our lives."

And it was, made even more incredible when, in the throes of passion, she cried out his name—his, not her dead husband's.

CHAPTER FIFTEEN

"BETSY . . ."

"Mm?"

"Let's get married."

It hurt her to say, "I can't," but she really didn't feel she had any choice.

"You said you loved me."

"I do, but—"

"But nothing. I love you, too. Let's get married."

"I can't. I'm . . . not sure."

Ben scooted around on the bed until he could rest his chin between her breasts. "Not sure we'd live happily ever after?"

"For openers."

"Neither am I."

His bluntness shocked her. "Then why . . . ?"

"Hey, I'm willing to take a shot at it. You know what they say—nothing's sure but death and taxes."

She stroked his throat with her fingertips. "I wish I could be that casual about it."

"I'm not casual—I'm realistic," he said fiercely. "The thought of marriage scares me as much as it does you, but damn, Betsy! Once in a while, you've got to take a chance, or what's the use of living?"

"Until I'm sure we can make it work..."

"Life doesn't come with guarantees, sweetheart." He covered her breasts with his hands and began gently kneading her sensitized flesh. "I'm willing to work at it."

"Are you... really?"

"I'd lay my life on the line for you, Betsy. You should know that. I'll love you and protect you and do my best to make you happy."

"I *am* happy." And she was. For perhaps the first time since her husband's death, she was truly happy.

He pressed his advantage. "Then say you'll marry me."

"I'm not a fighter, Ben."

"And I am, which is the only reason we're here like this now."

She had to smile at that. "Maybe, but I can't see a lifetime of fighting and fussing."

"Can you see a lifetime of *this?*"

He touched her confidently She shifted beneath his hands and mouth, not sure she'd be able to give him up after their passionate joining.

He rolled his tongue around her nipple, then withdrew. "Say you'll marry me or say goodbye." With both hands, he lifted her breast to his mouth and sucked the tip deep into his mouth, then withdrew again. "Those are your only two choices, sweetheart."

Sitting up between her legs, he touched the sensitive inner flesh of her thighs. "Decide now."

As if she had a choice.

HE LEFT just before dawn. Standing on her front porch, he pulled her against him and kissed her thoroughly.

"Damn," he murmured against her lips, "I hate to go."

"Me, too." A sudden thought occurred to her and she stiffened. "Oh, good grief!"

He tightened his hold on her. "What is it?"

"Chase! I have no idea what happened to him last night. He didn't even get a chance to see the café."

"He didn't come to see the café, he came to see you." Ben's lips stretched into a hard line, then relaxed. "I'd sure feel better if you'd stay away from him. Will you?"

She rested her cheek on his chest. "There's no need to be jealous of Chase," she murmured. "But I thank you for asking, instead of issuing an order or trying to start a fight."

He groaned. "Never suffer in silence, sweetheart. All you've got to do is speak up if you don't agree with me."

He made it sound so easy.

THE RING HE GAVE HER a few days later had belonged to his great-grandmother. "Julie says it's an old-fashioned setting, so if you'd like to have it changed..."

"Never!" She put it on her finger and held it out for him and everybody else at the Rusty Spur to admire. She wouldn't change it for anything in the world.

Even so, she resisted when he urged her to set a date, saying she could see no reason why they should hurry. They were committed to each other now, and the whole town knew and approved.

Plenty of time, she told him, basking in her joy.

Thinking he was doing the same.

HE WASN'T. He loved Betsy, he truly did, but always being on his best behavior with her was wearing him down. Never in his life had he known anyone who disliked and avoided conflict the way she did.

Unfortunately life on a ranch was nothing *but* conflict. It was man against nature, man against animals and, at the Straight Arrow, often man against woman. Up to this point, the woman had never been a wife, only a sister or grandmother or mother, but he had no reason to believe a wife would be any different. If *he* didn't drive Betsy nuts, the rest of his family would.

Was he doing her a disservice, giving her a false impression of what their life would be like? If he didn't love her so damned much... But he did, and so he kept pushing back the simmering resentment. Then on a sunny Sunday afternoon in September, it all came to a boil.

"HIGHER, DADDY, HIGHER!" Joey shrieked with laughter, and Ben gave the swing a mighty shove.

Nearby, Betsy propelled Lisa's swing with small measured pushes. The children had been pleased to hear they'd soon be brother and sister, although the concept of marriage obviously meant very little to them.

"Ben!"

Julie's strident voice emerging from the kitchen window of the cottage cut across the grain of the quiet scene. Ben and Betsy exchanged startled glances; then he turned toward the house.

Betsy started after him. "You kids stay here in the yard," she directed. "We'll be right inside talking to Aunt Julie if you need us."

Julie waited in the kitchen, feet planted wide and fists on her hips. She looked mad enough to eat nails—and she also looked as if she'd been crying. "Say I told you so and be done with it!" she shouted at Ben.

Betsy frowned. "What is it, Julie? What's happened?"

"Nothing much. My life's over, that's all." And Julie collapsed into tears in Betsy's comforting arms.

It occurred to Ben that anger had served his sister better than sympathy.

The story came out between sobs: Julie and Scott were finished.

"It's all your fault!" she accused her brother, dashing tears away. "You never liked him—don't deny it!"

"Who's denying it?" Ben looked nothing so much as relieved. "You're better off without him."

"That's not for you to say."

"Hey, if your brother can't tell you the truth...?"

"But it's not the truth! He's the only man I'll ever love," she sobbed.

Ben made a rude noise. "Julie, you're twenty-one years old and you've got plenty of time. Everybody knows that engagement was a mistake. At least now it won't be fatal. Truth is, you wouldn't know love if it spit in your eye."

"I would! I do!" Julie dried her tears on the hem of her shirt. Then his words seemed to sink in. "What do you mean, everybody knows it was a mistake?"

"Just what it sounds like." He looked a little uneasy.

Julie whirled on Betsy. "You liked Scott, didn't you?" Taken aback, Betsy tried to sidestep. "Your feelings are what matter, not mine." Trying to slow the quick escalation of this quarrel, she searched for something soothing to add, some wisdom to impart. "Maybe this is just a lovers' quarrel. After you've both thought it over—"

Ben snorted. "Damn it, Betsy, leave well enough alone."

Julie moaned. "It's too late, anyway. He's gone, packed up and moved to Denver without me. His dad's going to close the video store, so Scott won't have any reason to come back."

"But why?" Betsy appealed for an explanation.

"Ben got hold of him, that's why. Who wouldn't cut and run after that?"

"You must be mistaken. Ben wouldn't—"

"Hell yes, I would. I did."

Betsy turned to him, unwilling to believe. "Surely you didn't . . . threaten him?"

He shrugged, his eyes hard. "What I said to him might have been called threatening in some circles. He was shooting off his mouth, telling his low-life friends what a hot little number Julie is. I took exception— *strong* exception."

Julie's cheeks blazed bright red. "That's a lie!"

Ben froze. "I don't lie, Julie, and you damn well know it."

"Neither does Scott, and we never—" She bit off her words and turned away.

Then it was true, what Julie had told Maggie and Betsy. Ben wouldn't lie, but Betsy wasn't surprised to realize Scott would and had. He and Julie had broken up because she wouldn't sleep with him, and he'd found a face-saving way out. Betsy's heart went out to her sister-in-law-to-be. "You poor little thing!" she exclaimed. "You—"

"Don't baby her!" Ben snapped. "She thinks she's so grown up, let her act it."

"But—"

"Ben Cameron," Julie yelled, "why don't you mind your own business?"

"Please—" Betsy tried.

"Betsy *is* my business! I'm going to marry her."

The children entered the fray before anyone even noticed they'd come into the house. Both were in tears and talking at once.

Betsy looked from one to the other. "What's wrong with you two?"

"He hit me!" Lisa rubbed the back of her head. "I don't want him for my brother!"

"I didn't. The swing did," Joey explained. "She pushed me off! It was an accident."

Betsy knelt, drawing both children to her. "I'm sure neither of you meant to hurt the other," she soothed, checking Lisa's head; there was a bump but no blood. Nor did Joey have any obvious injuries. "These things happen. Why don't you make up, and I'll give you each a big glass of lemonade—"

"I hate him! He's mean!"

"Please, honey—"

"Lisa hates me and I won't never have a sister—"

"Now, Joey, that's not what she—"

"Stop it!"

Ben's angry voice cut through Betsy's attempts to mediate. "You're making things worse. Let them settle their own quarrels." He pulled Joey out of Betsy's arms. "You kids go on back outside and stop interrupting the grown-ups."

Betsy stood up slowly. Loud angry voices always tied her stomach in a knot. Holding herself under tight control, she placed a hand on each child's shoulder and steered them toward the back door. "Yes, go on outside," she urged. "I'll fix you a snack later. How does that sound?"

Lisa lifted her chin, her lower lip trembling. "I won't eat with *him* ever again," she said with finality. "He's mean."

"I am not mean!" Their loud voices faded away.

Julie resumed her attack on Ben. "Where do you get off driving away the man I love—loved, whatever."

"Then you don't object to having your name spread all over town as an easy lay?"

Betsy couldn't believe this. Apparently these two wouldn't quit until they drew blood. She pressed both hands to her temples and sucked in a shaky breath. It took every ounce of strength she possessed to say, "Please go, both of you."

Ben whipped his head around to look at her. "You throwing me out?"

"I'm throwing you both out."

"Don't do this," he said. "It's family business, and if you're going to be part of the family, you might as well get used to it."

"I'll never get used to it. All this fighting and un-happiness—"

"Some things are worth fighting for."

"No. No, Ben." Shaking her head in denial, she backed away.

He continued relentlessly. "If you love someone, you owe them the truth, even if it leads to temporary unhappiness—"

"Temporary?" Julie practically shrieked the word. "My life is ruined and you're talking temporary?"

Betsy stared at the two of them. "I can't deal with this now! Please *go.*"

For a moment Ben just looked at her. Then he said, "If I go, I won't be back."

She wondered if that was what she'd meant all along. She stood paralyzed with dread but unable to make a move toward him.

He laughed harshly. "Julie's not the only damn fool in the Cameron family." His intent gaze never left her face. "No guts, no glory," he said slowly. "I thought all you needed was a chance to find your backbone, but I was wrong. You should never have left California, Betsy."

He walked out, and she knew he'd gone to get Joey from the backyard.

Julie touched Betsy's arm. "He doesn't mean it," she said, not sounding too sure. "Ben's got a temper, but he gets over it."

Betsy shook her head, incapable of a coherent response. She clenched her right hand around her left, and Ben's engagement ring pressed into her flesh.

Joey and Lisa, holding hands, preceded Ben into the living room while faithful Erica frolicked at their feet. The children had obviously done what the adults couldn't: made up their quarrel.

Ben placed a proprietary hand on his son's shoulder and drew him subtly away. "Say goodbye to Lisa Marie," he ordered. "We've got to go home now."

Lisa appealed to her mother. "Please, Mama, can Joey stay? We'll be good!"

Betsy refused to look at Ben. "You *are* good, sweetheart."

Joey added his entreaties. "Please let me stay and play. I'll be good, too."

Betsy was sure Ben wouldn't be swayed by the boy's pleas. But this time, he surprised her—now that it was too late.

"Ask Lisa's mother," he said in a cool voice. "If Aunt Julie will give you a ride home later..."

Julie shook her head. "Sorry, Aunt Julie's going home with Daddy."

"In that case—" Ben shrugged "—I'm afraid—"

"But Aunt Maggie will be by later. You can go home with her, Joey." Julie added by way of explanation, "Maggie went to see Nancy about working part-time at the Spur. She's coming by later to pick me up."

Ben turned toward the front door. "Then you be good, Joey."

"I will, Daddy."

"Wait." Betsy stepped forward, holding out her left hand. Ben responded automatically, and she dropped his great-grandmother's ring into his exposed palm.

For a moment he stared at it. Then he said, "If that's the way you want it."

That's not at all the way I want it, she longed to cry. *It's the way it is.* "I want the same thing you want," she said. "Goodbye, Ben."

When he'd gone, Julie let out a long unhappy sigh. "I'm sorry," she said, edging toward the door. "I feel responsible."

"You're not." All Betsy wanted now was to be alone.

"But you love each other."

"Apparently love isn't enough." Betsy pulled herself together enough to add, "I'm sorry about Scott." It was a lie, but a kind one.

There seemed nothing more to say. Julie followed Ben out, and Betsy was alone.

THE CHILDREN HUDDLED in the backyard, heads close together. "We could go live in the forest like Hansel and Gretel," Lisa Marie suggested, darting an offended glance toward the house. "Big people are mean."

"Yeah, mean." Joey looked at the trees ringing the small meadow beyond the back fence. It looked scary. He wasn't sure he'd like living in the forest like Hansel and Gretel, maybe meeting a witch who ate disobedient little children.

"I like gingerbread," Lisa said dreamily, "but I never saw a gingerbread house. Do you like gingerbread?"

"It's okay."

"If the witch throws you in a cage, I'll save you," Lisa offered. "Can we go now?"

Joey figured he'd have to think about that a little longer—and think about how angry his father would be if he caught them before the witch did.

"BETSY, YOU CAN'T DO this," Nancy said.

Maggie added, "Ben's in love with you, for heaven's sake, and we were under the impression you love him, too."

Betsy, tossing clothing into a suitcase, tried to tune them out. "I'm doing what I have to do," she said. "Ben doesn't care. He made that perfectly clear."

Maggie shook her head. "You're wrong. He cares so much it scares him. But he can't change what he is, even for you. He tried. Lord knows, he tried."

"What he is, is stubborn and judgmental." Betsy didn't even have to close her eyes to see him, to feel his anger and disappointment. "Hasn't *he* ever made a mistake?"

Maggie frowned. "You mean nobody's told you?"

Nancy shook her head. "It wasn't my place."

"Told me what?" A cold chill skittered down Betsy's spine. "About Crystal? I know all about that."

Maggie's lips tightened. "Crystal wasn't really Ben's mistake. He was hers. No—I'm talking about our dad."

Betsy sat down hard on the bed. "Ben never talked much about him."

"That's understandable, since he feels responsible for Dad's death."

Betsy dug cold fingers into the quilt. "Tell me."

"Dad was an alcoholic. By the time Ben was seventeen, he already carried a lot of responsibility as the oldest son. He took on way too much, but he never complained—until one day he just lost it. He blew up at Dad and took off with a carload of his buddies, stayed out all night drinking beer and talking big like boys will. Ben'd never done that before."

"They got into trouble?"

"There was trouble, but not the kind you mean. It was Dad. He was drunk, which wasn't unusual, but drunk or sober, he was still a cowman. He saddled up and rode out to check the herd, which was what Ben had refused to do. The horse came back with an empty saddle.''

Knowing Ben, loving Ben, the implications were immediately clear to Betsy. She felt the sting of sympathetic tears.

Maggie nodded. ''Nothing on four legs could throw Dad when he was sober, but that was no consolation at all to Ben. He came home the next day with a hangover of his own and his tail between his legs, but it was too late. He blamed himself, regardless of what anyone else thought or said. Since then, no one has ever been able to find a single instance of Ben Cameron shirking his duty. He *is* a stubborn man, and he rarely cuts anybody any slack. But he learned the hard way what it means to shirk responsibility. He's not selfish, he's scared—scared he'll let down those he loves. Can't you try to understand?''

SOMEWHERE ON ARROW ROAD, Ben interrupted his furious monologue to draw a deep breath. He'd been lamenting Betsy's lack of spunk and spirit, but before he could pick up the thread of his complaints, Julie jumped in.

''You want to shut up and listen for a change?'' she demanded. ''Just because you're Cupid's answer to Dudley Do-Right doesn't mean everyone else is or even should be. Betsy may not be tough, but she's no pushover, either. Crystal was tough and look how that turned out.''

That shook him because it was true. ''Damn it, Julie—''

"I'm not finished!" She waited until she had the floor again before going on. "Betsy Ross is the best thing that ever happened to you. Why'd you turn tail and run?"

Hurtling down the road at ninety miles an hour *felt* like running. But had he turned his back on her out of cowardice? Maybe he *didn't* have the guts to take the emotional risks involved.

Julie wasn't through with him. "You know you've just driven her out of town," she said more quietly.

"I don't know any such thing."

"The hell you don't. Go back now, or you're going to lose her forever. It's as simple as that."

A forever without Betsy? Even if it meant risking everything, even if he ultimately lost, it was in his nature to fight for what he loved. Hanging a U-turn that left his sister clinging white-faced to her seat, he gunned the engine and headed back to town, praying he'd be in time.

"SHH!" JOEY PRESSED a finger to his lips, cautioning Lisa to silence. She nodded, blue eyes wide and expectant. Satisfied, the boy slipped the bolt from the gate and gave it a shove. It swung open easily.

Taking Lisa's hand, Joey led her through. Once outside the fenced yard, they paused. Lisa glanced at Joey, impatient to go on, but the boy was looking uncertainly at the dark and brooding forest.

Joey knew that *things* lived in the trees, scary things like bears and wildcats and probably witches and monsters. If they went in there, it would be up to him to protect Lisa, who was, after all, only a girl. He swallowed hard. "Maybe we shouldn't run away today," he suggested in a small voice.

"We have to!" Lisa's whisper was strident. "When Mama gets her suitcase packed, we'll be going away. I want to stay with you and Aunt Nancy and Erica and Roger and . . . and all."

"Me, too," he agreed miserably, "but—"

Erica chose that moment to shoot past, brushing against Joey's legs. The shaggy pup halted in the path ahead, plumy tail waving cheerfully. It made Joey feel better, because he didn't think Erica would let anything hurt them. Of course, Erica was a lot smaller than that big cat Joey had seen in the tree. But hadn't Aunt Julie once said Erica had the heart of a lion?

Resolutely Joey started forward. Lisa went with him willingly, her chubby hand clutching his confidently.

Betsy sat on the edge of her bed, shoulders drooping. After a moment she said, "You're right, Maggie."

"Right about what?"

"About me. About Ben. I wish he'd told me."

"He's too ashamed to talk about it," Maggie said. "He never intends to let anyone down again, which makes him seem bossy and preachy sometimes. But it also makes him rock-steady, a man you can count on. Honey, you've got to take the bitter with the sweet, as Granny says."

Betsy shivered. "Have I been living in a fairy tale?"

Nancy sat beside Betsy on the bed and patted her hand. "In a lot of ways…yes, I think maybe you have been. Real people aren't perfect."

Betsy had to think, had to figure out why she so often disappointed herself. But it was growing dark; first she needed to call the children in and feed them, go on with all the small ordinary tasks.

Leaving Maggie and Nancy in the kitchen making coffee and sandwiches, Betsy went out the back door. Her mind was a million miles away—or maybe only a few, with Ben wherever he was. "Lisa Marie!" she called. "Joey, time to come in!"

The yard was empty, the gate open. Glancing around with concern, she spotted them hand in hand, hurrying toward the trees with Erica dancing around them.

They knew better than to leave the safety of the yard! She started forward, but movement in a big tree beside the trail caught her eye. She looked up. On a limb in a tree halfway between her and the children lay a great yellow beast. The lazy switch of its tail had drawn her attention. As she stared in frozen horror, the mountain lion leapt lightly to the ground.

There was no time to seek help, no time to avoid action, certainly no time to run away somewhere to "think about it." With a shriek of pure terror, that most nonconfrontational of women looked around frantically for a weapon. All she saw was a rag mop leaning against the side of the house. Grabbing it, she took off down the trail as fast as she could.

The children had whirled around at Betsy's scream, huddling in each other's arms in abject terror while the lion bounded toward them. At their feet, little Erica growled, then launched himself to meet the charge of an animal big enough to swallow him in a single gulp.

The lion skidded to a stop as if uncertain about the foolhardy creature confronting it so fearlessly. Before it could make up its mind, Betsy attacked from the rear, swinging the mop like a saber.

Confused, the tawny beast turned to catch a solid *whop!* in the face from the rag mop. Snarling and spitting, it struck out with an enormous paw. Betsy refused to retreat. Fighting back fiercely, she jabbed and poked with her weapon, simultaneously screaming at the kids to run.

Spitting and hissing, the lion swiped at the mop again. Curved talons delivered a glancing blow to Betsy's right arm. Crimson droplets of blood flew. Fighting for all their lives, she felt no pain, more concerned that the children remained frozen to the spot.

Two more voices joined hers: Maggie and Nancy had arrived, but Betsy dared not count on anyone but herself. Erica's frenzied barking added to the cacophony as the little dog attacked the lion from the rear.

The timely arrival of reinforcements tipped the scales. With a bloodcurdling scream, the cougar took off for the trees at warp speed, leaping gracefully over Erica in its haste to make tracks.

Shrieking hysterically, Joey and Lisa Marie bolted for the safety of Betsy's arms. She grabbed them in a ferocious hug, her blood still boiling with rage—and some of it dripping down her arm and onto the ground. She ignored Nancy's attempts to tend her injury; she couldn't even feel it. She had no time for that! How dare any creature attack her darlings? She would fight a rampaging elephant in their defense.

"Betsy!"

A new deeper voice joined the mix. Twisting around on her knees, Betsy saw Ben and Julie charging toward the little group. He'd come back! Rising, she took a joyous step toward him, but Joey's cry stopped her.

"Daddy!" The boy darted past, running to meet his father. Ben grabbed Joey in a fierce hug, but his anxious gaze was on Betsy.

Whose heart was in her throat. The danger was past, but instead of collapsing with relief, she rose on her toes like a fighter seeking an opening. Drunk on adrenaline, she confronted Ben squarely.

Ben leaned down to kiss Joey's tear-streaked cheek before starting toward Betsy. Apparently noticing the blood on her arm for the first time, he stopped short, his face registering alarm. "You're bleeding. Let me..." He tried to take her in his arms.

He no doubt thought she'd faint at the sight of a little blood. Betsy gave him a shove. "So what?" she shouted. "This time I didn't panic. I didn't run away!" She gave him another shove and he retreated.

"Hang on a minute." Hands held like a shield, he fell back yet another step before the magnificence of her anger. "What are you mad at me for? I wasn't even here!"

"I'm mad at you because you were right! Sometimes you have to fight, because some things are worth fighting for and there won't always be someone else around to do it."

Grabbing his shirtfront with both hands, she hung on. "I've had it, Ben Cameron. This is your last chance, do you hear me? Once and for all, do you love me, or did you just want to sleep with me? Because I'm warning you, I'm not a fighter, and if that's what you want, I'm not it. You'll have to take me as I am or not at all."

"Love to—if you'll return the favor."

Her lips parted in astonishment. That was it—the key: *Take me as I am.* She was too shocked to speak.

"I love you," he said. "You may not consider yourself a fighter, but a woman who can beat the hell out of a mountain lion with a mop is nobody's pushover unless she wants to be."

Betsy gasped, the events of the past few minutes finally sinking in. "I did, didn't I," she said, her voice hoarse after all the yelling she'd done. "What have I got to be afraid of? I am woman. I can do anything, even handle *you!*"

Smothered in his embrace, she dimly heard Lisa Marie's voice. "I bet this means we're not moving away, Joey. I bet this means we'll all live happily ever after. I bet this means..."

The rest of it was lost, for Betsy Ross, slayer of dragons, fainted dead away.

EPILOGUE

IT WAS SNOWING at the Straight Arrow Ranch on the last day of October, a little more than two years later. Snug and warm inside the ranch house, Ben stood before the television set in the upstairs family room, smaller than it had been with new partitions that had added a couple of postage-size bedrooms for the children. Abruptly he called to six-year-old Lisa Marie. "Come see what's on television, honey."

Lisa, Joey, Erica the dog and Roger the cat responded. The children were already dressed in their Halloween costumes: Lisa a ballerina and Joey—what else? Ben thought proudly—a cowboy. Erica sported a colorful ruff around his neck while Roger's collar was decorated in crazy-making orange and black crepe paper streamers.

The image of Evan Ross flashed across the television screen. "That's my other daddy!" Lisa exclaimed. She peered closely at a film she'd seen many times before.

Ben left them to it, strolling downstairs to the kitchen where Betsy fed the baby under the watchful eye of Grandma Cameron. Cat—short for Catherine—gurgled and flashed her dimples at Daddy. Uptairs he could hear Joey and Lisa fighting over the emote control, over who got to sit in Daddy's chair, over who got to hold the dog.

Betsy smiled at her husband, relinquishing the spoon to Grandma, who took over the feeding chore happily. Other voices came from deeper inside the house: Julie, engaged to an engineer from Albuquerque and planning a Christmas ceremony around what she insisted upon calling "the most beautiful wedding gown in the world"; and Jason, well on his way to making a name for himself in rodeo—with his brother's blessing—yelling at each other; Chuck's low rumble and Maggie's lighter voice calling, "Betsy, be sure and remind Nancy and John about supper here Saturday night, okay?"

All of it the normal give-and-take of life in a big family, Betsy thought; not the idolized family of her dreams but the real thing—and so much better than she'd ever imagined.

Ben lifted her hand to his lips. "Sure you want to risk gettin' snowbound drivin' into town in this weather just so the kids can engage in legalized extortion? Wouldn't you rather stay home, get to bed early and . . . ?"

She grinned at his view of trick-or-treating. "You know I would," she said serenely, "but I can't let you weasel out on the kids. Duty before pleasure, sweetheart. Besides, Aunt Nancy's expecting us."

In fact, Nancy was keeping the Rusty Spur open tonight, offering free coffee and doughnuts for all comers and treats for the children. Betsy had made the doughnuts earlier in the day in the snazzy new kitchen paid for by proceeds from the sale of Evan's diamond ring. The Rusty Spur was not only in the black, it was thriving, thanks to the draw of freshly baked goodies.

Planting a light kiss on Ben's cheek, she added, "Besides, I've already told Joey and Lisa they can bring Erica and Roger, since they're dressed for the occasion." She added quickly, "You don't mind, do you?"

"Mind?" He slid his arms around her waist and whispered in her ear, his gaze on Grandma diligently feeding the baby and pretending not to listen. "You're offering me kids, critters and Cupid, instead of a very long, very *personal* night in the sack with the woman I love, and you ask if I mind?" His laughter held promise of treats to come. "What's to mind?"

What, indeed? As he herded kids and critters through gently falling snow to reach the four-wheel-drive Jeep Cherokee that had replaced Betsy's BMW, he reminded himself that they had plenty of time. Betsy Cameron would be in his bed—and in his heart—tonight, tomorrow night, the night after that and the night after that . . . forever.

HARLEQUIN SUPERROMANCE®

WOMEN WHO *Dare*

They take chances, make changes
and follow their hearts!

Once a Wife
by Patricia Keelyn

The Past—1985

Diana Colby's life is a mess. Her husband, Reece, has been
disinherited. Her infant son has been diagnosed with juvenile
diabetes. She's just found out she's pregnant again—and she's
only seventeen years old. So, when Reece's mother offers to
look after Diana's husband and child if only Diana will leave
them, she feels she has no choice. She also knows she'll regret
her decision for the rest of her life.

The Present—1996

Eleven years have passed. Diana's made a new life, but has
never forgotten her first love or her child. When Diana receives
a message that her son, Drew, needs her, she knows she must
go back. But returning brings with it a whole new dilemma.
How can she face Reece again after deserting him? And how is
she going to tell him about his daughter, Lissa, the child he
never knew he had?

Watch for *Once a Wife*
by Patricia Keelyn.

Available in March 1996 wherever
Harlequin books are sold.

WWD96-2

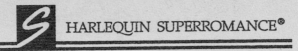

HARLEQUIN SUPERROMANCE®

MARRIED TO THE MAN
by Judith Arnold

Jane Thayer has it all. Or she will as soon as she rids herself of one little problem—an ex-husband she didn't know she was still married to. Her fiancé will never understand. So Jane does the only thing she can do. She goes to New Orleans to track down Cody Sinclair, a man she hasn't seen since their wild and reckless youth.

Cody's *still* wild and reckless. A photojournalist for a major newspaper, he's a magnet for trouble…and women. Right now he needs a lawyer—Jane. The woman who wants to be his *ex*-wife. But suddenly he's not so sure that's a good idea. Jane wants to talk about it, but Cody has other things in mind….

First Love, Last Love

**Available in March, wherever
Harlequin Superromance novels are sold.**

UNLOCK THE DOOR TO GREAT ROMANCE AT BRIDE'S BAY RESORT

Join Harlequin's new across-the-lines series, set in an exclusive hotel on an island off the coast of South Carolina.

Seven of your favorite authors will bring you exciting stories about fascinating heroes and heroines discovering love at Bride's Bay Resort.

Look for these fabulous stories coming to a store near you beginning in January 1996.

Harlequin American Romance #613 in January
Matchmaking Baby by Cathy Gillen Thacker

Harlequin Presents #1794 in February
Indiscretions by Robyn Donald

Harlequin Intrigue #362 in March
Love and Lies by Dawn Stewardson

Harlequin Romance #3404 in April
Make Believe Engagement by Day Leclaire

Harlequin Temptation #588 in May
Stranger in the Night by Roseanne Williams

Harlequin Superromance #695 in June
Married to a Stranger by Connie Bennett

Harlequin Historicals #324 in July
Dulcie's Gift by Ruth Langan

Visit Bride's Bay Resort each month wherever Harlequin books are sold.

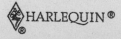

Yo amo novelas con corazón!

Starting this March, Harlequin opens up to a whole new world of readers with two new romance lines in SPANISH!

Harlequin Deseo
- passionate, sensual and exciting stories

Harlequin Bianca
- romances that are fun, fresh and very contemporary

With four titles a month, each line will offer the same wonderfully romantic stories that you've come to love—now available in Spanish.

Look for them at selected retail outlets.

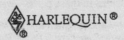 HARLEQUIN ®

SPANT

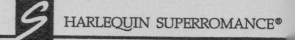

HARLEQUIN SUPERROMANCE®

From the bestselling author of
THE TAGGARTS OF TEXAS!
comes

Cupid, Colorado...

This is ranch country, cowboy country—a land of high mountains and swift, cold rivers, of deer, elk and bear. The land is important here—family and neighbors are, too. 'Course, you have the chance to really get to know your neighbors in Cupid. Take the Camerons, for instance. The first Cameron came to Cupid more than a hundred years ago, and Camerons have owned and worked the Straight Arrow Ranch—the largest spread in these parts—ever since.

For kids and kisses, tears and laughter, wild horses and wilder men—come to the Straight Arrow Ranch, near Cupid, Colorado. Come meet the Camerons.

THE CAMERONS OF COLORADO
by Ruth Jean Dale

Kids, Critters and Cupid (Superromance#678)
available in February 1996

The Cupid Conspiracy (Temptation #579)
available in March 1996

The Cupid Chronicles (Superromance #687)
available in April 1996